Tales of Valhalla

Also by Martyn Whittock and Hannah Whittock

1016 and 1066: Why the Vikings Caused the Norman Conquest
The Anglo-Saxon Avon Valley Frontier: A River of Two Halves
The Viking Blitzkrieg: AD 789–1098

Also by Martyn Whittock

A Brief Guide to Celtic Myths and Legends
A Brief History of the Th ird Reich: The Rise and Fall of the Nazis
A Brief History of Life in the Middle Ages

Tales

of

Valhalla

NORSE MYTHS & LEGENDS

MARTYN WHITTOCK AND
HANNAH WHITTOCK

PEGASUS BOOKS
NEW YORK LONDON

TALES OF VALHALLA

Pegasus Books, Ltd.
148 West 37th Street, 13th Floor
New York, NY 10018

Copyright © 2018 by Martyn Whittock and Hannah Whittock

First Pegasus Books paperback edition January 2020

First Pegasus Books hardcover edition September 2018

First published in United Kingdom by Robinson, an imprint of Little, Brown Book Group

Library of Congress Cataloging-in-Publication Data is available.

ISBN: 978-1-64313-337-9

10 9 8 7 6 5 4

Printed in the United States of America
Distributed by Simon & Schuster
www.pegasusbooks.com

To Neal, Elizabeth, Lesley and Debbie.
Remembering our fun times in Brussels. HEW

Contents

Part Two: Norse Legends

Introduction

THE NORSE MYTHS have gained widespread attention in the English-speaking world. This is largely due to a great interest in the myths and legends that lie behind the world of the Vikings (the Norse) and also through a Scandinavian diaspora (especially in the United States), which has communicated these myths to the wider world.

That there is such a widespread interest is demonstrated by the appearance of Norse mythological themes in popular culture. Films such as *Thor* (2011), *Thor: The Dark World* (2013) and the *Avengers* films featuring Thor (the latest being *Avengers: Age of Ultron*, 2015) demonstrate the enduring interest in reworkings of – and spin-offs from – Norse mythology. These particular films are adapted from the Marvel Comics superhero, whose creators (Stan Lee and Jack Kirby) based their character of Thor on the Norse mythology of the thunder god. Furthermore, the 'Middle Earth' of Tolkien (as seen in both *The Lord of the Rings* and *The Hobbit*) is heavily indebted to Norse/Germanic mythology.

This is nothing new, since these stories have been 'quarried' and adapted across time and culture. From medieval Icelanders celebrating their Viking roots as they recorded these myths, to William Morris's poem, *Sigurd the Volsung*. From Wagner's *Der Ring des Nibelungen* (*The Ring of the Nibelung*), to J. K. Rowling's werewolf, Fenrir Greyback. From the twentieth-century manipulation of Norse mythology by the Nazis and their allies, to modern commercial and cultural references to Norse myths in order to promote sports teams, beer, restaurants and much else. Clearly, Norse mythology continues to influence a range of aspects of modern culture.

The question is: what are the ancient stories that lie behind these later recreations and reinterpretations? This books aims to both provide a *retelling* of these dramatic stories and also *set them in context* so that their place within the 'Viking world-view' can be understood. These are not new translations of the myths and legends. This is because there already exists a number of academic translations from the Old Norse language; and also because the accounts – even when expertly translated – can still be difficult to follow. Instead, these are freely worded retellings that are based on the original accounts but which present them in an accessible way as stories that can simply be read as such. They have been chipped out of the matrix of (mostly Icelandic) medieval accounts, in much the same way that a fossil-hunter disentangles one dinosaur fossil from the bones held within a mass of rock. As a result, the single stories and accounts can then be explored by a modern reader.

The stories in question are Norse *myths* (stories, usually religious, that explain origins, why things are as they are, the nature of the spiritual) and, to a lesser extent, *legends* (stories that attempt to explain historical events and that may involve historical characters, but are told in a non-historical way and often include supernatural aspects). Between them they take us into the mental world of the early medieval Viking Age.

With regard to language, Old Norse used letters that are no longer used in Modern English. In almost all cases we have translated these letters into modern English ones. So, to give an obvious example, we have anglicised Óðinn to the more familiar form of Odin. However, very occasionally, they will appear when referring to a source, personal name or place name that employs these, along with modern Scandinavian letters not used in English when they appear in modern place names, etc. The one exception is Æsir (one of the two families of Norse gods), where we have used this form due to its frequent use in many modern sources, rather than the anglicised form of Aesir.

With regard to written sources, we have referred to them in an anglicised form, so *Grimnir's Sayings* rather than *Grímnismál*. Where a word, phrase or source is given in Old Norse it is always accompanied by a translation such as: *Heimskringla* (*Circle of the World*) or the personal name Bodvar Bjarki (*bjarki* means 'little bear'). Occasionally a medieval manuscript's name is given without translation (such as the *Codex Regius*) because this is the usual convention.

In 2013 and 2014, co-author Martyn Whittock visited Iceland, Denmark, Norway and Sweden as part of the research for this book (including exploring the manuscript evidence in the Culture House exhibition in Reykjavik). Hannah Whittock (with a First and an MPhil. from Cambridge in Anglo-Saxon, Norse and Celtic studies) has brought a detailed knowledge of the Old Norse texts and their themes to the project, along with skills in reading Old Norse (the language of the original accounts).

We are much indebted to the scholars, whose expert translations have assisted us in our own freely worded retellings of these myths and legends, and a selection of these are listed in a Select Bibliography at the end of this book. Readers who wish to study these myths in the context of the literature within which they were first recorded can access them in these translations.

Any errors, of course, are our own.

Martyn and Hannah Whittock

I

Who were the 'Norse'?

B EFORE WE EXPLORE a selection of Norse myths and legends, it is helpful to understand something about what is covered by the term 'Norse'. Where and when did they live and what was the geographical spread of their influence?

The term 'Norse' is used to describe the various peoples of Scandinavia who spoke the Old Norse language between the eighth and thirteenth centuries AD. While it had eastern and western dialects it would have been generally mutually understood across the range of areas within which it was spoken. A third recognisable form was spoken on the island of Gotland.

The Old Norse language later developed into modern Danish, Faroese, Icelandic, Norwegian and Swedish. In addition, there once existed the so-called Norn languages of Orkney and Shetland that are now extinct. It was, essentially, the language of the Vikings. Consequently, this book is basically about the myths and legends of the Vikings.

The Vikings and the extent of their settlement

The term 'Viking' is itself a controversial one. At the time, it described more of what one *did* (raiding, pirating, adventuring) than what one *was*.[1] The later Old Icelandic verb used to describe 'moving, turning aside' was *víkja* and this word in Old Norse may have developed the sense of 'seafarers far from home'. Old Norse Scandinavian written sources describe a pirate raider as a *víkingr* and a raiding expedition as a *víking*.[2] It did not originally have an ethnic meaning but it has come to have that in modern usage. Consequently, today we use the term 'Viking' to describe Scandinavians of the so-called 'Viking Age'. It is in that sense that we will use it in this book.

The Viking Age lasted from the late eighth century until about 1100. It was in this period of time that people from Scandinavia first *raided* and then *settled* in a wide arc of territory that stretched from Russia in the east to Greenland and the coast of North America in the west. They raided both sides of the English Channel and settled in Normandy, eastern and northern England and the northern and western isles of Scotland, and established a Viking kingdom in Dublin. It was these peoples who colonised Iceland, the Faroes and parts of Greenland. More distant raids even reached Spain and into the Mediterranean.

From the tenth century onwards, we see the emergence of kingdoms in Denmark, Norway and finally Sweden but nation-building took time and borders were fluid and changeable for many generations. For this reason, when we use the terms 'Denmark', 'Norway' and 'Sweden' it is to describe loose early political units, not the distinct nation states with which we are now familiar.

With regard to North America, the sagas refer to exploration of a region called 'Vinland'; although there is some debate about whether the references to '*vínber*' ('wine berries') indicate wild grapes or other plants. The name 'Vinland' is first recorded in the writings of the German medieval chronicler named Adam of Bremen, in his *Description of the Northern Islands* (written *c*.1075), in the German form '*Winland*'. He implied that it referred to 'wine', hence 'grapes'. This name then appears in the thirteenth-century account in *The Saga of the Greenlanders*. Its use there suggests that what was in mind was *vínber*, a term used variously for grapes, currants and, perhaps, bilberries. In addition, it has been suggested that the term '*vínviður*' ('grape-vines') mentioned in *The Saga of the Greenlanders* should actually have been '*viður*' ('wood'), in which case '*vínber*' need not have referred to grapes but, rather, to berries growing on trees.[3] This leaves the matter open of whether the thirteenth-century Norse accounts refer to 'wild grapes' (the wine-making plants of Adam of Bremen's earlier account) or some other wild berry that could be fermented in order to make wine. This is important because it may help explain exactly how far south along the eastern seaboard of North America the eleventh-century explorers reached. Clearly, they did not find wild grapes growing at L'Anse aux Meadows in Newfoundland, which currently is the only archaeologically attested Norse site on the North American continent.[4] This is why it is certain that L'Anse aux Meadows was not Vinland. However, that site did contain clues pointing to more southerly explorations carried out by the Norse settlers who built the houses discovered there. These clues were in the form of butternuts (or white walnuts) found at the site. Since these are native to the eastern United States and south-east Canada, it suggests that Vinland may have been as far south as the St Lawrence River and parts of New Brunswick, since this is the northern limit for *both* butternuts and wild grapes.

There is one other possible literary reference to Vinland in the form of a line on the Hønen Runestone from Norderhov, Norway (sadly now lost). The line in question reads in a runic inscription in Old Norse: '*Vínlandi á ísa*' ('from Vinland over ice'). However, it may be better interpreted as representing: '*vindkalda á ísa*' ('over the wind-cold ice').[5] Either way, it does not give us a geographical fix on the actual location of the Vinland mentioned in the thirteenth-century sagas.

What seems clear, though, is that other evidence for Norse activity in North America is either a hoax or based on material (i.e. coins) that reached North America long after the Viking Age and tells us nothing about the places visited by real Norse explorers centuries earlier. It seems that, later, some settlers of Scandinavian origin (for example, in Minnesota) were so keen to publicise their Scandinavian roots – and celebrate earlier medieval connections to their new home – that some of them fabricated 'evidence' in order to proclaim it. The Kensington Runestone, from Minnesota, is in this category. However, we may surmise that in the future further, legitimate archaeological evidence for Norse settlement on the eastern seaboard will be revealed and this will add to the persuasive evidence already amassed from L'Anse aux Meadows.

The evidence for Norse mythology: literature

Most of what we know about Norse myths comes from two later medieval sources: the thirteenth-century *Prose Edda* and the *Poetic Edda*.[6] The term 'Edda' may be derived either from the Old Norse word *óðr* (poetry) or the name of a character found in one of the poems in the *Poetic Edda* or from the Latin *edo* (I compose). Its use in the titles of these two collections is due to terminology employed by later scholars. These two sources tell us most of what we now know about Norse mythology. The clues found in *skaldic* poetry, sagas and place names will also be assessed and compared with the evidence in the *Eddas*. For Norse legends, we depend on sagas, again mostly from thirteenth-century Iceland.

The *Prose Edda* (also known as *Snorra Edda* or the *Younger Edda)* is widely believed to have been written by Snorri Sturluson, an Icelandic chieftain, in the early thirteenth century. Snorri is also the author of *Heimskringla* (*Circle of the World*), a collection of sagas about the Norwegian kings. These sagas contain a large amount of skaldic poetry – especially skaldic praise poetry – and are an important source for this type of poetry. Skaldic poetry is one of the two main forms of Old Norse poetry and is a highly complicated poetic form usually reserved for writing historical or praise poems. Unlike other forms of poetry from this period, skaldic verse is very much attributable to specific poets or *skalds*. Skaldic poetry makes extensive use of *kennings*, which are a poetic tool whereby figurative language is used in place of a more concrete single-word noun. These figurative compounds often contain references to the Norse mythological world. Snorri also makes reference to a large number of kennings and explains their origins in his *Edda*.

The *Prose Edda* was written in Icelandic and is unusual for early medieval treaties on poetry in that it is written in the vernacular and is also about poetry that itself was written in the vernacular. There are seven surviving manuscripts. Of these, six are from the Middle Ages and the seventh dates from around 1600. None of these manuscripts is the same, with each having different variations, and all of them to some extent are incomplete. The four main manuscripts are: the *Codex Upsaliensis*, *Codex Regius*, *Codex Wormianus* and *Codex Trajectinus*.

The first three of the four main manuscripts were composed in the fourteenth century. The *Codex Upsaliensis* is the oldest surviving manuscript and was written in the early fourteenth century. This manuscript has the only reference to the title of the first part of the *Prose Edda*, *Gylfaginning* (*The Tricking of Gylfi*) in Old Norse, which we will later come across as we explore the myths. It is also an illustrated text. The *Codex Regius* is a little later and was written in the first half of the fourteenth century. It is the most complete of the four manuscripts, and seems the closest to the original. For this reason, it is used as the basis for most editions and translations of the *Prose Edda*. The *Codex Wormianus* was written in the mid-fourteenth century. This manuscript also contains several other pieces of work on poetics including the *First Grammatical Treatise*, which is a twelfth-century work on the phonology of Old Norse, and *The List of Rig*, which is an Eddic poem. The sixteenth-century *Codex Trajectinus* is the final manuscript and is a copy of an earlier thirteenth-century manuscript.

The *Poetic Edda* is a collection of anonymous Old Norse poems that focus on Norse mythology and the Germanic heroic world. These are all Eddic poems – the second main form of Old Norse poetry. This poetic form is generally looser than skaldic verse, although it does employ alliterative verse and some kennings. The majority of Eddic poems are contained in the *Codex Regius* and many of the poems it contains are only found in this manuscript. The *Prose Edda* does quote some of these poems – such as *The Seeress' Prophecy* – but these are only fragments and do not feature the poems in their entirety. Although this manuscript was not written until the 1270s in Iceland, it is widely accepted that it records poems from before the conversion to Christianity. However, these poems can be very difficult to date, particularly in relation to each other, and it has also proved difficult to ascertain exactly where they were originally composed.[7]

Another source of Old Norse poetry is 'manuscript AM 748 I 4to',[8] which is a fourteenth-century vellum manuscript containing a number of poems, including *Baldr's Dream*. Other than *Baldr's Dream*, the other poems it contains are also found in the *Codex Regius*.

Finally, a rich source of Old Norse literature is the *sagas*.[9] The Norse sagas are generally classified using titles that indicate their thematic content: 'The Kings' Sagas'; 'Sagas of Icelanders'; 'Short Tales of Icelanders'; 'Contemporary Sagas'; 'Legendary Sagas'; 'Chivalric Sagas'; 'Saints' Sagas'; and 'Bishops' Sagas'. These were written in Iceland and are mainly in prose, although some of them do contain both skaldic and Eddic poetry embedded in the text. Apart from the 'Legendary Sagas', such as *The Saga of the Volsungs*, these are often realistic and at least loosely based on real individuals living in Iceland. They feature tales about the migration to Iceland, early Viking voyages and raids, and feuds and disputes in Iceland. The characters in these stories are often very human in their portrayal and, despite the extreme situations they find themselves in, relatable. As we will see, they include some legendary material that appears later in this book.

The evidence for Norse mythology: archaeology

Archaeology can be used to compare the evidence from Viking Age graves, carvings and artefacts with the picture that we get of Norse beliefs from the later written evidence. So, we find 'Thor's hammers' used as pendants across Scandinavia and in Britain;[10] birds accompany a mounted warrior (possibly Odin and his ravens?) on decorated Vendel-style helmets unearthed in Sweden;[11] an amulet in the shape of a woman carries a drinking horn (a valkyrie?) from Öland, Sweden;[12] a warrior struggles with two bears on a bronze plaque from Torslunda, Sweden, which may also show human-animal hybrids;[13] a carving of Odin's eight-legged horse, Sleipnir, comes from Gotland;[14] there are elite ship burials in Norway, Sweden and the British Isles; sacrifices of animals and occasionally of people have been found. All of these echo themes found in the later written myths and corroborate something of what they reveal about Norse beliefs in the Viking Age.

In a similar way, runestones from Denmark, Sweden and Norway reveal beliefs through the pictures engraved on them, as well as in the brief runic messages carved on them. Runes revealing religious beliefs, and belief in magic, have also been found cut into bone, on weapons and other items. From these the names of gods and religious practices can be compared with the ideas recorded in the literature. However, while there clearly is evidence for common beliefs across a wide 'Norse culture area', we should not expect uniformity, as the beliefs were not codified or policed by a common religious hierarchy.

Other surviving clues

Early Anglo-Saxon settlers originally worshipped similar gods to other groups of north-west Germanics and Scandinavians and so religious beliefs beyond the Scandinavian homelands can be traced and compared. While names differed slightly (Old Norse *Odin* and *Thor* appear in Old English as *Woden* and *Thunor*), there is a general assumption that the beliefs were similar across the northern world; although it must be admitted that our evidence for Anglo-Saxon pagan beliefs is thin. Nevertheless, aspects of these northern beliefs can still be identified outside Scandinavia: from the English words for 'thunder' and 'Thursday' (both containing the Old English form of the Old Norse name Thor) and Wednesday (meaning 'Woden/Odin's day'), to place names that record the worship of these Scandinavian deities in England, such as the name of the Wansdyke (Woden/Odin's dyke) earthwork in Wiltshire and the many Grim's Ditches (formed from the word *grima*, 'the masked one', another name for Woden/Odin).

In the ninth century, invading Vikings reintroduced their form of these gods to England and elsewhere until they later converted to Christianity. As a consequence, there are scenes illustrating Odin's fight with the wolf at Ragnarok (the end of the world) carved on a cross from Kirk Andreas, Isle of Man; Thor fishing for the Midgard serpent is carved on a standing cross at Gosforth, Cumbria, which also seems to be decorated with a valkyrie; Regin forging Sigurd's sword and Sigurd roasting the dragon's heart can be seen on a stone cross from Halton, Lancashire.[15] Anglo-Saxon written sources also refer to the raven-banners, which represented the companions of Odin and which also appear in the Viking myths, and were carried by Viking armies.[16]

Across the Viking diaspora from Sweden to Iceland, the names of Norse gods and goddesses – as well as references to elves, dwarfs and dragons – appear in the landscape. These reveal the way that these beliefs influenced the outlook and the 'mental maps' of farming communities and can be compared with the documentary evidence to form a more rounded picture of Viking Age beliefs.

However, it is from the *written* traditions – most first recorded in thirteenth-century Iceland – that we get the detail regarding these earlier myths; and the retelling of these stories is the aim of this book.

2

The impact of Christianity
on Norse mythology

T HE WRITING DOWN of Norse mythology occurred princi-
pally in the thirteenth century, in Iceland, when Snorri
Sturluson compiled his *Prose Edda*; and it was then that the
Poetic Edda was also written down, mainly in the *Codex
Regius*.[17] This work was done by practising Christians in a
country which had officially been Christian for over 200 years.
It is therefore possible to debate how much this is an accurate
representation of pre-conversion beliefs and how much we are
viewing Norse mythology through a medieval Christian lens.
The key point is that none of the evidence for Norse mythology and Norse religion was written down by believers who
lived in the Viking Age.[18] The same, of course, is similarly true
for all our evidence for Celtic mythology and also for Anglo-
Saxon pre-Christian beliefs. The Vikings are not alone in
having their beliefs later recorded by those who no longer
subscribed to them.

The work and ideology of Snorri Sturluson

Snorri Sturluson's *Edda* was composed as a textbook for the traditional art of writing skaldic poetry. His *Edda* addresses the content, style and metres of traditional Viking poetry and due to that is also greatly concerned with pre-Christian mythology. The Norse mythological stories are mainly found in the section entitled *The Tricking of Gylfi*, where we hear about the beginning and the end of the world, as well as various other tales about the gods. The part called *The Language of Poetry* also contains mythological stories as examples to explain the origins of the poetic form called kennings. These stories are based on older, traditional poems and possibly oral prose stories, although the process of oral transmission means that they are likely to have been greatly adapted/corrupted from when they were first composed. It also seems that Snorri himself adapted these stories and – with the addition of his *Prologue* – attempted to neutralise them to make this pagan past acceptable to a Christian present.

Snorri outlines his attitude towards the pagan past in his *Prologue* and uses it to set the mythology within the social context of his day, basing it 'on a historical interpretation rather than an ideological or mythical one'.[19] The beginning of the *Prologue* reads very similarly to Genesis and he then goes on to discuss how God became neglected by mankind. The *Prologue* then moves to highlight a belief in animism or natural religion whereby those who had not been exposed to Christ – due to their predecessors moving away from God – sought to explain creation but were unable to do so due to a lack of divine wisdom. There is a clear distinction made between knowledge of God that had been gleaned through natural observations and that acquired through grace. Despite this, both are presented as heavenly gifts from God and as such it is a sympathetic attempt to record the beliefs of his Viking Age antecedents without prejudice, while still maintaining the false nature of it.

Snorri then moves on to discuss the movement of Odin and his brothers from their homeland of Troy to Scandinavia where they set up their own kingdom. This links the Scandinavian pagan past not only with the biblical past but also back to the classical past, which was socially acceptable within medieval Christian society. The narrative is concerned with the seeming greatness of Odin but he is not portrayed as a warrior-god but as an ancient man to whom people wrongly began to offer worship and sacrifices. In contrast to this central role of Odin in the *Prologue*, the character of Thor is neutralised in both the *Prologue* and in *Ynglinga Saga*, which is also thought to have been written by Snorri. Thor is placed in the genealogy in a way that diminishes his importance compared to that of Odin. Since Thor was seen as a counter-force to Christ by many Christian missionaries, it may be that, as Odin was less powerful and potent in the mind, then it was safer to promote him as an analogue to Christ. As we will explore in later chapters, the way the beginning of the world is presented in *The Tricking of Gylfi* seems to suggest that Snorri adapted the traditions to make them more familiar to a Christian audience.[20]

In *The Language of Poetry*, Snorri discusses the pagan past in relation to the kennings used within skaldic poetry and to provide the readers of his treatise with an understanding of where the origins of these kennings lay. Despite the initial references to the Æsir as gods at the beginning of *The Language of Poetry*, Snorri employs 'euhemerism', where the pre-Christian gods are explained as transformed by later traditions from what were originally just powerful humans, to make them more socially acceptable and to reduce their potency. He justifies the telling of the myths as giving examples and explanations, and suggests that these stories should not be viewed as mythology but rather understood so that they can be used in poetry. He references the telling of the stories with the quoting of verse from various major poets. The implication is that these stories may not be true but that it was still socially acceptable to use them within poetics as it is an ancient, traditional form of oral communication that has been used by a long line of poets before him. He demonstrates a strong defence of the poetic tradition yet he cannot and does not want to promote it as a belief system. This shows the intellectual balance that Snorri needed to achieve.[21] It is this emphasis on the kennings rather than mythology itself that helps to remove its sting: Snorri's *Edda* is not a catalogue of pre-Christian mythology; instead, it is a treatise on poetry, which is heavily reliant on pagan mythology and which adapts and uses it for his own polemic purposes.[22] This means that he has no problem with denying the authenticity of the stories as the stories are not his primary concern. Nevertheless, for later readers he provides an insight into the earlier Norse mythology.

Evidence from Adam of Bremen

Although most of the information about Norse mythology comes to us through either the *Prose* or the *Poetic Edda*, information about the way the gods were worshipped comes through a number of other, different, sources. Adam of Bremen, a German chronicler and monk writing in the second half of the eleventh century, records gods named Thor, Wotan (Odin) and Frikko (Freyr) being worshipped at the temple at Uppsala.[23] Interestingly, though, it is Thor rather than Odin who is recorded as the chief god. Odin is also depicted mainly as a god of war rather than a god of poetry that we see in the later sources. This trio of gods ties in with the writings of the Roman historian Tacitus, from the first-century AD, although he uses Roman names: Hercules, Mercury and Mars (the last more often thought to equate with the Norse god Tyr).[24]

Possible Christian influence on the sagas

In the sagas, there are several characters who have particular devotions to different gods. One of these is the main character, named Hrafnkell, in *Hrafnkell's Saga*. This character is so dedicated to the god Freyr that he is nicknamed *Freysgoði* or Freyr's chieftain. Not all characters have such a firm devotion to one god and, in *Egill's Saga*, Egill Skallagrímsson 'converts' from Thor to Odin. This may, though, be coloured by Christian ideas of devotion to one particular God.

A contemporary voice?

In the absence of native, written records from the age of conversion, skaldic poetry offers us the closest it is possible to get to the thoughts and feelings of those who lived through the Viking period. However, in a pre-literate society, oral tradition and transmission was the only way to preserve verses and this means that the skaldic verse that has been preserved had undergone many stages of transmission before it was written down in the form that it currently is in. Although the tight, metrical rules favoured the accurate memorisation and passing down of skaldic stanzas, the manuscripts give plentiful evidence of corruption and variation. This means that we cannot take for granted that the verses that we have are the original utterances of the skalds (poets), although it does seem likely that in most cases we are getting the general sense of what the original skald said. The work of the skalds is often concerned with the lives and deeds of great men and, once the complex kennings are stripped away, the verses often amount to little more than 'the king is a good warrior who has killed many men'. However, what is of particular interest with regard to the preservation of original mythology lies in the kennings themselves, as it is often within these that clues can be found about both the pagan religion and the faith of the convert kings.

All of this means that having a truly accurate picture of what eighth-, ninth- and tenth-century Scandinavians believed is very difficult to achieve. The best evidence comes from the poetry – both Eddic and skaldic – but even with this the years of oral transmission mean it is hard to know whether it has survived completely intact. As we will see in the *Seeress' Prophecy*, even in one of the most well-known Old Norse poems, there can be parts of the poem that seem to have a later Christian interpolation.[25] What is consistent across all the sources, however, are the names of the gods and we can be fairly certain that these were the gods that the people of early medieval Scandinavia worshipped, even if we cannot be completely certain of the exact belief system. And the stories, though transmitted through Christian writers, still provide significant amounts of information concerning traditions associated with these gods and goddesses.

Part One: Norse Myths

3

The origins of the world

FOUND IN THE collection of Norse myths known as the *Prose Edda*, and particularly in the section called *The Tricking of Gylfi*, there are many tales of the adventures of the Norse gods and giants from the beginning of life to the building of the bridge Bifrost, between Asgard and earth.

The purpose of *The Tricking of Gylfi* seems to be to provide a background for the accounts of the kennings (usually compounding two words to indirectly describe an object), which are found in *The Language of Poetry*, another section of the *Prose Edda*. The nature of the gods and their presentation is very different from that in the *Prologue* of the *Prose Edda*. While in the *Prologue* the characters of Odin and Thor are presented simply as grandiose humans, in the main body of *The Tricking of Gylfi* they – along with many others – are repeatedly and clearly referred to as gods and are firmly separated from the realms of humanity. In addition, the compiler, Snorri, was seeking to explain most, though not all, of the Norse mythology. He collected information about different topics and placed them in roughly chronological order triggered by questions. The presentation of these stories by Snorri seems to suggest that he adapted them to make them more familiar to a Christian audience. Snorri refers to Odin as 'All-Father' to provide a synchronisation between paganism and Christianity, something which is later reinforced by the description of him as living through all the ages and ruling all the kingdoms. The three speakers can be seen to represent the Trinity. Calling them 'High One', 'As High' and the one on the highest throne 'Third' can be seen to imply a sense of unity and equality that is a defining feature of the Christian Trinity. The names of all three of the speakers are also given as names for Odin in the lists of Norse poetic synonyms known as *heiti*, and this seems to confirm the sense of unity attributed to these three characters.

The Tricking of Gylfi is punctuated throughout with Eddic poetry. This is reminiscent of the poetic forms found in the version of the mythology known as the *Poetic Edda*. The prose version is based upon the stories outlined in the poetry. Although by no means the only source, the largest source of this poetry is *The Seeress' Prophecy*, found in the *Poetic Edda*. Although similar in many ways to *The Seeress' Prophecy*, there are several differences in the presentation of the information and Snorri seems to have been trying to draw it more into line with Christian ideology. However, despite some similarities between biblical stories and the mythological tales, the vast majority of them are completely at odds with Christian teaching and the actions of the gods are not at all 'God-like' in the Christian sense of the word. Odin is neither omnipotent nor omniscient; he has to sacrifice his eye in order to gain wisdom; and he is powerless to prevent his own total destruction by

Fenrir the wolf. As such, he is greatly diminished in comparison with Christ, who transcends death. In this way, the purpose of the account was clearly to diminish pagan beliefs even as they were being retold.

* * *

The tricking of King Gylfi of Sweden and the creation of Zealand

Long ago in the land that we now call Sweden, there lived a king named Gylfi. One of the stories about him tells how once a wandering woman came to his court and seduced him. As a reward, King Gylfi granted her a piece of land in his kingdom. The land was as much as could be ploughed with four oxen over one day and one night. It was to be her 'ploughland'. Now, this wandering woman was no ordinary mortal. Instead, she was one of the divine Æsir. She was called Gefion and she was married to a giant. She went to the north, to Giantland, and there she selected four strong oxen to do her ploughing. These were no ordinary oxen for they were in fact her sons whom she had transformed, and they were half-giant, half-Æsir. These great oxen pulled the plough with such strength that it sliced deeply into the land and broke its connection to the earth beneath it. As a result, it was dragged away into the sea by the oxen that were pulling the plough. Away to the west they hauled it, until at last it came to rest in a large inlet of the sea. Gefion halted the oxen there and called the land that had been planted in the sea Zealand, meaning 'sea-land'. A great hole in the ground had been left in the place from which that land had been uprooted and this filled with water to become Lake Mälaren in Sweden. It can still be seen today that the bays of the lake are the same shape as the headlands of Zealand and this bears witness to how the lake was formed long ago.

The story of Gefion was known to the poet Bragi the Old who composed a verse that reminded his listeners that,

> Gefion happily took from Gylfi a great piece of land
> And the steaming oxen made of it a part of Denmark.
> Each of the oxen had eight eyes and four heads
> And the land they stole was rich in meadows.

Now, King Gylfi was intelligent and also a magician. He was astonished at the way that the Æsir always got their own way and he wondered why this was so. He asked himself: was this because of their own skills and ability or were the gods particularly favourable to them? He was determined to discover the answer and so he decided to travel to Asgard, the home of the gods. He decided to go in secret and in order to do this he took on the appearance of an old man. But the Æsir had the gift of prophecy and were able to outwit him. They knew that he was coming and were determined to trick him; not all would be as he perceived it to be! For the Æsir would meet him in various disguises.

King Gylfi in Asgard: the questions posed by 'The Wanderer'

When the old wandering man – who was of course King Gylfi – at last reached Asgard, he was amazed at its size and its grandeur. But what impressed him the most was the great hall that stood in the centre of the city. It was called Valhalla, which means 'hall of the slain', though some say its name means 'shield-hall'.

As he approached the hall, his attention was caught by a man standing there who was juggling – but doing this with seven knives. The knife-juggling man asked King Gylfi his name. Now King Gylfi did not wish to give himself away so he replied that his name was 'The Wanderer', though some say his name was 'Way-weary' but it means much the same. He said that he had been long on the road and asked if he could shelter for the night and whose hall it was at which he was seeking shelter? To this question the knife-juggler replied that it was the hall of their king. But with regard to the king's name, the traveller should ask that himself.

As Gylfi was led into the hall he noted that it was spacious with a great many chambers and that those within were engaged in many activities from gaming and drinking to fighting each other in combat. Seeing his curiosity, the knife-juggler warned him that he was to proceed with great caution when he entered a room for he would not be able to predict whether an enemy was lurking within or not.

As last Gylfi came upon three thrones with three men seated on them and the thrones were ranked one above the other. At this sight Gylfi asked his companion the name of the king of this hall and was told that the one who sat on the lowest throne was the one and his name was 'High One'; another was named 'As High' and the third (who sat on the topmost throne) was named 'Third'. Gylfi asked the king named 'High One' if there were wise and knowledgeable people living in the hall. 'High One' replied that there were indeed but that it would cost Gylfi if he turned out to be less knowledgeable that the ones whom he questioned.

Who is greatest of the gods?

Undeterred by this warning, Gylfi asked his first question: 'Which god is the highest and most ancient of all gods and goddesses?' To this, 'High One' replied that this most ancient god was the one known as 'All-Father' but that in Asgard he was known by twelve other names.

Then Gylfi asked his second question: 'Where is the dwelling place of this god and what works and wonders has he performed that demonstrate his power?' To this, 'High One' replied that the 'All-Father' was alive in all ages and rules over every living thing. To this, the man on the second throne – who was named 'As High' – added that this ancient god made all that exists and everything that lives whether it be on the earth, flies in the sky or in any other realm. When he had added this, the one named 'Third' spoke up and told Gylfi that the greatest work of the ancient god 'All-Father' was the creation of people and the spirit within each person. It was this spirit that would outlive the body of mortals, which was doomed to decay. Of these mortals, those who were worthy would go on to live with 'All-Father' after they died, in the place known as Gimle, the most beautiful place on earth. On the other hand, the wicked would be condemned to Hel and Niflhel, which was located in the ninth-world.

Then Gylfi asked his third question: 'What did All-Father do and where did he live before the making of all things?' To this question, he was given the reply that 'All-Father' then lived among the frost-giants.

The origins of the frost-giants and of Odin

Then Gylfi asked his fourth question: 'When and how did all things come into being and what existed before this?' To this, the one named 'High One' answered that this was before time or anything else existed. There was then simply a great void and no life.

To this, the one named 'As High' added that before earth was made, there came into existence the place called Niflheim with a great spring at its centre and from this flowed ten rivers. Near this was Hel-gates. The one called 'Third' explained that before earth existed there was to the south a flaming region called Muspell and from this place, at the end of the world, would come Surt who would defeat the gods and burn up all things with fire.

Then Gylfi asked his fifth question: 'How were things before people grew in numbers?' To this the speakers, combined, told him of great poisonous rivers encrusted with ice and from which vapours rose. The northern part of this was covered in thick ice while the southern part melted with the heat from Muspell. At the point where ice and heat met, there the melting drops took on the form of a man and his name was Ymir. He was a frost-giant and from him are descended all the frost-giants. These frost-giants remembered their ancestor Ymir with their own name for him and this name was Aurgelmir.

Then Gylfi asked his sixth question: 'How did other people come into being and was Ymir one of the gods?' To this, the one named 'High One' answered that Ymir was not a god but that he and all frost-giants were evil. Ymir sweated while he slept and from his sweat under his left arm there was formed a male and a female; and a son grew from the sweat of his legs and it was from these that the race of frost-giants came.

Then Gylfi asked a seventh question: 'Where did Ymir live and on what did he eat?' To which he received the reply that when the ice continued to melt and drip it formed a great cow, whose name was Audhumla, and from its udder there flowed four rivers of milk. These fed the giant Ymir.

Then Gylfi asked his eighth question: 'What did the cow feed on?' The answer that he received explained the origins of the god Odin, for he was told that the cow licked salty rocks, and from those melting rocks appeared a man named Buri. From Buri's son – who married a giantess – came three sons. And the eldest was called Odin the other two were named Vili and Ve. Odin and his brothers became rulers of all that is.

The making and structure of the universe

Now Gylfi thought about these different races that had come into being in ancient times: the frost-giant descendants of Ymir and the god-descendants of Buri who had appeared when the cow licked the salty rocks. Gylfi wondered how these ancient races got along. The answer that he received was that Odin and his brothers killed the frost-giant Ymir and from his body there flowed so much blood that it drowned all the other frost-giants, except one who escaped with his family and servants. And so the race of frost-giants continued. After Ymir was killed, his body was taken by Odin and his brothers and from his body they made the earth; from his blood the sea and all the lakes; from his bones the rocks; and from his teeth the tumbled broken pieces of rock that lie on mountainsides. The sea (made from Ymir's blood) surrounded all the earth and confined the earth in the middle of that great sea, that few if any can cross. From Ymir's skull they made the sky, which had four corners and under each corner they set a dwarf. These dwarfs' names were: Austri (which means 'east'), Vestri (which means 'west'), Nordri (which means 'north') and Sudri (which means 'south'). The stars they made from the sparks of fire that burst from Muspell, the place of fire. The clouds they made from Ymir's brain.

Then 'High One' explained that the earth is a great circle and beyond it lies the great sea. The giants live on the shore of that great sea but they are prevented from entering the other places of the earth because a great hedge was established that was made from the eyelashes of Ymir. That mighty hedge is named Midgard, that is the 'middle enclosure' or, as some call it, 'Middle Earth'. This is the place where people live. The first people were made by Odin and his two brothers from pieces of wood they found on the seashore. A man was formed from this wood and named Ask; a woman was formed and named Embla. Each one of Odin and his brothers gave gifts to these newly formed people: one gave life; the second gave consciousness and movement; the third gave speech, hearing and sight.

In the centre of the world was formed Asgard, within which the gods and goddesses made their home. Within Asgard, Odin set up his throne, with his wife named Frigg. From them the divine family of the Æsir are descended. That is why Odin is known as 'All-Father', for he is father of all gods and men. The first god to be born was Thor, who was extremely strong and could overcome all living things.

Odin All-Father made Day and Night. Night was the daughter of a giant and she was dark in colour. She had three husbands in succession and the last was Delling of the Æsir. From their marriage a son was born whose name was Day and who was bright and attractive in appearance because he was half-Æsir. Odin All-Father took Night and Day and gave each a chariot drawn by horses. And as they rode across the sky they gave rise to day and night. From Night's horse, Hrimfaxi, the saliva dripping from his bit forms the dew. From Day's horse, Skinfaxi, light streams forth from his mane.

Sun, Moon, the bridge Bifrost and the end of all things

Hearing all of this, Gylfi, who is known as 'The Wanderer', mused on the origins of the sun and moon and how they are kept in their course. Then 'High One' explained that Moon and Sun were children of a man named Mundilfaeri. Moon was his son and Sun was his daughter. Because the gods considered their father arrogant they seized his children and put them in the sky. There Sun drives the chariot that is day and Moon guides the moon through the night.

Sun rides fast across the sky because she is pursued by a great and terrible wolf named Skoll. And another wolf, named Hati Hrodvitnisson, pursues Moon. And one day they will catch them both. These wolves are from the forest named Iron-wood, where lives a terrible giantess – a trollwife – whose giant sons are all in wolf-shape. From this family of giant-wolves will come one who will drink the blood from all who die and will go on to consume the heavenly bodies and cast blood across all of the sky. On that day the sun will cease to shine.

At that time, destruction will come out of Muspell, the place of fire. Riding on horses, those who advance from Muspell will break the bridge that connects heaven and earth. That bridge is called Bifrost and is seen in the rainbow. It was well made by the gods but it will break when the sons of Muspell ride out, for nothing that exists will be able to withstand them.

4

The order of things

FOUND IN THE collection known as the *Prose Edda*, and in a section called *The Tricking of Gylfi*, these stories tell of the courts of the gods, the structure of the universe, the nature of fate and the hierarchy of the gods. The *Poetic Edda* also contains a poem, called *The List of Rig*, which gives a complementary supernatural explanation for the origins of the human social order.

In *The List of Rig*, a god called Rig creates the three different classes of mankind – Thrall, Farmer and Lord. In Old Norse, the word *thrall* (*þræll*) was used to describe a slave. In Old English the corresponding term was *theow* (*þēow*). The poem is found in the fourteenth-century *Codex Wormianus*, which also contains a copy of Snorri Sturluson's *Prose Edda*. The name Rig is likely to come from the Irish word for king, *Ri*. This may suggest that the Old Norse poet spent some time in the Viking kingdoms of the Irish Sea region. It is even possible that the poem was originally Celtic in origin due to this use of the name Rig. Rig is often assumed to be an alias for the god Heimdall, but this association is not completely certain. The identification with Heimdall is not found within the poem itself but, rather, in the prose introduction, which was added when the *Codex Wormianus* was written in the fourteenth century. The poem *The Seeress' Prophecy* refers to the 'offspring of Heimdall' in its opening line and this would also seem to suggest a role for Heimdall in the creation of mankind. It may therefore be that the later fourteenth-century prose introduction is trying to marry the two traditions and to create a single coherent narrative from the two. This may represent the intention of the original writer of *The List of Rig* or it may be the imposition of a later idea on the earlier work. Heimdall was the watchman for the gods and other traditions located his residence as being near the bridge Bifrost, linking Asgard (home of the gods) with Midgard (Middle Earth).

It is interesting to note that 'King', who emerges at the end of the poem, is the youngest son of 'Lord' and is marked out by his knowledge of runes and his relationship with Rig. This raises the idea of a king who is chosen by the gods rather than a simple father–son succession. This assertion of the divine origins of kingship may represent an ideology rooted in pagan Viking Age concepts. Alternatively, since the idea of divinely sanctioned kingship is one often found in medieval European Christian societies, it may represent a later Christian reworking of the earlier mythological material.

* * *

The journey of King Gylfi

King Gylfi of Sweden went to Asgard, the home of the gods, in order to discover the secrets of the Æsir. While there he asked many questions of three mysterious rulers named 'High One', 'As High' and 'Third'. Because Gylfi did not wish to give himself away, he said that his name was 'The Wanderer'. And it was in this guise that he sought out the secrets of the Æsir.

He first discovered how the universe came into being, how the frost-giants, the gods and people were created. He learned how the various parts of the universe were structured and how they would one day come to an end in terrible violence. He then went on to discover how society was organised and ordered within the universe that had come into being through the actions of fire and ice and the interaction of gods and frost-giants.

The temple, court and metalworking in Asgard

Odin, known as 'All-Father', appointed rulers to govern Asgard and also the fate of people. Together they then built a huge temple in the centre of Asgard, in the place called Gladsheim. In this temple stood thirteen thrones: one for Odin and twelve for his associates. Its appearance both inside and out was made gleaming by gold. As well as Gladsheim, they built a hall in which the goddesses lived. This was known as Vingolf.

After this, they established forges and metalworking equipment with which they made all the other tools that they required. They went on to be craftsmen in all kinds of materials: stone, wood and metal, and were goldsmiths who made all the furniture and every utensil out of gold. It was a golden age.

Soon that golden age would be challenged by the arrival of women from Giantland but first the gods established their thrones and the courts over which they ruled, and they first debated among themselves the fate of the dwarfs.

When the world had been made, the earth had been formed from the flesh of the giant Ymir. In that flesh living creatures had appeared in the same way that maggots appear in rotting meat. It was the decision of the gods, sitting in the temple of Gladsheim, that these beings should gain thought and the appearance of men but that they should remain inhabitants of earth and rocks. This was the origin of the dwarfs. The first dwarf was named Motsognir and the second was named Durin. Some dwarfs lived in the soil and some lived in the rocks.

The ash tree Yggdrasil

The holiest place of the gods of Asgard was centred on the ash tree known as Yggdrasil. It was there that they held court. That tree is biggest of all trees and its branches extend across the whole world. Of its roots, three support it and are of great length.

One of the roots of Yggdrasil grows into the realm ruled by the gods of the Æsir.

Another of its roots grows into the land of the frost-giants. Beneath this root there is Mimir's Well. Its water contains wisdom and knowledge and the master of that well, Mimir, is wise because he drinks from the well. Odin All-Father went there and for a single drink gave up one of his eyes as payment.

The third root grows deep into Niflheim. Beneath that root lies the bubbling and boiling spring of Hvergelmir [this is the source of many rivers]. There the dragon Nidhogg gnaws at this root of the tree. This third root extends far – into heaven – and another well lies beneath it. This is the very holy well of Weird. The gods hold court there and each day the gods of the Æsir ride to that place over the bridge Bifrost, which links heaven and earth. The best horse that Odin rides is eight-legged Sleipnir. Ten other horses he also owns. But the horse that once belonged to the god Baldr was burned when he was cremated. The god Thor walks to where the court is held, wading rivers to reach there.

The maidens who shape the fate of men

The red in the rainbow is the fire that burns on the bridge called Bifrost (that links earth to heaven). Otherwise the frost-giants and the mountain-giants could cross it. Protected on the other side are the beautiful places of heaven. One of the most beautiful places is a hall that stands beside the ash tree, Yggdrasil. In that hall live three maidens named Weird, Verdandi and Skuld. These are the norns and they shape the fates of people. Other norns visit each person when they are born to shape the course of their lives. The norns are drawn from three types of being: some are divine and are of the Æsir; some are elves; and the third group are drawn from the dwarfs. Good norns shape the destiny of those whose lives turn out well, while evil norns shape the destiny of those who experience misfortune in their lives.

The norns live beneath the ash tree and in its branches there sits an eagle who has knowledge of many things and, what is more, between the eyes of the eagle sits a hawk named Vedrfolnir. Up and down the trunk of the ash tree runs a squirrel named Ratatosk. He carries messages of ill will between the eagle and the dragon, Nidhogg. That is not all that troubles the ash tree. Four stags run in its branches and eat its leaves. These are named: Dain, Dvalin, Duneyr and Durathror. In addition, there are huge numbers of snakes living around the dragon, Nidhogg, who eats away the ash tree from below. Not only this, but one side of the tree is also rotting.

To try to save the ash tree, the norns that live beside Weird's Well draw water from it every day and also mud that is around the well and pour it over the ash tree in order to protect its branches from decay. The water from that well is so holy that it makes white anything that comes into contact with it. Furthermore, the dew that falls from the tree is sweet like honey and bees feed on it. Two swans also feed there, in the well itself, and from them are descended all the swans that exist.

The other amazing sites found in the realm of the gods

In the realm of the gods there are many amazing places. One, called Alfheim, is the home of the 'light elves'. The 'light elves' are bright in appearance, bright like the sun, and this is reflected in their nature. Beneath the ground, in contrast, live the 'dark elves'. These are blacker than pitch and this is reflected in their nature, too.

Other fair palaces are Breidablik and Glitnir; the last one is made from red gold and it has a roof shingled in silver. Another palace that is roofed in silver is Valaskialf, which is a palace of Odin's and in that place sits his throne that is called Hlidskialf. From that throne, Odin All-Father can see across the whole world. Even greater is the palace known as Gimle; it shines brighter than the sun and it shall survive the eventual destruction of heaven and earth when that occurs. Those who die and are good will go to live in that enduring place.

Gimle will survive the destruction of heaven and earth because there are other heavens beyond that in which the gods now live. One, called Andlang, lies south of and above the one lived in by the gods and yet another, called Vidblain, lies above it. It is in this third heaven that Gimle is situated and for now only 'light-elves' live in these places.

There is more to say about the order of things. From the north of heaven comes the source of all wind, when the giant eagle, Hraesvelg, flaps his wings. And with regard to the origins of summer and winter: the summer is born from its father, Svasud, and winter is born from Vindloni, the stern and cold-hearted one.

The ordering of the society of the Æsir

There are in number twelve divine Æsir. Of these Odin is the highest. Other gods submit to him as children submit to their father. For this reason, he is known as the 'All-Father'. He is married to Frigg, who knows the fate of all people. Odin is also the father of warriors slain in battle and it is his decision as to where they shall live in Valhalla. For this reason, he is also called 'father of the killed'. He is also known as 'god of the hanged' and 'god of prisoners' and 'god of cargoes'. And by many other names. These reflect the names by which he is known by different people in the world.

Below Odin stands Thor. He is the most outstanding of the other gods. Called 'Thor of the Æsir', he is stronger than any other god or man. His hall, which is called Bilskirnir, is located in Thrudvangar. This hall is larger than any other and has a great many chambers. Thor travels in a chariot that is drawn by two goats. These goats are named Tanngniost and Tanngrisnir.

Thor is also known for three of his possessions. The first is his hammer, Miollnir, the skull-smasher. Well do the frost-giants and the mountain-giants know it! Second is a girdle, which doubles his strength whenever he puts it on. The third and last is a pair of iron gloves that he wears whenever he wields his hammer. Of Thor, many stories are told.

Among the Æsir there are many other gods and goddesses too. Odin's second son (Thor being his first) is Baldr. Handsome and shining with bright light, he is praised by all. His eyelashes are so white that there is a white plant named after them. Though he is the wisest of the Æsir and merciful and speaks well, nothing that he pronounces ever comes to pass. In his home, Breidablik, there is nothing impure.

Another of the gods is Niord, god of wind, sea and fire. To him, in his home in Noatun, are offered prayers by those going on a journey or venturing out onto the sea to fish. Niord is not himself of the race of the Æsir. Rather, he is of the Vanir, and he was given as a hostage to the Æsir as part of the truce that brought peace between the Æsir and the Vanir. His wife is Skadi who is a giantess. Skadi wanted to live in the mountains, but Niord preferred his home by the sea. To resolve this, they divided their time between these two places; though Niord said he was disturbed by the howling wolves in the mountains and Skadi complained she was disturbed by the shrieking of the seagulls on the coast. So unhappy was Skadi that she left the seaside and went to live in the mountains, which is why she is known as 'ski-lady'. Left behind on the coast, Niord then had two children: Freyr, the ruler of rain, sun and what grows on the earth; and Freyia, who chooses half of all warriors killed in battle – the other half are taken to Odin's hall – and drives a chariot drawn by two cats. Those seeking peace and prosperity pray to Freyr; while people pray to Freyia about love. High-born ladies are called by a title that comes from her name.

Another god is Tyr. He is the warrior-god, courageous and prayed to by those going into battle. Those warriors most skilful in the arts of war are called after him ('Tyr-courageous'). Due to his wisdom, wise men are named after him too ('Tyr-wise'). Tyr only has one hand. This is because his other hand was bitten off by the wolf, Fenrir. When the Æsir chained up Fenrir, it was Tyr who placed his hand in the wolf's mouth as a pledge that Fenrir would eventually be released from his chain. When the Æsir did not do so, Fenrir bit off the hand of Tyr. That is why the wrist is now called the 'wolf-joint'.

Another god is Bragi, god of language and poetry. Both men and women who are skilful in speech are named after him ('Brag-man', 'Brag-woman'). His wife, Idunn, is keeper of the apples that the gods eat in order to remain young. Because of this, they will remain youthful until Ragnarok.

Other Æsir are Heimdall the holy, with golden teeth, who was born from nine maiden-sisters. He is watchman for the gods and lives near Bifrost in order to guard it against any mountain-giant who might try to cross the bridge and reach the realm of the gods. His horse is called Gulltop. Sleeping less than a bird, his eyesight is as keen at night as it is during the day and he can see a great distance. So keen are his senses that he can hear grass growing and wool growing on the back of sheep, despite them happening far below him on the earth. His trumpet is called Giallarhorn and its notes ring out so loud that they can be heard everywhere in all the different worlds.

The god Hod was very strong but blind. The gods would rather not talk of him because he did terrible things (unwittingly killing his brother, Baldr, and he was then himself killed in revenge by the god named Vali).

Vidar the silent is almost as strong as Thor and a defender of the causes of the gods, regardless of dangers.

Vali is fearless in combat and the son of Odin and the goddess Rind (a giantess). He is a very good shot with the bow (he avenged Baldr by killing Hod).

Another good shot with the bow and a skilled user of skis is Ull, the step-grandson of Thor. As well as being a fearsome warrior he is also beautiful in appearance. Those facing single combat will pray to Ull for assistance.

Those in legal difficulties pray to Forseti, the son of Baldr and Nanna. His hall is called Glitner, with its walls and pillars fashioned from red gold and its roof shingled in silver. In it he judges legal disputes between the gods and between men.

How the god Heimdall created the different orders of people

In an ancient time, the powerful god named Heimdall, who also goes by the name of Rig, journeyed along the green roads that run across the land. On his way, he called at three houses and while there he gave rise to the succeeding generations of the different social orders of people.

The first house that Heimdall (Rig) came to was lived in by an old couple. They were peasants and they welcomed Heimdall with heavy coarse bread and boiled calf. When night came Heimdall slept between them on their bed. He stayed for three nights and then left. After nine months, the old woman gave birth to a child. He was dark in hair colour and complexion and she named him Thrall. He grew to be strong but ugly and he was skilled in making things for the farm and in labouring. He married a girl whose name was Slave and their children are all those who labour for others as slaves. Their children had names such as Weatherbeaten, Lazy, Grey, Loud-noise and Talker.

The second house that Heimdall came to was lived in by a good-looking, elderly couple. He had a well-trimmed beard and she was dressed in the head-covering and smock of a farmer's wife. He was skilled at turning wood and she was skilled at spinning thread. When night came, Heimdall slept between them on their bed. He stayed for three nights and then left. After nine months, the old woman gave birth to a child. He had a ruddy complexion and she named him Farmer. He grew up skilled in ploughing, working with the cattle and building farmhouses and barns. He married a girl named Daughter-in-Law and they set up home together and their children are all those who farm the land. Their children had names such as Blacksmith, Trimbeard, Fighting-man, Wife and Sensible.

The third house that Heimdall came to was lived in by a handsome couple. The man was skilled with the bow and the lady wore the brooch and blouse of a noblewoman. Her face was bright and her skin was white. They welcomed Heimdall with fine bread and roasted pork and wildfowl. They drank wine together from fine goblets. When night came, Heimdall slept between them on their bed. He stayed for three nights and then left. After nine months, the lady gave birth to a child. He had blond hair and a bright look and she named him Lord.

Lord grew skilful in using the bow and the shield and in riding horses. Heimdall returned and taught him the runes and said that Lord was his son. Lord went on to conquer in war, he killed his enemies and he became overlord of nearby settlements. He grew rich and rewarded warriors. Lord married a girl – the daughter of Chieftain – who was wise and beautiful. Their children had names such as Son, Noble and Descendant. Their youngest son they called King. He knew the runes and had wisdom in many areas of life. He was strong and could understand the language of birds. So skilful did be become in the knowledge and use of runes that he became known by the name of Rig, his grandfather. As King rode through the woods, a crow reminded him that it was his destiny to lead armies and to learn from those who could steer ships and wield swords in war.

5

Loki the trickster and his children

AGAIN FOUND IN the collection known as the *Prose Edda*, and in a section called *The Tricking of Gylfi*, this tells of the trickster god, Loki, and his terrible children. The character of Loki is central to Norse mythology and to the group dynamics of the gods. Loki is the half-brother of Odin and they share the same mother. However, while Odin's father, Bor, was one of the Æsir gods, Loki's father was a giant. This means that Loki enjoys the peculiar distinction of belonging to the worlds of both the gods and the giants, who are natural enemies of each other. It is this uncertainty and conflict between the two sides of Loki's ancestry that contributes to his complex nature. Despite the fact that the poems of the *Poetic Edda* were a major source for Snorri as he compiled the *Prose Edda*, their representations of Loki are not always the same.

Loki is presented in both of the two Eddas as having an evil nature. In *The Seeress' Prophecy*, in the *Poetic Edda*, Loki is described in Old Norse as '*Lægiarnliki Loki*' ('That evil-loving Loki') and this view of Loki as evil fits with the description in *The Tricking of Gylfi*, which says that, 'Loki has a handsome and pleasing appearance, but he is evil in character, and he behaves capriciously'. However, while the *Poetic Edda* does portray Loki as evil, it does not seem to focus so heavily on the manifestation of this evil in the forms of tricks and mischief making. On the other hand, the poetic kennings that *The Language of Poetry* (in the *Prose Edda*) lists as being used for Loki all seem to highlight this sly streak in his character. By calling Loki the 'enemy of the gods', Snorri suggests that, despite being half-god and half-giant, his loyalties lie with his paternal ancestry. This is in contrast to Thor whose mother was a giantess and is always shown as completely loyal to the Æsir. This suggests that it is the father's blood that determines how the offspring will ultimately behave. The juxtaposition of outer beauty with this inner evil and moral ugliness may also reflect Loki's mixed parentage.

The manifestation of Loki's evil nature is also apparent in the monstrous brood he fathers. *The Tricking of Gylfi* highlights the important role Loki plays in fathering the creature ultimately responsible for the destruction of Odin. Snorri reminds us that all of these children will play an important role in the end battle: with the Midgard serpent killing Thor, and Hel providing her father with the crew of his ship. Since Snorri states that the reason for their evil nature is the evil nature of their father, it therefore also appears that Loki is being held accountable for the behaviour of his children.

* * *

The nature of Loki

There is one among the Æsir considered by some people to be the most disgraceful of all the gods and people; the one who is the cause of the Æsir's misfortune and the one from whom all deceits come. His name is Loki. His is the son of the giant, Farbauti, and his mother is Laufey. He has two brothers, named Byleist and Helblindi.

Loki is handsome on the outside but evil in his character. He cannot be trusted and is cunning above all others and skilled at trickery. It was his usual way to cause trouble for the Æsir and then to get out of the problem by use of tricks.

The children of Loki

Loki had many children by different women. From the one named Sigyn he had Narfi. From the giantess Angrboda he had Fenrir the wolf, Jormungand the Midgard serpent, and Hel.

These three children of Loki were brought up in Giantland. The Æsir feared that these three would be the root cause of much misfortune. This was for three reasons: prophecies stated that they would be the cause of disasters; their mother, a giantess, was an enemy of the Æsir; their father, Loki, had a nature that could not be trusted.

In order to prevent these disasters, Odin All-Father ordered the children of Loki brought to him. When the gods brought Fenrir the wolf, Jormungand and Hel before Odin, he decided the fate of each one of them.

Jormungand the serpent, Odin threw into the deep sea that surrounds the world. This is known as the Midgard ocean and, for that reason, Jormungand is known as the Midgard serpent.

There, in that great ocean, Jormungand grew in size until he was so long that his body encircled the whole world and his tail met his jaws and he gripped his tail in his jaws. It is said that when he releases his tail the world will end.

Hel was thrown into Niflheim (a realm made before the world and with a great spring at its centre, and from this flowed ten rivers; nearby was Hel-gates). There she was given authority over nine worlds, where she rules over those who die from sickness and old age. In that realm, she lives in a hall called Eliudnir and Hunger is the name of the plate she uses for her food, Famine the name of the knife with which she eats, Stumbling is the name of the threshold of her hall, Sick-bed is the name of her bed, Misfortune is the name of the curtains that surround her place of rest. Hel herself is easily recognised for she is half black and half the colour of flesh. Her look is fierce and her gaze downcast.

Finally, Odin allowed the wolf, Fenrir, to live among the Æsir. But of all the Æsir, only the god Tyr dared approach that wolf, so fierce was it. Only Tyr dared to feed it. Each day the wolf grew larger and stronger and the Æsir feared that it would do terrible things as the prophecies had foretold. So, they planned how best to restrain it so that it could not wreak havoc among them.

The binding of the wolf, Fenrir

In order to prevent Fenrir from bringing destruction on them, the Æsir fashioned a chain strong enough to hold that wolf. The chain they called by the name: Leyding. The Æsir challenged the wolf to try his strength with that chain. Now the wolf looked at the chain called Leyding and decided that, strong as it was, his wolf-strength was stronger. So he submitted to being chained, but with one great kick he shattered the chain.

Undeterred, the Æsir fashioned a second chain. This one they called Dromi. Once again, they challenged the wolf to be chained and, to persuade him, they said that he would gain great fame if he could break free from such a strong chain. Now, Fenrir considered the chain and thought how strong it looked but he also knew that he had grown stronger since he had shattered the first chain. Emboldened by this thought he submitted to being chained a second time, for he considered that the fame he would gain by breaking the chain was worth the risk of letting the Æsir bind him. And once he had been chained a second time, he once more exerted all his strength and he shattered the second chain as, earlier, he had shattered the first! And that is why men will say 'Freed from Leyding' and 'Shattering Dromi' to describe something that has been achieved by way of great effort. When they say this, they are recalling these deeds of Fenrir.

The Æsir began to fear that they would never be able to bind the great wolf. It was at that point that Odin All-Father chose one of the trusted servants of Freyr to carry out a special task. Now Freyr – the ruler of rain, sun and what grows on the earth – was one of the gods of the Æsir but descended from the race of the Vanir through his father, Niord, god of wind, sea and fire. The servant of Freyr was named Skirnir and Odin sent him down into the realm of the black-elves where dwarfs were tasked with making a third chain – one that would finally bind Fenrir. That chain was called Gleipnir and it was made from three things that otherwise were impossible to find. These were: the sound of a cat's footstep, the beard from a woman and roots from under a mountain. And these were combined with tendons from a bear, the breath of a fish and the spit of a bird. Together they made a chain that was as soft and smooth as silk but was of immense strength.

The ribbon-like fetter, Gleipnir, was brought to the Æsir and they were well pleased with it. They called the wolf to meet with them on an island in the middle of Lake Amsvartnir. The island was called Lyngvi. There they showed Gleipnir to Fenrir and declared that it was stronger than it looked but that they were sure that the wolf could tear it. Fenrir looked carefully at the ribbon-like silk fetter and declared that, as it stood, there would be little fame gained in tearing free from such a chain, but that he wondered if there was more to it than met the eye and so was reluctant to try it on. To this the Æsir replied that if he could not break it then the Æsir would no longer fear him and would release him. This promise by the Æsir did not reassure the wolf, who replied that if he was bound by the ribbon-chain and could not break it, then he doubted that the Æsir would rush to free him! But he did not want his courage questioned and so he asked that one of the Æsir would place his hand in his jaws as a pledge of goodwill on both sides.

The god Tyr loses his hand to Fenrir

None of the Æsir was keen to place their hand into the jaws of the great wolf for they knew he would bite it off if the ribbon-like chain held him firm. At last, the god Tyr acted and put his right hand in between the great jaws of the wolf. Then Fenrir submitted to being bound with the ribbon-like Gleipnir.

Once the band was on him, the wolf kicked as he had done before. But the harder he kicked the more firmly did the band hold him. Now at last he was held and bound. All the Æsir laughed to see the wolf finally restrained. The only one of the Æsir who did not laugh was Tyr, because the wolf bit off his right hand!

The restraining of Fenrir

Now that the wolf was bound, the Æsir secured him with a cord that they threaded through a huge piece of rock. They then took that rock and secured it firmly by driving it deep into the ground. As if that was not enough, they then took another great piece of stone and pegged the other rock into the ground with it. This rocky peg was driven even further down into the ground. As they secured it, the wolf lunged at them with its great open jaws and tried to bite them. But the Æsir took a sword and forced it upright between his jaws, so that it wedged the jaws open. With this done, the wolf could not savage them. He howled wildly and from his mouth enough saliva flowed to form the Hope river. And this is how it will be with Fenrir, the son of Loki, until the day of Ragnarok.

Even though that wolf was prophesied to eventually cause the death of Odin All-Father, the Æsir did not kill him. Had they done so, they would have polluted their sanctuary with the blood of the wolf and this they did not do from respect for that place. And so Fenrir waits – chained, jaws fixed apart and howling – until the day when he will finally break loose at the end of the world.

6

The goddesses of the Asyniur, the valkyries and the wife of Freyr

INFORMATION ABOUT THE female deities is found in a number of places in Norse literature. These include: the *Tricking of Gylfi* section of the *Prose Edda*; a poem called *Thrym's Poem* in the *Poetic Edda*; *Eulogy on the House*, a skaldic poem that is only partially preserved in the *Prose Edda*; and *Sorli's Story*, a short story in the later and extended version of *The Saga of Olaf Tryggvason*, which itself survives in the Icelandic manuscript known as *Flateyjarbók*, as well as in other places in both the *Prose* and *Poetic Eddas*. The story of Freyr and Gerd is also found in the Icelandic manuscript *Heimskringla*, in which Freyr was considered a king of Sweden and founder of the royal Yngling dynasty. The female deities are almost always beautiful and, while important figures, tend not to play an active or leading role in the stories in which they appear.

The valkyries are a particularly interesting female dimension to the Norse mythological world. They are the choosers of the slain who live in Valhalla but are sent to earth to collect those warriors chosen by Odin. However, as an intermediary is used to convey Odin's wishes, there is a possibility of these wishes being subverted. Valkyries are often depicted as semi-divine beings but they can also be royal princesses who decide to take on this role. Valkyries can fall in love, and can protect and bring good luck to their chosen hero in battle. The warriors, no matter how brave or strong they are, do not have the ultimate control; this control over victory, glory, life and death is left in the hands of women who belong to both the mythological and human world. This enables the hero to initially escape death, but he is not able to escape it for ever and his involvement with the valkyries inevitably leads him onto a collision course with previous lovers or family members. This is a common theme in the Eddic heroic poems, with those of Helgi Hundingsbane, in particular, built around the love and battles of the hero and his valkyrie lover, leading to his ultimate demise.

* * *

The goddesses of the Asyniur

Among the divine race of the Æsir there are both gods and goddesses. Properly speaking, the Æsir are the gods and the Asyniur are the goddesses. Of these goddesses, the highest is Frigg. She lives in a place called Fensalir, which is a very beautiful place indeed. She is married to Odin All-Father and is the mother of the god Baldr, who was killed as a result of Loki's cruel trickery.

Also high in rank and next to Frigg is Freyia. She is married to Od and their daughter is Hnoss. So beautiful is Hnoss that anything beautiful or of great value is described as being '*hnos-sir*' (treasured). When Od went travelling he left Freyia behind and she was lonely and wept tears of red gold. So much did Freyia miss Od that she went after him to try to find him. For this reason she is known by many names, for she took on different names among the different people where she travelled. To some she became known as Mardoll, to others Gefn or Syr. Freyia is known as the Lady of the Vanir (those gods and goddesses of fertility who made alliance with the Æsir after the war between them ended in a truce and then lasting peace).

On her neck Freyia wears a necklace called *Brisingamen* or Brising's necklace. It was this necklace that broke and fell from her neck when, in great anger, she heard news from Loki that Thrymr, king of the giants, demanded to marry her. She loaned it to Thor to wear when he impersonated her and went to Thrymr's court in her place. This necklace was also once stolen by Loki but Freyia enlisted the assistance of the god Heimdall (whom some consider a member of the Vanir) to find it. Finding Loki in the form of a seal, Heimdall took on seal-shape too and regained the necklace for Freyia. Some say that Freyia was also wife of Odin All-Father and it was in that role that she first gained possession of the necklace. According to this tale, one day in Asialand, Freyia came upon the cave of the dwarfs Alfrig, Dwalin, Berling and Grer. Seeing they were making a beautiful necklace she offered them gold and silver for it. But the price they demanded was to spend one night each with her. So great was her desire for the necklace that she slept with each of them for one night. In return she was given *Brisingamen*. The trickster and troublemaker Loki discovered her secret and told Odin, her husband, who was furious. He demanded that Loki should get the necklace and bring it to him. This Loki did by entering her room in the form of a fly, then changing into a flea and biting her as she slept until she restlessly turned and revealed the lock on the necklace, which Loki then unlocked and stole. Odin would only return it to her if she would cause two groups of warriors to fight each other for ever; a curse that would only be broken when a Christian (the later king named Olaf Tryggvason) would slay them and cause them to remain dead.

Other goddesses are found among the Asyniur. One, named Saga, lives in Sokkvabekk, a large palace. Another is a goddess of healing and this is Eir. Her medical skills are renowned. A virgin goddess is Gefion and all women who die as virgins become her attendants. Another virgin goddess is Fulla. Her hair flows freely and she wears a golden headband. Fulla is a close companion of Frigg. She carries Frigg's treasure-casket, takes care of her shoes and knows all her secrets. Siofn concerns herself with love and directs the minds of men and women when they fall in love. From her name men describe love between people by the word '*siafni*'. Those whose marriage union has been forbidden pray to the goddess Lofn, for she is so kind-hearted that she can persuade Odin All-Father or Frigg to allow it to take place, even if previously it was banned. For this reason, her name is used in the form '*lof*' (permission) when describing such unions and '*lofat*' (praised) is used when something is particularly noteworthy and of good report. Contracts between men and women that are made in private are called '*varar*', after the goddess Var. For she is highly attentive to such oaths and contracts and makes them a matter of her personal concern. Nothing escapes her close attention in such matters. For this reason, a woman who discovers a secret is described as using the word '*vor*' (discovered). And Var punishes all who break such oaths and contracts. The goddess Syn is guardian of doorways of the hall and of assemblies where things are in dispute. To declare 'no' to something at such an assembly is therefore called 'syn' (refute) after her. Those whom Frigg wishes to protect are placed under the protection of the goddess Hlin; from her name those in refuge are described as being in 'hleinir' (refuge/protection). Those who are wise are called 'snotr' (wise) after Snotra, the goddess of wisdom. Finally, there is the goddess Gna. Riding a horse named Hofvarpnir, which can cross the sky and sea, she is sent on journeys by Frigg. As a result, if something is very high, people say it is 'gnæfa' (towering), after her, because she is seen flying across the sky on Hofvarpnir. The mother of Thor, named Iord, and Rind, the mother of Vali, are also considered to be of the Asyniur.

The valkyries and Valhalla

Others among the goddesses of the Asyniur are those called valkyries. They serve in Valhalla and serve drinks to those warriors chosen to live there. They include those named Hrist, Mist, Skeggiold, Skogul, Hlokk and Reginleif. The valkyries are sent by Odin to attend every battle that occurs. There they decide who shall live and who shall die; who shall be defeated and who shall be victorious. Those valkyries called Gunn, Rota and Skuld (who is a norn) are those who decide among the warriors who will die. The norns rule the destinies of gods and people.

Those chosen for Valhalla are many in number and great is the amount of food they eat. Yet they always have enough for they are fed from the boar named Saehrimnir. It is cooked each day and yet is whole again that evening! So there is food enough for all that mighty crowd of warriors – yet there will still not be enough of these fighting men to withstand the wolf, Fenrir, when he breaks free at Ragnarok.

Odin himself, though, does not eat, for wine is both food and drink to him, though he gives meat to his wolves named Geri and Freki; while the two ravens that sit on his shoulders – named Hugin and Munin – whisper to him of all that they have seen between dawn and the evening feasting-time, as they fly out over the world.

But to return to Valhalla – the place to which the valkyries bring the slain – on its roof feeds a goat from whose udders flows mead to the warriors, and a stag from whose antlers drips enough water to be the source of many rivers. And the hall is so large that it is entered through five hundred and forty doors. And from these doors the warriors shall pour forth on the day that the wolf comes. Until that day comes, these warriors of Odin All-Father pass the time fighting each other by day and, come evening, they ride back to Valhalla and feast together on the meat from the boar named Saehrimnir.

Gerd: the most beautiful of women, the wife of Freyr

Though not of the Asyniur, the daughter of the mountain-giant Gymir and his wife Aurboda was considered the most beautiful woman in the world. Her name was Gerd. One day, she was spied on by the god Freyr of the Vanir. He went into the place called Hlidskialf, where he was not allowed to go since it is Odin's throne, and from that place he was able to look into all worlds. Gazing towards the north, he saw a woman approaching a great and beautiful hall and when she opened the door he saw that light flooded from her over the sea and sky and, having seen her, he went away downcast because he desired her so much. His father, Niord, noticed he was grief-stricken and sent his servant Skirnir to discover why Freyr was so unhappy. It was this same Skirnir who had been sent by Odin All-Father to secure the making of the fetter, named Gleipnir, that was used to bind the great wolf, Fenrir.

On asking Freyr what ailed him, Skirnir discovered the reason for his unhappiness and Freyr commanded him to go to the north and seek out the hand of the woman for him and to do so whether her father allowed it or not. Skirnir agreed but asked that he might take Freyr's sword with him to defend himself. Now this sword was like no other; it would fight on its own without even being held in the grip of its owner. It is for this reason that when Freyr later fought the giant Beli he was armed with nothing more than a deer's antler; and it was with the antler that he killed that giant. Far more serious, though, would be his lack of this sword when in time he would face Ragnarok without it. At that time the sons of Muspell will ride out and break the bridge Bifrost and wage war on the Æsir. Then will Freyr wish he had his famous sword in his grasp.

When Skirnir went to woo Gerd, he returned with the news that she would come to Freyr in nine nights' time to marry him, though Freyr found it a very long time to wait for the woman to come. In time she came, though, and married him and some say that they began the royal dynasty of the Ynglings in Sweden. Some say she only came after Skirnir threatened her, while some say she came willingly. In this manner, Gerd, the mountain-giantess, became one of the goddesses and was married into the race of the Vanir.

7

The cunning of Loki and
the adventures of Thor

FOUND IN the *Tricking of Gylfi* section of the *Prose Edda*, this tells of the trickery of Loki, and of a journey of Thor and Loki, and then of Thor alone, with the mischief and adventures that accompany these events.

These stories show frequent references to Thor's magical hammer, Miollnir. It is depicted as a fearsome weapon, which can crush skulls and level mountains. The *Prose Edda* tells us that it was made by dwarfs and it has become the symbol most commonly associated with Thor. Miollnir seems to have been used as a pendant or amulet by some followers of Thor during the early medieval period. It is interesting to note, though, that they are most often found in areas of strong Christian influence and may be a reaction to the wearing of crosses by Christian converts. If correct, this reveals another way in which Viking Age religious behaviour was affected by the interaction with Christianity.

Utgarda-Loki (or Utgard-Loki) is a major figure in these stories.

He is the ruler of a castle called Utgard in Giantland and is himself a giant. His name literally means 'Loki of the castle Utgard' and he is called this to distinguish him from Loki who is also travelling with Thor. This story does not appear in the *Poetic Edda*.

The appearance of giants in these stories reminds us of the complex interconnection between gods and giants in Norse mythology. The relationship encompasses some grudging cooperation (as in the fortress building) and even sexual relations (not apparent in these particular accounts); but is usually also associated with simmering threat and fear (as in the need for a fortress against the giants, Thor's killing of the giant-builder, the encounter with Skrymir and humiliation in the hall of King Utgarda-Loki). In such conflicts, Thor was traditionally seen as the enemy of the giants and his hammer was used against them to devastating effect.

These stories also show Thor battling twice with the Midgard serpent (in other accounts named Jormungand). This is the creature that will ultimately destroy him at Ragnarok. In Norse mythology, the Midgard serpent is a sea serpent fathered by Loki with a giantess (Angrboda) and it is so large that it encircles the entire world. Thor will encounter the Midgard serpent three times, the final time being at Ragnarok, the end of the world, when they will destroy each other. The encounter during the fishing trip seems to have been a fairly common motif in Viking Age art and appears on a number of picture stones. One of these is the Ardre VIII stone, which is a stone from the eighth or ninth century from Gotland in Sweden. If the picture really is the fishing trip with Hymir, then this shows the story to have been in existence for at least several hundred years before first being written down in the *Prose Edda*.

* * *

The tricking of the builder of a fortress

Long, long ago . . . when the gods had only just built Midgard and Valhalla, they were approached by a builder, who promised them that he could construct for them a fortification so strong that no mountain-giant or frost-giant could break into it, even if they had succeeded in getting through the boundary of Midgard. Furthermore, he said that he would be able to complete the construction in just three seasons of building. But the price of such a building would be high. He asked for Freyia as his wife and ownership of both the sun and the moon.

At this, the Æsir met together to discuss his terms and they made a counter-proposal to him. This was that he would get the payment that he demanded – but on condition that he completed the work in one season only. They would give him just one winter to build it and if it was not completed on the first day of summer then the builder would receive no payment whatsoever. In addition, no man was to assist him in the construction of the fortification.

The builder considered this counter-proposal. He replied that he would accept it if the Æsir would allow him just one assistant and this was the help of his stallion, which was named Svadilfaeri. The Æsir thought about this and, on the advice of Loki, they accepted this request.

On the first day of winter the building began. By day the builder worked on construction and by night he hauled stone to the site using the stallion, Svadilfaeri. The stones he hauled were enormous. Indeed, the stallion was twice as strong as the builder, and the Æsir saw that the builder was very strong indeed.

It should be noted that giants – for such the builder was – were fearful of being among the Æsir in case Thor arrived home while they were there, for Thor was a slayer of giants. It was for this reason that when the original contract to build the fortification had been agreed, it had been guaranteed by oaths and the witnessing of it by many powerful witnesses. It was only then that the giant-builder felt safe to go about his business, even though Thor was away killing trolls in the eastern mountains.

To return to the building . . . that winter the walls and gateways of that fortification rose at astonishing speed. And it was built so well that no enemy could ever break into it. Finally, just three days from the start of summer, the fortress was almost completed. This caused great concern among the gods of the Æsir because they knew that if it was completed by the start of summer then the details of their agreement meant that Freyia would go from Asgard into Giantland and, furthermore, the sun and the moon would be lost from the sky and would become the possession of giants. They looked for someone to blame for their dilemma and decided that it was the one who had persuaded them to agree to the builder's demands in the first place. Having considered this, they decided that the one to blame was Loki, son of Laufey. After all, it was Loki who was usually responsible for most evil things that occurred and it was he who had persuaded the gods to allow the builder the use of the stallion, Svadilfaeri. Consequently, they threatened Loki with death if he did not find a way to get them out of their difficulties. Loki was afraid because he could see that the gods were prepared to attack and kill him and so he swore oaths that he would free them from their obligation to pay the builder, whatever the cost to him personally.

That evening the plan of Loki to disrupt the building was revealed in the form of a mare who galloped out of the woods to distract the stallion, Svadilfaeri. The plan worked, for the stallion broke free of his harness, abandoned the hauling of stones and made off after the mare who galloped back into the woods. The builder ran after them but could not catch or control his horse. And so, all night, the stallion pursued the mare and the builder pursued them both and no work was done on the fortification. The next day the work was behind schedule for lack of stone hauled to the site. The builder realised that, with time running out, he was not now going to complete the work and he was furious, with a terrible rage.

Seeing the way he raged, the Æsir knew for certain that the builder was none other than a mountain-giant. Since the Æsir were ancient enemies of the mountain-giants they decided that the agreement they had made with the builder was null and void. They considered themselves no longer bound by the oaths that they had sworn and so they called on Thor to settle matters with the mountain-giant builder in the traditional manner. In no time at all, Thor returned and was wielding his giant hammer, Miollnir, the skull-smasher. With that mighty hammer he 'paid' the builder all right and that was with a blow so violent that it smashed his skull to pieces. And so, instead of the promised payment to him of Freyia as his wife, and ownership of both the sun and the moon, the giant received a payment of death. He was not to return to Giantland; instead he was sent down into Niflhel, that is 'misty Hel' (the lowest level of Hel, the place of the dead). In this way the gods went back on their oaths and Freyia – the wife of Od – was not given to be the wife of one of the giants.

Though the Æsir were spared from paying the builder, Loki had to pay a price for the tactic he had used to distract the stallion. For it was Loki who had appeared in the form of the mare. While he was in the form of the mare he had distracted the stallion to the extent of being mated by it. As a result, he gave birth to a foal, and this was no ordinary foal for it was the best horse of all horses owned by gods and by men. It was grey in colour and had eight legs and it became Sleipnir, the horse used by Odin All-Father.

Thor goes on an expedition with Loki

The gods have access to such strength and magic that they are hard for their enemies to overcome. Take the creation of the great ship called Skidbladnir, for example. Made by dwarfs and owned by Freyr, it is large enough to contain all the Æsir with their weapons and always gains a fair wind – yet it can be folded up and carried in a pocket! Such a ship is a reminder of the magic at the disposal of the gods and yet, even so, once Thor got into such a difficult situation that it almost overcame all his magical strength. It is a story that is not often told, for all declare that Thor is the mightiest, and yet it happened this way, even to him.

The story began when Thor and Loki went off on a journey together. They set off in Thor's chariot drawn by two goats (named Tanngniost and Tanngrisnir). After a day's travel, they stopped at the house of a peasant for the night. Thor killed both his goats, skinned them and prepared them for the evening meal. Thor and Loki were joined by the peasant, his wife and their children. The farmer's son was named Thialfi and his daughter was named Roskva and they shall play an important part in this story. When the goat stew was being eaten, Thor took the two goatskins and laid them on the floor beside the fire; he told the peasant and his family to throw the bones – from which they had eaten the meat – onto the goatskins. But unbeknown to Thor, Thialfi the peasant farmer's son split the ham bone in order to get at the juicy marrow inside. Only after doing that did he throw it onto the goatskin.

That night everyone went to sleep but Thor was the first to wake. Before dawn he dressed and raised his hammer, Miollnir, over the goatskins. At once, the goats were restored to life and stood up – but one was lame in its rear leg. Thor knew exactly what had happened; that the bone had been broken by one of the peasant family. He was terribly angry: his brow hooded his eyes and his hands were white as they clutched his hammer's handle in fury. All in the peasant family were utterly terrified and went down on their knees and begged Thor to have mercy on them. When he saw the depth of their terror his anger subsided. In payment for the damage to the goat's leg he accepted the gift of the young people – Thialfi and Roskva – to become his servants; and they have remained his servants ever since.

Thor and Loki, accompanied by Thialfi and Roskva, left the farmstead and travelled eastward to Giantland and even beyond there as far as the great sea. They left the goats behind and walked the way that led there. When, finally, they reached the sea they journeyed over it to a distant land and, at last, the four of them made landfall there. A little way inland was a thick wood and they journeyed through it until evening. They needed somewhere to stay but there was nowhere to be seen.

At last, after travelling through the trees in the dark, they came on a place of shelter. In the gloom they could only make out that it seemed a long building and the doorway into it took up the whole of one end. So in they went and settled down to sleep. In the middle of the night they were woken by a great earthquake. Thinking that perhaps great enemies were approaching, Thor called his companions and they moved further down the building until they found a side-chamber. Into it they went and Thor kept watch at the entrance, armed with his hammer, Miollnir. But no enemies came – and so there they passed the night, with Thor on guard. Round about them echoed great noises throughout the night: rumblings that made the earth shake.

At dawn, Thor went outside and saw a huge giant asleep on the ground. He was enormous and it was his snoring that had sounded like the rumbling of an earthquake in the night. Even Thor felt fear and clutched at his magical power-belt, called Megingjorth, and so increased his mighty strength, which is called his As-strength. Yet for once he was afraid to wield his skull-crushing hammer!

The giant looked at him and Thor asked him his name. The giant replied that he was called Skrymir. He recognised Thor of the Æsir and asked what he was doing with the giant's 'glove'? At that, Thor realised that the building in which they had spent the night was merely the glove of this giant and that the chamber into which they had retreated was merely the thumb of that huge glove!

The giant, Skrymir, asked if Thor and his companions would like to travel with him and he offered to carry their provisions – along with his own – in the bag that he carried on his back. Thor agreed and so they set off.

After a day's walk they rested, come evening, under a large oak tree. Skrymir went to sleep but left his bag full of

provisions open for Thor and his companions to help themselves to what was within and to have their supper. But Thor
could not untie a single one of the knots which secured that
bag no matter how he pulled on them or sought to shift the
strap-ends. Even mighty Thor could not open the bag. Soon he
became very angry. In his fury he reached for his hammer,
strode over to the snoring Skrymir and struck him on the head
with Miollnir, the skull-smasher. But not only did it not smash
his skull, it did not even hurt him in the slightest. Instead, he
merely stirred from his sleep and asked if a leaf had drifted
down onto his head! He asked if Thor and his companions had
eaten and were ready to sleep. Thor said that they were and
they settled down under another oak tree. They were all afraid
of the giant.

In the middle of the night, Thor resolved to finish off
Skrymir, who snored so loudly that the forest shook. Thor
struck him hard on the middle of the head and his hammer
sank deep into the head of the giant. But Skrymir just woke
and asked if an acorn had fallen from a tree and struck him.
Thor replied that it was midnight and there was time to get
back to sleep.

A third time Thor determined to kill Skrymir. This time he
waited until just before dawn and then he rushed at the deeply
snoring giant and drove his hammer down into the giant's forehead. The hammer went in as far as the handle. At this, Skrymir
woke and wondered if a twig had been disturbed by a roosting
bird and had fallen on his head!

Skrymir said that it was time to get up and continue journeying. He told them that the fortress called Utgard lay ahead
and in it there lived bigger creatures than himself; for he had
heard how Thor and his companions were whispering about his

great size. He warned them to be careful how they acted for these giants would not put up with insolence or pride from such tiny people. If they could not do that then it would be better that they turned back. However, if they were resolved to go on to Utgard, they should strike out for the east but he himself was heading north to the mountains.

Journeying on, they reached a vast fortress at noon and it was so tall that they struggled to look up at it. Even Thor could not force open its doors but they managed to squeeze through its bars and so made their way to a great hall. Within that hall there were large people sat on benches and a king named Utgarda-Loki (not to be confused with Loki). He greeted them mockingly and referred to the diminutive size of Thor and the inability of his party to impress those assembled in the hall.

At this challenge Loki spoke up and said he doubted that anyone there could eat food faster than he could! King Utgarda-Loki accepted Loki's challenge and called forth one of his retainers who was called Logi. A trencher was brought and topped with much meat and Loki and Logi were set at either end and ate towards each other. They met in the middle but, while Loki had consumed all the meat off the bones, his rival – Logi – had eaten meat, bones and trencher!

This had not started well and King Utgarda-Loki asked if there was another feat that Thor's party might excel at? Thialfi replied that he was a very fast runner and so was set to race one of King Utgarda-Loki's retainers, who was named Hugi. But Hugi won the race so convincingly that he met Thialfi as he ran back! A second time Thialfi was beaten, although he was fast on his feet. A third time Thialfi was also convincingly beaten by Hugi. And so the second contest was lost as the first had been.

Then King Utgarda-Loki asked Thor at what feat he excelled. And Thor replied that he could compete at drinking with anyone. And so a drinking horn was brought and King Utgarda-Loki said that it could be drunk in one go, or perhaps two; but never more than three gulps were ever needed. Now the horn was long but not really that big and Thor felt confident. But when he took his first deep drink (until he was forced to stop to breathe), it looked as if he had taken only a little from the horn. The second drink was a little better. And the third great gulp made more of an impression on the contents of the drinking horn . . . but still it had not been emptied.

King Utgarda-Loki then asked if Thor might be able to excel at something else, for so far he felt that the claims of the Æsir had disappointed him. Thor was determined to go on, though, and so King Utgarda-Loki challenged him to lift his cat, a thing done easily by the young retainers in that hall. And so a grey cat appeared but, try as he might, Thor could not lift it up, for the cat arched its back and not a paw was lifted from the ground; when at last Thor could raise it no higher, at that point just one paw had been raised!

Thor grew angry and demanded that someone should come and fight him! King Utgarda-Loki said that since Thor was so small, nobody in the hall would lower themselves to this contest, so Thor should fight an old woman named Elli who was summoned to the hall. It was that ancient old woman against Thor of the Æsir, but she bested him! Try as he might, he could not make her lose her footing. On the other hand, she was skilled in wrestling and soon Thor was forced down on one knee. Yet another contest had been lost.

Since it was late, all then retired to bed and, early in the morning, Thor and his companions dressed and made to leave but King Utgarda-Loki cheerfully laid food and drink before them and walked with them a short distance when they left. As they walked, he asked Thor what he thought of his time in the fortress of Utgard? And Thor replied that he had been humiliated and dishonoured by the contests.

Then King Utgarda-Loki revealed that Thor and his companions had been tricked in these encounters. Otherwise Thor would have been too strong and his companions would have succeeded. For King Utgarda-Loki was the same person as the giant Skrymir that Thor had met in the forest. The bag had been fastened with magical wire and when Thor had wielded his hammer, Skrymir had secretly moved a mountain into the way to receive Thor's blows. Then, in the hall at Utgard, other tricks had been played. Logi, who outconsumed Loki, was really named 'flame' and appeared in the form of a man, and that was why he could consume trencher, bones and meat. Hugi, who outran Thialfi, was really named 'thought' and appeared in the form of a man and could race faster than a man can run. The drinking horn was connected to the sea and Thor had lowered the sea level in that contest! The cat was really the Midgard serpent in disguise and he is so huge that he encircles the earth and even raising that 'cat' by one paw was an amazing feat. And the old woman was old age whom nobody can defeat. That was why she had forced even Thor to one knee.

When he discovered how he had been tricked, Thor raised his hammer to wreak vengeance but King Utgarda-Loki was gone and the fortress of Utgard had vanished. At this, Thor led the way back to his own hall at Thrudvangar but he resolved that he would meet again with the Midgard serpent and once more enter into a trial of strength with it.

Thor and the giant, Hymir, fish for the Midgard serpent

It was not long before Thor set out to get revenge on the Midgard serpent that he had failed to lift in the hall of King Utgarda-Loki. He was so eager to do this that he set out without a companion and without his chariot pulled by the two goats (Tanngniost and Tanngrisnir). On this journey he changed his appearance to that of a young boy and in this disguise he set out across Midgard. He travelled until one evening he arrived at the home of a giant who was named Hymir, where he stayed the night. The next day he asked if he could accompany Hymir on a fishing trip. Hymir was not impressed with the assistance he might get from one so young and small but, nevertheless, he agreed. Nor did he think the young lad would much appreciate the discomfort of staying out fishing for as long as Hymir was inclined to do.

Thor was angry and thought of using his famous hammer on the giant but held himself in check, since he needed to reserve his strength for what he intended to accomplish on the fishing trip. Hymir told him to find his own bait and so Thor tore off the head of an ox, named Himinhriot, that belonged to Hymir.

Together, Thor and Hymir rowed out to sea and Hymir was impressed with the strength of Thor's rowing. Indeed, when Hymir was ready to stop, it was Thor who insisted that they rowed even further out from the shore. At this, Hymir became alarmed and said that instead of taking his usual catch of flatfish he feared that they might meet the Midgard serpent in such deep water. But Thor rowed further, much to the displeasure of Hymir, who was now alarmed at how far they had travelled out to sea.

At last, they reached a point where Thor threw overboard his ox-head bait and it sank to the seabed. It was there that the Midgard serpent seized that bait, and the huge hook within it dug into the mouth of the serpent. The serpent pulled away in alarm and Thor's hands came down on the side of the boat with a great crash. At this, anger rose in Thor and he summoned up his As-strength from within himself and braced himself so hard that his feet tore through the bottom of the boat and he stood on the seabed. So braced, he hauled the serpent up to the boat. There Thor glared at the Midgard serpent and the serpent glared back at Thor and spat poison!

The giant Hymir panicked to see the serpent hauled to the boat and the water cascading in. In his fear he drew his knife and, instead of cutting bait, he cut Thor's fishing line. And that, just as Thor was raising his hammer to strike the Midgard serpent! Thor threw his hammer after the serpent and some say it struck it on the head and killed it, while others think that the Midgard serpent escaped and still lies in the sea that surrounds the world. What is certain is that Thor then struck Hymir and the blow threw him head first into the sea. Thor, on the other hand, waded back to the shore.

8

The killing of Baldr and the punishing of Loki

FOUND IN the *Tricking of Gylfi* section of the *Prose Edda*, these stories tell of how the god Baldr was killed, along with the punishment of Loki and the end of the world. Other references to the killing of Baldr are found in the *Poetic Edda*, in *Baldr's Dreams*.

Loki's role in the death of Baldr is represented very differently in the two Eddas. In the *Prose Edda*, Loki is clearly held responsible for the death of Baldr, while in the *Poetic Edda* there is no mention of Loki in connection with his death. One of the Old Norse poetic kennings used for Loki in *The Language of Poetry* is 'Ráðbani Baldrs' ('cause of Baldr's death'); while the description of Baldr's killing in *The Tricking of Gylfi* shows Loki was not pleased when he saw that Baldr was unharmed by things thrown at him and that, due to this, Hod took the mistletoe and threw it at Baldr, at Loki's instigation.

The *Prose Edda* also more explicitly says that, 'It was certainly an achievement of Loki to not only cause Baldr's death, but also ensure that he was not released from Hell.' Both *The Language of Poetry* and *The Tricking of Gylfi* imply it is Loki and Loki alone who is responsible for the death of Baldr. He deliberately seeks out the one weapon that can kill Baldr and, in his typical trickster role, tricks Hod into being the person who will ultimately deliver the blow. Then his refusal to weep means that Baldr cannot be raised from Hell, which only compounds his guilt. Snorri's version of the killing of Baldr leaves us in no doubt as to who is responsible for Baldr's death, and Hod is portrayed as an innocent who is duped into being a part of Loki's plan. This appears to be consistent with the character of Loki as he has been portrayed all along by Snorri: as a player of tricks who seems to be seeking the destruction of the gods.

However, in contrast, there is no mention of Loki as instrumental in Baldr's death in the *Poetic Edda*. In *Baldr's Dreams*, it is Hod who is held solely responsible and this version of the story seems to suggest that Loki was not involved at any point. The poet does not discuss the reason why Hod killed Baldr, but the complete absence of Loki from the story suggests that, as far as the author of *Baldr's Dreams* was concerned, either Loki did not play an important role or that, as Hod was the perpetrator of the crime, the guilt for it was ultimately his. This is in contrast to Snorri who seems happy to lay the blame for every wrongdoing, and especially those related to the end of the world and the destruction of the gods, firmly at Loki's feet.

* * *

The killing of Baldr

The god known as Baldr the Good (a son of Odin) dreamed strange dreams which seemed to indicate that his life was in danger. At this the Æsir gathered together and they discussed what it was that they should do in order to protect Baldr. In order to do this they thought of all the kinds of things that might threaten Baldr and they then endeavoured to ensure his protection from all these threats. The goddess Frigg (wife of Odin All-Father) sought out solemn promises from all these threats so that Baldr would not be harmed and, in this way, she secured for him protection from fire, water, iron and every type of metal, stones, earth, trees, all diseases, all animals and every kind of bird, all snakes and all poisons. When this was finally completed, Baldr was safe from all dangers. As a result, it became a sport among the Æsir to have Baldr stand before them and throw rocks at him, fire arrows at him and strike him with weapons. But nothing harmed him. He was safe from all these dangers. All the Æsir thought that this was amazing.

There was, though, one of the Æsir who was not amused by these games and who was displeased that nothing harmed Baldr. This was Loki, son of Laufey. Moreover, he was determined to change this state of affairs. He changed his appearance to that of a woman and in this form he went to visit Frigg in the place called Fensalir. There the 'woman' (who was really Loki) discussed with Frigg what would be taking place when the Æsir next assembled. It turned out that at this next assembly – as often when the Æsir gathered – they would be testing Baldr's invulnerability. This time they would be shooting arrows at him.

At this news, Loki asked Frigg if *everything* had sworn the oath to protect Baldr. To this question, Frigg replied that not *everything* had sworn the oath. There was one thing and one thing only that had not sworn the oath. This was something called mistletoe, which grew to the west of Valhalla. It was just a young shoot, too young to be worth making swear the oath.

At this Loki was off. He went to find that shoot of mistletoe and, when he found it, he picked it and fashioned it into an arrow. With that mistletoe-arrow in his hand, he went to the assembly of the Æsir that Frigg had earlier spoken about.

When Loki reached the place of assembly, he noticed that the blind god, Hod, was standing at the edge of the crowd who were firing arrows at Baldr. Sidling up to him, Loki asked him why he was not taking part in the fun of firing at the invincible Baldr? Hod replied that he was not taking part for two reasons. The first was that he could not see Baldr and the second reason was that he had no weapon.

Loki soon 'solved' these problems for Hod. He first gave Hod the mistletoe-arrow and then told Hod exactly where to fire it, so that the arrow flew in the direction of Baldr. He reinforced his point by saying that, if Hod did not fire the arrow, he would not be honouring Baldr as others were doing. He said this because the Æsir believed that by celebrating the invincibility of Baldr, they were doing him great honour.

As a result of Loki's intervention, Hod fired the mistletoe-arrow straight at Baldr. Loki made sure that his aim was true and so the arrow that Hod fired flew with unerring flight towards Baldr. It struck him and it passed right through his body. Baldr fell dead; it was the worst deed that any god or man ever did. When Baldr fell, the Æsir were struck dumb with shock and horror. They were frozen to the spot but looked at each other with outrage at what had been done and determined on vengeance against the one who had killed Baldr.

The attempt to reclaim Baldr from Hel

Although the Æsir were determined to avenge Baldr, they could do nothing because their assembly was sacred and a place of sanctuary, where no act of vengeance could occur. Instead, they wept inconsolably, they were so struck with terrible grief. The god who was most stricken with grief was Odin. This was because he realised more than the others the dreadful harm that Baldr's death would cause for the Æsir and how terrible was the loss.

Finally, Frigg spoke up and asked if there was anyone among the Æsir who would ride the road that led to Hel and would there beg for the life of Baldr, and offer any amount of ransom if only Hel would release Baldr and allow him to return to Asgard, the home of the Æsir. If anyone would do this, they would win Frigg's love and her favour, so greatly did she wish for the return of Baldr.

There was only one who took up the request made by Frigg. This one was Hermod the Bold, who was also the son of Odin. The eight-legged horse of Odin – Sleipnir – was summoned and Hermod mounted that swift steed and spurred it towards Hel on his mission to save Baldr, his brother, from death.

Meanwhile, the Æsir lifted Baldr's body and took it to the sea, where his ship was moored. This was called Hringhorni and it was the largest ship in the world. The Æsir intended to conduct Baldr's funeral on board this mighty vessel. But the ship could not be made to move.

At this setback the Æsir sent to Giantland for help to launch the ship. It was the giantess Hyrrokkin who answered their call and rode to them on a wolf controlled by vipers acting as reins. When she dismounted, Odin ordered four warriors to steady her mount. These were berserkers, who fought without fear or self-control in battle. But even the four of them were not strong enough to hold the wolf-mount of Hyrrokkin. Instead, they were forced to strike it and force it to the ground.

When Hyrrokkin reached the ship she was so strong that she pushed it out to sea with one touch and sparks flew from the rollers beneath the ship and the land shook, as with an earthquake. At this, Thor's anger flashed against the giantess and he made as if to crush her head with his hammer: Miollnir, the skull-smasher. But the other gods restrained him with their pleas on behalf of the giantess.

When Baldr's body was placed on his ship, his wife – Nann Nepsdaughter – collapsed with grief and died. Her body was placed on the ship and burned alongside that of her husband. As the pyre was lit, Thor blessed it with his hammer, While he was doing this a dwarf ran in front of him and Thor kicked him into the fire, so that he too burned, along with the bodies of Baldr and Nann.

Beings from across the lands and worlds came to attend the funeral of Baldr. There was Odin with Frigg, the valkyries and Odin's two ravens, Hugin and Munin; Freyr was there in his chariot drawn by a boar; Heimdall was there on his horse and Freyia was accompanied by her cats; there were frost- and mountain-giants. On that pyre Odin laid a great gold arm ring alongside Baldr's horse, which wore its fine harness.

While all this was happening, Hermod the Bold rode on his mission to Hel to try to reclaim the life of Baldr. He rode for nine nights, through dark valleys that were so deep that they were black like night. At last, he approached Gioll Bridge with its covering of bright gold. There he came face-to-face with the warrior-maiden, Modgud. As he approached, she asked him his name and his parentage. She was intrigued because the bridge responded to his footsteps as earlier it had done to the footfall of five regiments of dead warriors. However, it was clear that Hermod was not dead and so Modgud asked what business he had riding the road that led to Hel, for it was a way reserved for the dead. To her question of what brought him there, he replied that he came looking for Baldr and wondered if Modgud has seen him pass that way? To this she said that, indeed, she had seen Baldr and that he rode the way of the dead that led down and to the north and was the way to Hel.

At this news, Hermod spurred his horse over the bridge and rode on until he reached the gates of Hel. There he adjusted the horse's saddle and rode it at the locked gates and drove it to leap high over them. Once over the gates he rode up to the hall that lay within the defences and dismounted and went inside. There he saw Baldr, his brother, sitting in a place of honour within the hall.

In the morning, Hermod begged Hel to allow him to take Baldr back to Asgard and he explained that everything and everyone was weeping over Baldr's death. To this, Hel replied that, indeed, he could take Baldr if it could be proved that *everything* and *everyone* was indeed mourning him. But if so much as one thing refused to do so, then Baldr could not return.

So Hermod returned to the Æsir in Asgard with the agreement made by Hel – and its condition. At this, the Æsir sent messages across the world to beseech all things to weep for Baldr and so free him from Hel. And all things did this; everything wept for Baldr. They wept as frost weeps when the sun shines on it. All things wept . . . with one exception. Deep in a cave the messengers of the Æsir found a giantess and she refused to weep. For, she said, she had gained nothing from Baldr, living or dead, and Hel could keep him. That giantess, we may presume, was Loki in disguise.

The punishment of Loki

The gods were furious that Loki had both caused the death of Baldr and had also contrived to ensure that he could not be ransomed from Hel. Realising that they meant to punish him severely, Loki ran away and hid inside a mountain in a building that he constructed so that it had four doors. This was so that he could look in all directions to see if the gods were coming after him. But still he did not feel safe from the anger of the Æsir. So, by day, he transformed himself into a salmon and hid beneath Franangr waterfall. Despite this, he still did not feel safe and wondered what things the Æsir might do to catch him in his watery hiding place. While sitting in his house with its four doors he picked up linen threads and, as he pondered how he might be caught, he tied them into the form of a net. This was the first time that anyone had made such a thing. He did this as he sat before a fire.

But at that moment he saw that the Æsir were approaching; for Odin had seen his hiding place. At this, Loki threw the net into the fire and ran down to the river. Changing himself into a salmon once more, he leapt in.

Back at Loki's four-doored house, the Æsir had arrived and the first to enter was Kvasir, the wisest of them all. He looked at the fire and saw in it the ashes of the net and he guessed from their shape that they were a device for catching fish. Learning this, the Æsir worked together to create such a net for their own use. Once it was made they took it to the river, for they had guessed that Loki was hiding there. They threw in the net and

Thor took one end and the rest of the Æsir took the other end. Together, they dragged the net through the water in order to catch Loki. But Loki realised what they were doing and swam ahead of the net and hid between the stones on the riverbed. A second time the Æsir dragged the net because they sensed that Loki was in the water. This time the net dragged along the bed of the river and Loki was forced to leap over it and escape back under the waterfall. Otherwise, he would have been forced into the sea and easily captured. A third time the Æsir pursued him in the river; but this time Thor waded into the middle of the river while the other Æsir pulled the net towards the sea.

Loki now saw that he was in desperate danger. Whether he swam into the sea or jumped the net to swim back to the waterfall, he was doomed. For the Æsir would catch him in the open water of the sea and Thor would catch him if he attempted to swim back up the river. But it was to the waterfall he attempted to go; he leapt the net once more in an attempt to get there. As he did so, Thor seized him but Loki slipped through his grasp. But, although Loki slid between his fingers, those fingers closed around his tail. That is why the body of a salmon still grows slimmer the closer to the tail, for that is where Thor gripped Loki.

So that was how Loki was caught. The Æsir took him to a cave and there they took three slabs of rock and punched a hole through each one. Then they brought Loki's sons, Vali and Narfi, to the cave. Vali they turned into a wolf and Narfi they tore into pieces. With Narfi's guts they tied Loki to the three stones: one was under his shoulders, one was under his loins and the third was placed behind his knees. As they did so, the binding-guts turned to iron and Loki was held fast. Then a poisonous snake was suspended over him so that its venom dripped into his face. But Loki's wife, Sigyn, tried to help him by catching the poison in a bowl and she still does. But when the bowl is full she goes to pour it away and then the poison drips into Loki's face once more. At this Loki convulses in agony and that is what is called an earthquake. There he will lie – chained beneath the dripping poison – until the end of the world; until the day called Ragnarok.

A myth-poem: How Odin rode into Hel to discover the identity of Baldr's killer.

As well as the story recounted in *The Tricking of Gylfi*, in the *Prose Edda*, there is also a poem called *Baldr's Dreams* that is found in the *Poetic Edda*. This account explains how the Æsir responded to the terrible dreams that Baldr was having and is recounted in a shortened form here in order to give an insight into its content.

> The Æsir came together to discover the cause of Baldr's terrible dreams.
> Then up stepped the one who sacrificed himself for men, Odin,
> who saddled Sleipnir and rode him down to Hel,
> where he was met by a barking dog all covered in blood.
> But Odin undeterred by this rode on to reach Hel's hall door.
> On the eastern side the seeress lay within her grave
> where Odin recited a spell to awake the dead and so she rose up unwillingly.
> She spoke, 'Who has woken me? Who has brought me back along this road?

'I, whose grave has felt snow, rain and dew. Long dead have
    I so lain.'
Odin then hid his name and said he was called 'Wanderer'
and 'Wanderer' asked which warrior was soon expected
    there,
who was soon to travel to the hall of Hel and be welcomed?
Then, in reply, the seeress spoke, 'The mead stands ready
    here for Baldr,
and his coming will be distress for the Æsir.'
So 'Wanderer' asked who would it be that would kill Baldr
    and
deprive Odin of his son?
He learned that Hod would do this deed and in his anger
    'Wanderer' asked
who would revenge himself on Hod for such a death as
    Baldr's?
Then 'Wanderer' heard how Odin would have another son,
    by Rind,
who less than one day from his birth would fight
and would not wash his hands nor comb his hair until the
    vengeance
act was done and Baldr's killer brought to the funeral fire.
Then 'Wanderer' asked a question of the secret knowledge
    of the seeress
and she guessed his name and declared him to be,
    'Odin-ancient-sacrifice',
who alone could visit her and no one else would ride that
    road
and meet her there until the day that Loki would be loosed
and destruction fall on all the gods.

9

The kidnapping of Idunn
and the origins of poetry

AGAIN FOUND IN the collection known as the *Prose Edda*, but this time in the *Language of Poetry* section, are journeys of the Æsir gods Odin, Loki and Haenir; the kidnapping of Idunn due to the misdeed of Loki; the origins of poetry; and the gaining of poetry by Odin.

The Language of Poetry shows Snorri attempting to systematise traditions and to create a single narrative out of the complexity of Old Norse mythology. Snorri discusses the pagan past in relation to the kennings used within skaldic poetry (composed at the courts of Norse rulers), in order to provide the readers of his treatise with an understanding of where the origins of these kennings lay. There are several other accounts of the origins of poetry: *The Sayings of the High One* in the *Poetic Edda*; and carved on the Stora Hammars III stone (Larbro Parish, Gotland, Sweden, *c.* 700). However, neither of these is as complete as Snorri's version of the story.

The story about the origins of poetry comes close to the beginning of this section of the *Prose Edda*. This is because it is necessary to explain the original in order to give a background to the wide range of kennings that Snorri sets out later. Kennings were a key part of the tool kit of a skaldic poet, allowing him to demonstrate his skill and understanding of the pantheon of Norse mythology. The origin of poetry starts with an internal dispute between the Æsir and the Vanir and moves onto a dispute between dwarfs and giants. The ability to compose poetry is presented as being highly prestigious and only the most powerful people in the myth (the Æsir) are able to utilise the mead – both the giants and the dwarfs lack the ability to culturally benefit from it. This gives a particular status to human poets as, even though they are only benefitting from Odin's cast-offs, they are still able to use it, which is more than the other races are able to do.

Poetry is strongly associated with Odin and his continual search for wisdom. However, it is not enough to solve Odin's troubles with the giants and interestingly there are no accounts of Odin himself actually using kennings.

* * *

The loss of the goddess Idunn and her recovery

One day, three of the Æsir set out on a journey. These were Odin, Loki and Haenir. They crossed the mountains and the wild places and soon they were running short of food. At last, they made their way down into a valley where they found a herd of oxen grazing. They killed one of the oxen and prepared to cook it. They built an earth-oven to do this and placed the ox inside; but when they opened the door they found that the ox was not cooked. They tried a second time and again it was not cooked. They could not understand this and discussed among themselves why the ox would not cook. As they talked they heard a voice from the oak tree under which they were sitting. Looking up, they saw a huge eagle perching on the branches of the tree. The eagle told them that he was the reason why the ox was not being cooked and that, if they would but grant him his fill of the meat, he would cause the ox to cook for them. The three gods agreed, and so the eagle flew down and began to tear away huge chunks from the ox.

At this, Loki became very angry and seized a piece of wood with which he struck the eagle. The eagle flew upwards and the piece of wood was stuck at one end to the eagle and at the other end to Loki. Up and up the eagle flew and Loki thought that his arms would be torn from his shoulders. He shouted to the eagle, begging it to release him. But the eagle was in no mood to do so and would only free Loki if Loki would find a way of enticing the goddess Idunn out of Asgard and get her to bring her magical apples with her. It was these apples that kept the gods young. Loki agreed and the eagle freed him.

Nothing much else happened on that journey but, when the three gods finally made their way back to Asgard, Loki put his plan into action. He persuaded Idunn to leave Asgard with him and come out to a forest. In order to achieve this, Loki told her that he had found fine apples growing there and suggested that she bring her own apples with her to compare with the ones that he had found.

When Loki and Idunn reached the forest, the eagle swooped down. Now, that 'eagle' was really a giant by the name of Thiazi, who had taken on the form of an eagle. He seized Idunn in his talons and flew away with her. He carried her to his home in Thrymheim.

The loss of Idunn affected the Æsir very badly. Without her apples they began to grow old. So, they gathered together to ascertain what had happened to her. The last time she had been seen, they agreed, was when she had left Asgard in the company of Loki. So they compelled Loki to appear before them and threatened him with torture and death if he did not resolve the situation. At this, Loki was terrified and offered to go to Giantland to search for Idunn. He asked Freyia to change him into the form of a falcon (for this was one of her attributes) and, in this form, he flew to Giantland, to the home of Thiazi.

Now, the giant was out at sea, fishing, and Idunn was alone in his hall. Realising his chance, Loki changed her into the form of a nut, clutched her in his claws and flew off with her. When Thiazi returned he found that Idunn was gone. At once, he took on his eagle-form and flew after Loki. The wingbeats of the eagle were so strong that they caused a storm to form around him.

From Asgard, the Æsir saw the falcon (which was Loki) approaching, with the eagle in close pursuit. To save the falcon they brought huge piles of wood-shavings and threw them at the base of the wall of Asgard. When the falcon reached the spot it dropped down to the foot of the wall with the eagle close behind. But as the falcon dropped, the eagle missed it as it struck after the bird. At the same time, the Æsir set fire to the wood-shavings so that a great sheet of flames leapt up. The eagle plunged into the fire, its feathers burst into flame and it crashed to the ground. As it did so, the Æsir seized their chance: they leapt forward and killed the eagle. And this was how they killed Thiazi, a tremendous deed that is still spoken of.

This would have been the end of the matter but Thiazi had a daughter, named Skadi, and she was determined to avenge the death of her father. She dressed for war and marched towards Asgard. When she approached the walls of that fortress, the Æsir offered her compensation to buy her off; and the first thing they offered was that she would be allowed to choose a husband from among the Æsir. But she would choose him from his feet alone and would not be allowed to see any more of him. She agreed and when she saw one of the Æsir, whose feet were beautiful, she was sure that it must be Baldr and so she claimed him for her own. But the feet were those of Niord of Noatun, the Vanir god of the sea. In time, though, they parted because she did not want to live beside the sea with its busy seafarers; and he did not want to live in the grim and cold mountains.

The terms of the compensation agreed by Skadi the giantess included the stipulation that the Æsir would have to make her laugh. She was sure that they would be incapable of doing this. But that was before Loki got to work. He took a piece of string and tied one end around the beard of a nanny-goat and the other end he tied around his own testicles. Once that was done, the nanny-goat and Loki tugged at that cord and they pulled back and forward with both of them squealing. At this sight – and as Loki suddenly landed in her lap – Skadi laughed out loud. And so the reconciliation between her and the Æsir was achieved. Furthermore, Odin took Thiazi's eyes and threw them up into the sky and they became two new stars in the night sky.

The father of the giant, Thiazi, and the origins of poetry

Now, Thiazi – the one killed by the Æsir – was the son of Olvaldi. This Olvaldi was rich and owned a great deal of gold. When Olvaldi died, his three sons divided up their inheritance among themselves and they did it in this way. Each took a mouthful of his gold in turn and they continued in this fashion until it was all divided up. That is why, among the many names used to describe gold, is this one used by human poets: 'the speech of giants'. In this way secret language is used to speak of it. Another poet may call it simply 'words', another will call it 'giant speech' but they are referring to gold and hiding the reference to it within these phrases. This secret language is what is known as poetry. Now, poetry came into existence in this way . . .

Once, long ago, the gods of the Æsir and those of the Vanir were locked in bitter conflict. At last, they called a truce and talked of peace. This peace deal was sealed when all the gods spat into a cauldron and mingled their spit. Then they dispersed but this symbol of peace between the gods remained. From this mingled spit was formed a man, named Kvasir. He was wise and travelled widely, dispensing knowledge. But when he met two dwarfs – brothers named Fialar and Galar – they murdered him. His blood they poured into vessels and mixed it with honey. This became such a powerful liquid that any who drank from it became wise in poetry or other forms of knowledge. The dwarfs told the Æsir that Kvasir had suffocated under the weight of his own wisdom. In this way the dwarfs were left in possession of the powerful mead of poetry.

Now, by and by these two dwarfs invited a giant and his wife to stay with them; that giant was named Gilling. One day they went out to sea with Gilling but the boat struck a reef, over-turned and the giant drowned. The dwarfs, though, managed to right the boat and made it back to shore. When they told the giant's wife what had happened, she was grief-stricken and could not be consoled. She wept so much that the dwarfs grew tired of her lamenting and Fialar suggested that she step outside and look towards where Gilling had drowned, in order to find some consolation. When she did so, Galar (who had climbed up above the doorway) dropped a millstone on her head and silenced her crying. This was how she died.

The son of Gilling was a giant named Suttung. He heard of how his father and mother had died and he went to the home of the dwarfs and seized them as his prisoners. Taking them out to sea, he reached a rocky reef that the sea covered at high tide. As punishment he left the dwarfs on the rocks to die by drown-ing. At this, the two dwarfs begged him for mercy and offered to pay him compensation for the death of his father. The price they offered was the mead that they had made from the blood of Kvasir mixed with honey. Suttung accepted this compensa-tion and took it home with him to a place known as Hnitbiorg. There he placed it in the safe keeping of his daughter, Gunnlod. As a result, poetry is sometimes known as 'Kvasir's blood', 'drink of dwarfs', 'dwarfs' transport' (since they were saved from drowning by trading it), 'Suttung's mead' or 'drink from Hnitbiorg'.

Now, this drink of poetry passed into the ownership of the gods – the Æsir – in this way. Odin, known as All-Father, went on a journey. He came to a hayfield where nine slaves were at work. He offered to sharpen their scythes and they were pleased at the offer. When he had completed the task the slaves were so pleased with what he had done that they offered to buy his whetstone from him. Odin agreed but said that they should offer a reasonable price, though he did not actually name what that would be. The price, though, soon became apparent. Odin threw the whetstone up into the air and the nine slaves all sprang to seize it. But they were still holding their scythes and, as they went to catch the whetstone, they cut each other's throats with their scythes. Those slaves had belonged to a giant named Baugi.

That night Odin lodged with Baugi. Now, Baugi was the brother of Suttung who had gained the mead of poetry from the two dwarfs. Baugi was depressed because his nine slaves had killed each other and he had no other workmen. At this, Odin offered to do the work of the nine dead slaves and asked as payment one drink from the mead of poetry. Baugi said that such a decision could only be made by Suttung but he would try to persuade him. But when the matter was discussed with Suttung, he refused; he wanted to keep all the mead for himself. When this was conveyed to Odin he suggested that they try magic in order to gain access to the mead and Baugi agreed. Odin took an auger, of the type used for boring holes in wood, and told Baugi to drill through the mountain. This Baugi did, but the first time he stopped before he had drilled right through. Odin told him to do so again and this time he did indeed drill right through the mountain. Seeing this, Odin turned himself into the form of a snake and slithered into the hole that Baugi had drilled. As he did so, Baugi stabbed at him with the auger but missed.

Once through the mountain, Odin took on his usual form again and went to where Gunnlod was guarding the mead of poetry. There, he slept with her for three nights and after that she allowed him three mouthfuls of the mead. However, Odin's drinking was of such a volume that in three great gulps he had consumed all of the mead. Then he changed himself into the form of an eagle and flew swiftly away, pursued by Suttung who also took on an eagle's form. As Odin approached Asgard, the Æsir saw him and put out vessels into which Odin spat out the stolen mead. In this way it became the property of the Æsir. This is why poetry is sometimes called: 'Odin's discovery', 'Odin's drink' or 'Odin's gift'. It is also called the 'gift of the Æsir'. But not all the mead made it into the containers that were put out by the Æsir. For Suttung was flying so close to Odin that in his flight to escape him, Odin let some of the mead fall behind him and this did not become the property of the Æsir. This portion of mead is available to anyone and that is why even those who are not skilled poets might find that they can compose a riddle or a rhyme. They are benefitting from the mead that Odin let fall behind him as he fled from the eagle.

10

Adventures in Giantland

As with many of the Norse myths, this account of adventures in Giantland is found in the *Prose Edda*. It is taken from the *Language of Poetry* section, which contains stories of the adventures of Odin in Giantland and of battles between Thor and the giants. In Norse mythology, giants are the traditional enemies of the gods of both the family of the Æsir and that of the Vanir. In Old Norse, they are described as the *jötnar* (singular *jötunn*) who live in one of the nine worlds of the Norse cosmos. As a result of an ancient conflict, they had been banished there by the gods and goddesses of the Æsir. According to the Norse understanding of the origins of life and the universe, they were all derived from the first great giant, Ymir. All those of the first race of giants died when Ymir was killed by Odin and his gushing blood drowned them. All, that is, except two from whom the giant race was then repopulated. This new race of giants included frost-giants, fire-giants, wind-giants, mountain-giants and sea-giants.

In the Norse myths, the giants are frequently depicted as enormously destructive and voracious. In fact, the word *jötunn* seems to be related to the words 'to eat' and probably conveyed the idea of insatiable appetites and consumers of people. Trolls – also the enemies of the gods – were regarded as related beings. Giants are, not surprisingly, described as being of huge size and often hideously ugly. Some appear humanoid, while others are described as terrifying beasts with many heads or the appearance of a ravening wolf (for example, Fenrir). Giants were often associated with rocks and mountains, which was probably due to their association with the original formation of the world in its raw and rocky state. However, the mythology is complex, for some giants are described as sexually attractive and married to or partaking in casual relationships with the gods (involving both the divine families of the Æsir and the Vanir); some of the Æsir claimed descent from unions of this kind. In some of the stories the assumption seems to be that some giants were not of great stature. What is clear, though, is that the main theme in the relationship between giants and gods/goddesses is one of competition: whether that is over possession of beautiful women or a fine horse (as in the first story), or a trial of strength (as in the second story). Mutual antagonism and the threat of mutual destruction colours much of the relationship and, in this, Thor features as the most prolific of giant-killers.

* * *

The visit of the giant Hrungnir to Valhalla

While Thor was off attacking trolls in the east, Odin rode his eight-legged horse, Sleipnir, into Giantland. There he arrived at the hall of a giant by the name of Hrungnir. When the giant saw Odin approaching, he was impressed. He asked who it was that was riding this way, with a helmet of gold and a remarkable horse. Odin replied that he would bet his own head that no horse in the whole of Giantland was as good as Sleipnir. Now, Hrungnir too had a fine horse that was named Gullfaxi, which means 'golden mane', that ran well with fine strides. Onto it he leapt and rode after Odin, for he was angry at Odin's boasting and the slur it cast on the horses of Giantland. The chase went on for miles, with Odin always managing to keep ahead and Hrungnir close behind but never managing to overtake him. In fact, they raced so hard that they arrived back at Asgard and Hrungnir did not even realise that he had left Giantland far behind. Both horses galloped in through the open gates and Hrungnir found he was in the fortress of the gods who are known as the Æsir, at the hall called Valhalla.

Ahead of him were the great doors that led into the hall and, as he dismounted, the Æsir approached him and offered him a drink. Hrungnir was in no mood for pleasantries and demanded it in great quantities. As each of Thor's great goblets were brought out, he drained them with ease. Not surprisingly, he was soon very drunk. Now it was his turn to boast. To the assembled gods of the Æsir he boasted that he would pick up Valhalla and carry it back to Giantland; and as for Asgard itself, he would destroy it and the gods. Looking about himself in this drunken state he declared that, after he had killed the gods, he would take Freyia (goddess of beauty and love, Od's wife) and Sif (the golden-haired goddess of earth's fertility and wife of Thor) back to Giantland with him. Of all the Æsir, it was only Freyia who dared to bring him his drinks. At last, the Æsir grew tired of his drinking, his boasting and his threats. So they called out the name of Thor, that killer of giants.

Immediately, Thor appeared. He stormed into the hall and was furious to see a giant there, drinking and being served by Freyia as if he was one of the Æsir. Thor raised his great hammer and made as if to crush the skull of the giant. But Hrungnir was unafraid and replied that he was in Valhalla under the protection of Odin and, furthermore, that he carried no weapons. He chided Thor that it would be dishonourable to kill an unarmed opponent. Instead, he challenged Thor to meet him on the border of the territory of the giants and the Æsir, at Griotunagardar.

The single combat of Thor and Hrungnir and the whetstone lodged in Thor's head

Now, nobody had ever challenged Thor to single combat before and Thor accepted the challenge that the giant had thrown down. At this, Hrungnir galloped back to Giantland. When the other giants heard about the forthcoming duel they were very worried. This was because Hrungnir was the strongest of all the giants and the other giants feared what would become of them at the hands of Thor if he succeeded in killing Hrungnir. So, they built a giant of clay, called Mokkurkalfi, who could fight alongside Hrungnir when Thor arrived. He was tall and broad and his heart was taken from a horse. Even so, he was terrified when Thor appeared. Beside him stood Hrungnir; he was very strong with a heart, head and shield made from stone. Indeed, that is why the sign used for stone-carving is still called 'Hrungnir's heart'. Even his weapon, a whetstone, was a weapon of stone rather than of iron. Together, Mokkurkalfi and Hrungnir prepared to face the wrath of Thor.

As Thor approached, he sent on ahead his servant, Thialfi. He was the one who, along with his sister, became Thor's servant when Thialfi put himself in Thor's debt by breaking the leg-bone of Thor's chariot-pulling goat, in order to extract the marrow. When Thialfi saw Hrungnir, he tricked him by saying that Thor was tunnelling underground to reach him. At this, Hrungnir threw down his stone shield to protect his feet and relied on his whetstone alone to face Thor.

Then Thor hurled his hammer, Miollnir, at Hrungnir; and Hrungnir replied by throwing his whetstone at Thor. When the two weapons met in mid-air, the whetstone shattered into two pieces. One piece tumbled to the ground. From pieces of that broken rock are derived all the whetstones now used by men. The second piece embedded itself in Thor's head and he fell to the ground. However, Hrungnir was the one fatally injured, for Thor's hammer struck him on the head and shattered his skull. And so he died. As he crashed to the ground, he fell across Thor and pinned him to the ground. While this was happening, Thialfi easily dispatched the clay-giant, Mokkurkalfi. After he had done this, he went over to Thor and attempted to free him, but he was unable to shift Hrungnir. The Æsir too attempted to move the giant but, even with their combined strength, they could not lift his leg from Thor's neck. It was only when Thor's three-year-old son, Magni, arrived that Thor was freed. For that three-year-old lifted the giant's leg with ease and so freed his father.

Thor was so proud of what Magni had done that he promised him Gullfaxi, the giant's horse. It seemed a fitting gift to give to such a strong little boy, who had freed his own father.

But Odin intervened. He told Thor that it was wrong to give such a fine horse to the child of a giantess; for although Magni was Thor's son, he was born to the giantess, Iarnsaxa. Better, Odin declared, would it be if Thor gave such a horse to his own father (that is to Odin). But the horse went to Magni.

After that, Thor returned to his home at Thrudvangar but the whetstone remained lodged in his head. This remained the state of affairs until Thor received a visitor. This was a sorceress and her name was Groa, the wife of Aurvandil the Bold. When she saw the state of Thor's head, she chanted spells over him and the whetstone started to work loose. Thor was relieved at this and was grateful that the problem seemed on the way to being solved. In his gratitude to Groa, he decided to tell her a story involving her husband, for he felt that this would make her happy. Sometime before, as Thor recounted to her, he had rescued her husband, Aurvandil, out of Giantland in a basket carried on his back. In so doing, he had waded through the 'Ice Waves' rivers that are known as Elivagar and which flowed out from the great void of nothingness (called Ginnungagap, the 'great abyss'), which existed in the far north at the beginning of the world. The rivers were so cold that, as Thor carried Aurvandil south, it had this effect: Aurvandil's toe froze as it was hanging out of the basket. Seeing this, Thor broke off the frozen toe and threw it into the sky to become a star. This is still called 'Aurvandil's toe'. Thor went on to say that Aurvandil would soon be home with Groa, his wife. At this, Groa was so pleased that she forgot the words of her spells. As a result, the whetstone remained in Thor's head and did not come fully out. This is why it is still forbidden to throw a whetstone across the room of a house, for when this is done the whetstone that remains lodged in Thor's head moves, to his discomfort.

Loki's capture and the victory of Thor over the giant, Geirrod, without the use of his hammer, belt of strength and iron gloves

To return to the victory of Thor over Hrungnir . . . This was not the only triumph that Thor had over his enemies. Another such was when Thor visited the hall of Geirrod the giant. At that time, Thor was without Miollnir his hammer, his mighty belt and his iron gauntlets. This lack of his usual equipment was down to Loki and this came about in this way.

Loki had taken on the form of a falcon that was an attribute of the goddess Frigg. In this form, Loki-falcon had flown to Giantland and landed on the window sill of Geirrod's hall. But Geirrod spotted him and ordered one of his servants to catch the bird. It was no easy matter since the window was high up in the wall and the wall was hard to climb. This amused Loki and he resolved to let the servant climb up the entire height of the wall before flying off at the last minute to escape the servant's grasp. But when that moment arrived, Loki found that his feet were stuck and he could not get away. As a result, he was captured and brought down to Geirrod. Geirrod looked hard at the falcon and saw that there was something in its eyes that was different to any bird. In fact, he was convinced that the 'bird' in front of him was really a person in disguise. He demanded that the falcon answer his question as to who he was, but Loki kept quiet. Frustrated by the bird's silence, Geirrod locked him in a chest and there the bird was imprisoned for three months and starved. When the three months were over, Geirrod had the chest unlocked and the falcon brought to him. Once more, he demanded to know the real identity of the bird. This time, Loki answered him, for he feared that if he did not do so he would die of hunger in the locked chest. In order to gain his freedom, Loki promised the giant that he would get Thor to come to the hall – but without his mighty equipment. No hammer. No belt. No iron gloves. As a result, Loki was freed in order to go and fetch Thor and bring him into Giantland.

Thor answered Loki's summons and came into Giantland. There they spent the night in the hall of a giantess named Grid. She was the mother of Vidar the silent. Now, Grid advised Thor what kind of giant Geirrod was; how he was cunning and difficult to deal with. Seeing that Thor lacked his usual weapons she loaned him another belt of strength, some iron gloves and a staff. Setting out from there, Thor and Loki made to cross the wide river Vimur. Putting on the belt of strength and steadying himself with the staff, Thor waded out into the strong current and Loki clung onto his belt. As they crossed the river, the water began to rise and Thor saw that ahead was Gialp, Geirrod's giantess-daughter. She was blocking the river and it was her who was causing the level of the great river to rise. Picking up a large stone from the riverbed, Thor flung it at Gialp and struck her. At the same time, he grasped a rowan tree growing out of the riverbank and hauled himself up and out of the swirling current. That is why it is said that 'the rowan tree saved Thor'.

Having crossed the river, Thor and Loki were soon at the hall of Geirrod. There, they were given lodging in a goats' byre with only one seat to sit on within it. As Thor sat he suddenly found that the seat was rising up and threatening to crush him against the roof. Wedging the staff of Grid against the roof timbers, he forced the seat down hard. There was a scream and Thor discovered that beneath the seat were Geirrod's two daughters, Gialp and Greip. Both now had broken backs for they had been forcing the seat upwards before Thor put a stop to that.

Next, Geirrod called Thor into his hall. Awaiting him were games designed to test him. Geirrod picked up a molten lump of iron and threw it at Thor. Because Thor was wearing the iron gloves that the giantess Grid had given him, he was able to catch the glowing lump of metal and hurl it back at Geirrod. But Geirrod threw himself behind a pillar to protect himself. However, this did not save him, for Thor threw it with such force that it crashed through the pillar (although it too was made from iron), passed right through the body of Geirrod, then out through the wooden wall of the hall and buried itself in the ground outside.

And so – although due to Loki's capture and the manner of his release, Thor had been compelled to go to visit Geirrod without his hammer, belt of strength and iron gloves – through the assistance of the giantess named Grid he had succeeded in defeating Geirrod. Once more, it was Thor who had triumphed over the giants. Trolls or giants, Thor was their sworn enemy and many had cause to regret coming against him in a fight.

11

Stories of gold and of gods

F OUND IN THE *Prose Edda* and in *The Language of Poetry* are stories about the origins of gold and its association with the gods and the giants, with adventures and with vengeance. These stories sometimes use tales found elsewhere in the collections of myths in order to make these points. For example, the story of the otter-pelt, Fafnir and Sigurd also appears in Chapter 19 of this book, as does that of Hrolf Kraki in Chapter 23.

The high profile of gold in the mythology reminds us of how important it was in royal gift giving and in binding warriors to their lords in the Viking Age. As a consequence, a significant number of myths and associated poetic terms were connected to this precious metal.

Giants and giantesses (*jötnar* in Old Norse) are common characters in Norse mythology. The gods are frequently in opposition to the giants who they have banished to Giantland and refused entry to Asgard, the home of the gods. The relationship between the gods and the giants is a complex one with several of the gods, including Odin and Loki, partly descended from giants. There are intermittent quarrels with the giants, which see the giants trying to seize various treasures or goddesses and the gods then raiding Giantland (*Jötunheimr* in Old Norse) to get them back.

Dwarfs (Old Norse: *dvergr*), in contrast, are only ever portrayed as masculine. They work as smiths and produce various treasures for the gods – including some made out of gold. Their homes, in earth and rocks, also associate them with the mining of precious minerals. The *Poetic Edda* describes dwarfs as being the product of the primordial blood of Brimir (Ymir) and the bones of Blainn (see Chapter 17). The *Prose Edda*, though, has a different story and instead refers to dwarfs as similar to maggots, which grew in the flesh of Ymir before being given reason by the gods. Some of the norns (female beings who rule the destiny of gods and men) were thought to be descended from dwarfs (see Chapter 4). Incidentally, the traditional plural of 'dwarf' was 'dwarfs', not 'dwarves'. The latter form was popularised by J. R. R. Tolkien to describe beings of Middle Earth and has gained increased currency since then.

* * *

Gold is called by many names in poetry, such as 'Aegir's fire', 'Glasir's leaves', 'Sif's hair', 'otter-payment', 'Fafnir's home', 'Niflungs' treasure', 'Frodi's flour' and 'Kraki's seed'. Now these names are because of the stories associated with this precious metal. These are some of the stories that lie behind these names . . .

Gold described as 'Aegir's fire'

One day Aegir (the sea-giant) went as a guest to the halls of Asgard. When it was time to leave, he repaid the compliment by inviting Odin and the Æsir to come to visit him in three months' time. When the time had elapsed, the Æsir set off to journey to his hall. The Æsir who went were Odin, accompanied by Asyniur, Bragi, Freyia, Freyr, Frigg, Gefion, Idunn, Loki, Niord, Sif, Skadi, Tyr and Vidar. Thor, though, was not in that number since he was in the eastern regions killing trolls.

So, the Æsir reached the hall of Aegir. There they took their places for the feast and Aegir had light brought into the hall so that they could see as they ate and drank. Now, in Valhalla, where the Æsir lived, the light in the hall at feasts shone from swords but in the hall of Aegir the light shone from glowing lumps of gold. They shone so brightly that they illuminated the whole hall. It was as if fire was blazing there. As the feast got under way, Loki got into a dispute with the other gods and he also killed one of the slaves of Aegir. That slave's name was Fimafeng. This was not the only thing that stood out during that feast. A remarkable thing was that the feast served itself. Food arrived on its own, as did the drink and the knives and all that was necessary. It simply appeared at the mead benches. This is why gold is sometimes called: 'Aegir's fire'. Such is the way of poets that this has given rise to other names, too, that are linked to this. It is also known as 'fire of the sea' (since Aegir is a sea-giant), also 'fire of rivers and lakes' (since, as a giant of water, Aegir has also given his name to these stretches of water in poetry). Sometimes it is called 'fire of Ran' because she is the wife of Aegir and has a net that can catch any who sail on the sea. In this way her name is used as a substitute for that of Aegir himself.

Gold described as 'Glasir's leaves'

Gold is also called 'Glasir's leaves' because a tree by that name stands in front of the doors of the hall at Valhalla and its leaves are made from red gold. So this tree that grows before Odin's hall has also given poets a way of describing gold.

Gold described as 'Sif's hair'

Another name for gold is 'Sif's hair'. The story that lies behind this name involves the goddess Sif and how she was mistreated by Loki. Now, Loki, from his nature of causing trouble, had cut off all the golden hair of Sif. When Thor heard of this he was furious and seized Loki and threatened to break every bone in his body. But Loki, in fear of Thor's anger, swore an oath that he would employ black-elves to make Sif new hair that would be made so that it would grow as any other hair. It was to the sons of the dwarf Ivaldi that Loki finally turned and secured from them their agreement to make the golden hair for Sif. It was these skilled metalworkers who also made Odin's spear, which is called Gungnir; and the ship Skidbladnir, which is the finest ship in the world and belongs to the god Freyr (although some say it was made by Odin).

It was at this time that Loki had a bet with another dwarf, named Brokk, in which Loki wagered his own head against that dwarf's brother (Eitri) being capable of making three such amazing things as Sif's hair of gold, the spear of Odin and the ship of Freyr. Eitri pitted his skills against the task set him. First, he put a pig's hide into his blazing forge and urged his brother, Brokk, to keeping blowing on the flames until the heat had finished working on the pig's hide. At this point Eitri left his metalworking shop but Brokk kept on working the bellows. While Brokk did this, a fly landed on his arm and bit him; but Brokk kept on at his work and ignored the fly. When Eitri returned and pulled the pig's hide out of the fire it had been transformed into a boar with golden bristles.

Then Eitri put a lump of gold into the forge and again told Brokk not to rest from blowing the bellows on it. Again Eitri went out and again the fly returned; only this time it settled on Brokk's neck and bit him, twice as hard as before. Again Brokk ignored the fly and kept at his work. When Eitri returned he pulled a gold ring from the flames and that gold ring is called Draupnir, which has the property of multiplying itself into other rings: every ninth night, eight new rings drip from Draupnir and add to the wealth of Odin, its owner.

Finally, Eitri placed a lump of iron into the forge and again told Brokk to keep working the bellows, for the work would fail if there was even a single pause. Once more Eitri left the workshop and once more the fly returned. Only this time it settled on Brokk's face and bit his eyelids. The blood ran into Brokk's eyes and he could not see. Brokk was so distracted that he attempted to swat that fly, even as he was working the bellows. The fly flew off. At this point, Eitri returned because he knew that it had come close to everything in the forge being spoiled due to Brokk being distracted by the fly. Despite this, a hammer had been forged and Eitri took it and presented it to Brokk, along with the boar with its golden bristles and the magical ring.

These three amazing things were carried to Asgard by Brokk, so that the Æsir could judge their worth. And Loki also brought the golden hair, the spear and the ship to set against what Eitri had made. Those who sat in judgement were Odin, Thor and

Freyr, and their judgement was to be final, with no appeal against it. So the trial of the wondrous things began.

Loki gave the spear to Odin, the golden hair to Thor and the ship to Freyr so that they could judge their excellence; for the spear was unstoppable, the golden hair would root itself in Sif's head, and the ship would always find a fair wind and could be folded and carried in a pocket. To challenge this, Brokk gave the multiplying ring to Odin, the boar to Freyr and the hammer to Thor. Like Loki, he extolled their virtues: the ring multiplying every ninth night; the boar could race across the sky and the sea faster than the best horse and would shed light from its golden bristles; the hammer could strike as heavily as Thor wished, it would never miss its target, it would always return to him and it was small enough to be kept inside his shirt. Odin, Thor and Freyr conferred and were in agreement that the hammer was the greatest of all the remarkable works and that with it the frost-giants could be kept at bay. In consequence, they announced that the dwarf had won the contest and had defeated Loki. Faced with this defeat, Loki offered to pay compensation for his head in some way, but Brokk was not interested: he wanted Loki's *head*.

Loki was not going to wait for Brokk to cut off his head and so he sprang away. In his escape he was aided by the shoes that he was wearing, for they could carry him across sky and sea at great speed. But Brokk appealed to Thor for justice and Thor caught Loki. As the dwarf made to cut off Loki's head, Loki protested that the head belonged to the dwarf – but not the neck. At this Brokk stitched up Loki's lips – though not without difficulty and it finally required an awl to make holes in the lips – for this was the mouth that had challenged Brokk and his brother. And that is why gold is sometimes called 'Sif's hair'.

Gold described as 'otter-payment'

Once, Odin, Loki and Haenir were out exploring and they came to a river. Following its course to a waterfall, they came upon an otter. The otter had caught a salmon and was eating it. So relaxed was the otter that it did not sense the approach of the three members of the Æsir, so that when Loki threw a stone at it, the rock caught the otter completely by surprise and it was struck on the head. At this, Loki was very pleased, since in one action he had gained both an otter and a salmon. Picking up the otter and salmon, Odin, Loki and Haenir went on their way until they reached a farmhouse and went inside. This was the home of the magician, Hreidmar. The three members of the Æsir asked if they could stay the night. Furthermore, they explained that they carried their own provisions and showed Hreidmar the salmon and the otter. At this sight, Hreidmar called his two sons. They were named Fafnir and Regin. When they arrived, Hreidmar showed them the body of the otter, which he declared was their brother, and he told them that the Æsir had killed him. Incensed at the death of Otter, his two brothers seized the three Æsir and bound them tightly. Seeing the danger that they were in, the Æsir negotiated for their lives by inviting Hreidmar to name the price in treasure that should be paid by them as compensation for the life of his son. This was sealed with oaths.

Hreidmar skinned the otter and declared that the price he demanded for the life of his son was that the skin should be filled with red gold and, indeed, covered entirely with it. Only this would satisfy him. This was a great demand and so Odin dispatched Loki into the realm of the black-elves to seek out sufficient gold. Coming to a lake, Loki saw a fish that was actually the dwarf, Andvari. Seizing him as prisoner, Loki would not release him until the dwarf gave up all the gold that he had hidden in his underground home in the rocks. This amounted to a huge amount of gold. The dwarf had no choice but to do as Loki demanded. But as he paid over the gold he tried to keep back one solitary ring. But Loki spotted this and demanded that Andvari hand that over with the rest of the gold in his hoard. At this, the dwarf pleaded to be allowed to keep the ring, since it was a magic ring and from it he could, in time, cause more gold to accrue. Loki, though, was having none of it and demanded every last piece of the dwarf's gold. Faced with losing everything, the dwarf declared that whoever owned the ring would find it brought nothing but destruction. Loki was undaunted by the threat and said that this could indeed be so and that he, Loki, would tell whoever took the ring about its terrible power.

Loki took the gold back to Odin who gave it to Hreidmar – except for the ring. Odin thought it a thing of great beauty and so kept it for himself. Having received the gold, Hreidmar filled the otter-skin with it. When it was so full that no more gold could be pressed inside, Odin began to cover the outside of the pelt with gold. Soon the whole skin was covered with gold. The whole skin, that is, apart from one whisker. Seeing this, Hreidmar demanded that it too should be covered or the agreement that had been made with the Æsir would be null and void. In response, Odin took the ring and with it he covered the remaining whisker of the otter. In so doing, the agreement with Hreidmar was fulfilled since the otter-payment had been made in full.

This being done, the possessions of the Æsir were returned to them. Odin received back his powerful spear and Loki the shoes with which he could race across sea and sky. Then the

Æsir were no longer afraid of Hreidmar and so Loki pronounced the ring's doom on Hreidmar. And this was indeed so. The gold was the cause of Hreidmar's death. This is why some poets call gold by the name of 'otter-payment'. Others, mindful of the way that the gold was paid over and of the fate of Hreidmar, know it as 'metal of conflict'. Still others call it 'forced payment of the Æsir' in memory of the way that they had to produce the gold in order to save their lives.

Gold described as 'Fafnir's home'

This is how the gold taken from Andvari became the doom of Hreidmar. Once he had taken the gold, he refused to share any of it with his sons. For they had demanded some as compensation for the death of Otter, their brother. When Hreidmar refused them, they killed him, their own father.

With Hreidmar dead, the two brothers fell out among themselves. Regin demanded that Fafnir should share the gold with him. But Fafnir replied that, since he had killed his own father for the gold, he was not inclined to share it with his brother and that Regin should leave before he was killed. Following this threat, Fafnir put on a terrifying helmet that had belonged to Hreidmar and took up his father's sword, too. Regin fled away at the sight. Picking up the gold, Fafnir took it up to the heathland that is called Gnitaheath or 'Glittering Heath'. There he dug a lair for himself and the gold. With the gold hidden underground, Fafnir turned into a serpent and lay down on the gold (in the manner of dragons, who guard the gold within burial mounds).

Although Regin had not gained his share of the gold, he had not given up on it. He went to live at the court of King Hialprek of Denmark. There he became a craftsman making fine swords. While there, Regin became the foster-father to Sigurd, son of Sigmund, of the family of the Volsungs. Sigurd was renowned for his strength and his courage as a royal warrior who was descended from brave ancestors. Regin told Sigurd about the great hoard of treasure hidden on Gnitaheath and how it was guarded by Fafnir the serpent. Regin told Sigurd that he should go with him and win this gold. To this end, Regin forged him a sword, which was called Gram (meaning 'wrath') and which was so sharp that with it Sigurd cut Regin's iron anvil in two. Prepared for battle, the two set out for Gnitaheath and Fafnir's great hoard of gold.

There an ambush was prepared for Fafnir. Sigurd dug a trench in the place that Fafnir came down to drink. He hid in the trench and when Fafnir the serpent passed above him he drove his sword through the serpent's body. And so died Fafnir. With the serpent dead, Regin told Sigurd that he had killed his brother but that he would accept compensation in the form of Sigurd roasting Fafnir's heart for him. While Sigurd did this, Regin drank from Fafnir's blood and then lay down to sleep.

Meanwhile, Sigurd was still roasting the heart of Fafnir. Testing whether it was cooked, he burned his fingers on the juices that seeped out and so he put them in his mouth to cool. As the blood of Fafnir touched his tongue he suddenly found that he could understand the language of the birds in a nearby tree. One bird said how Sigurd would be wise to eat Fafnir's heart himself. Another bird spoke and said how Regin was plotting revenge against the warrior who had killed his brother.

Warned by the birds, Sigurd rose, drew his sword and killed Regin. Taking Grani, Regin's horse, Sigurd rode further onto Gnitaheath, until he came to the lair in which Fafnir had hidden the gold. Taking the treasure he placed it on the back of Grani and rode away with it. That is why some poets refer to gold as 'Fafnir's home', while others call it 'Grani's load' and yet others call it 'Gnitaheath-metal'.

Gold described as 'Niflungs' treasure'

After Sigurd gained the gold, he rode on until he came to a hall set on the mountain; and inside he found there was a sleeping woman. She was dressed in helmet and mail. Sigurd cut the mail from her and she awoke and told him that her name was Hild and that she was a valkyrie.

From there, Sigurd rode on to the court of King Giuki. He stayed there some time and married the king's daughter, Gudrun. Her brothers – Gunnar and Hogni – then swore oaths of brotherhood with Sigurd. The family of Giuki were known as the Niflungs. As a result of the oath of brotherhood, Sigurd accompanied them when they rode to seek a bride for Gunnar. This was Brynhild, the sister of Atli Budlason, whom some call Attila the Hun. Now, Brynhild's home of Hindafell was surrounded by fire and she had sworn to only marry the man who was brave enough to cross that ring of flames. Gunnar was determined to cross the fire but his horse refused to do so. Only Sigurd's horse, Grani, was prepared to do this but Grani would let nobody on his back but Sigurd, and he knew who Sigurd was no matter how well he was disguised. So Sigurd and Gunnar exchanged appearance. By so doing, the horse would cross the flames for he knew his rider was really Sigurd (even though he appeared to be Gunnar) and yet Brynhild would believe that it was Gunnar who had done so and therefore would consent to marry him. This is what happened but that night Sigurd placed his sword between them so that they had no sexual relations. In the morning, he and Brynhild exchanged gifts. He gave her the ring that had once belonged to Andvari, and she gave him a ring from her own treasure store.

In this way Gunnar won Brynhild and married her. But things did not go smoothly within that family because of a falling out between Brynhild (the wife of Gunnar) and Gudrun (the wife of Sigurd). And that arose from Brynhild's boasting. For one day she and Gudrun went to the river to wash their hair. While they were doing this, Brynhild said that she should not stand downstream from Gudrun and have Gudrun's soiled water to bathe in, for her husband Gunnar was braver than Sigurd. At this Gudrun retorted that in truth it was Sigurd who was the bravest for he had killed both Fafnir and Regin and seized their gold-hoard. Brynhild was not impressed and answered her that Sigurd had not dared to cross the barrier of fire at Hindafell; only Gunnar had dared do that. Gudrun then answered that the gold ring that Brynhild treasured was the same as one that Gudrun herself had been given by Sigurd and this was clear proof that it was Sigurd who had crossed the flames, slept with Brynhild and given her a ring. These rings had come from Fafnir's gold-hoard on Gnitaheath and only Sigurd owned that golden treasure now. At this, Brynhild fell silent, for she could make no reply.

Brynhild was bitter at what Gudrun had said and so she tried to incite Gunnar, her husband, to kill Sigurd and to include Hogni in the killing. But both men refused as they were sworn-brothers of Sigurd. Instead, they got their other brother, Gothorm, to do the killing. He stabbed Sigurd, but Sigurd threw his sword at him and it sliced him in half. As well as killing Sigurd, his three-year-old son Sigmund was also murdered at the same time. Brynhild then stabbed herself and was burned on the same funeral pyre as Sigurd. Gunnar and Hogni took Fafnir's treasure and ruled jointly. Brynhild's brother, King Atli Budlason, then married Gudrun, the widow of Sigurd. He invited Gunnar and Hogni to visit him but they feared for their gold and buried it in the riverbed of the River Rhine. It is there to this day and nobody has ever found it. King Atli Budlason fought and captured Gunnar and Hogni. He cut Hogni's heart from his living body and threw Gunnar into a snake pit. His hands were tied but he played his harp with his toes to lull the snakes to sleep. But one snake did not sleep and bit and killed him. This is why gold is sometimes called 'Niflungs' treasure', for Gunnar and Hogni were of the family of the Niflungs, and they had become the owners of the gold-hoard of Fafnir.

The killing of Gunnar and Hogni left their sister, Gudrun, bitter towards King Atli Budlason, her husband. In revenge, she killed her two sons by King Atli Budlason and fashioned cups out of their skulls. The outside of each skull she adorned with silver and gold. She placed mead in these skull-cups and mixed it with the boys' blood. Then she served it to her husband along with the boys' hearts that she had cooked. After the king had drunk the blood of his own sons and eaten their hearts, Gudrun told him what she had done with many bitter words. However, the mead was so strong that everyone in the hall fell asleep over the mead-tables and that night Gudrun killed King Atli Budlason and set fire to his hall. So died Atli (Attila) and his Hun nobles.

After this, Gudrun tried to drown herself in the sea but was washed ashore on the coast of Denmark, where she was found and married by King Ionakr. They had three sons and, like all the Niflungs, they had raven-black hair. In Denmark, Gudrun had with her the beautiful Svanhild, the child of Sigurd. She was chosen to be the bride of King Iormunrekk the Great, who some call Eormenric, of the Ostrogoths. But when he sent his son to fetch her, he and Svanhild decided to marry each other instead of Svanhild marrying old King Iormunrekk. When King Iormunrekk heard of this he had his son executed and Svanhild trampled to death under the hooves of his horses and the horses of his nobles.

When Gudrun heard that her daughter had been killed, she sent her three sons to kill King Iormunrekk but they fell out among themselves and two of them murdered the third because he was the favourite of their mother. When they reached King Iormunrekk, they cut off his arms and legs but, without their brother to assist them, they did not cut off his head and so his head alerted his men who stoned the two brothers to death. And so died the sons of Gudrun.

Gold described as 'Frodi's flour'

There was once a son of Odin by the name of Skiold. He lived in a place then known as Gotland but now called Denmark. His grandson was named Frodi. When Frodi became king, Augustus was emperor of Rome and it was during this time that Christ was born. Frodi was a powerful king who brought peace to the northern lands, which people referred to as 'Frodi's peace'. Nobody killed another, even if they had the right to exact vengeance; and a gold ring could lie on the ground and not be picked up. One day, Frodi went to Sweden to visit its king and while he was there he purchased two strong female slaves. He set them to work on a huge set of millstones that had been found in Denmark and which would grind out whatever was ordered from them. Now, Frodi ordered 'gold' and 'peace' but the overworked slave girls ground out an army and Frodi was killed when a sea-king (a Viking) came against him. This sea-king took the millstones and the slave girls and ordered them to grind out salt, but so much was produced that his ships sank and that is how the sea became salty. It was after that grinding of the millstones that gold is sometimes called 'Frodi's flour' for, had he succeeded, the slaves would have ground him out sacks of gold in the same way that flour is usually produced.

Gold described as 'Kraki's seed'

There was once a king of Denmark known as Hrolf Kraki (meaning 'long-faced Hrolf'). While he was king, the ruler of Uppsala in Sweden was King Adils, who had married the mother of Hrolf Kraki. He was at war with the king of Norway. They had agreed to meet in battle on the ice of Lake Vaeni and so King Adils called on Hrolf Kraki to support him. Now Hrolf Kraki himself was engaged in a war with the Saxons to the south and could not answer the summons himself but, instead, he sent twelve of his berserkers. In the event the battle led to the death of the Norwegian king and the berserkers asked for the pay that they had been promised by King Adils, along with treasure for their king, Hrolf Kraki. But King Adils refused any payment and those warriors left him feeling very angry.

When Hrolf Kraki heard of this, he gathered his army and sailed to Sweden. He and his berserkers rode to Uppsala where they were greeted by the mother of Hrolf Kraki. She took them to a hall where they were given drink and great fires were built for them. But the men of King Adils heaped so much wood on the fires that they threatened to burn Hrolf Kraki and his men.

But Hrolf Kraki was unafraid and actually added to the fires by throwing his shield onto the flames and his warriors did likewise. Then they took the Swedish retainers and threw them onto the fire too.

After this, the mother of Hrolf Kraki gave him much gold and told him that he should go. They did so, but were pursued by King Adils and his army. To divert them, Hrolf Kraki scattered gold on the ground in the same way that a farmer scatters seed and the Swedish soldiers dismounted to pick it up. But King Adils continued to pursue the Danish king and his warriors until Hrolf Kraki threw a gold ring to the ground and King Adils bent down to pick it up on the point of his spear. At this, Hrolf Kraki mocked him and said that, though he was greatest among the Swedes, he had grovelled like a pig to get the gold ring. And this is why gold is sometimes called 'Kraki's seed'.

Other names for gold

Gold is also known in poetry as 'fire of the arm', since it glows in warriors' arm rings; and 'fire of ice', since it can be white; and 'Rhine's red metal', recalling how it was hidden in that great river. In a similar way, gold is associated with noble people in various ways, such as calling a man 'gold-breaker', because a warrior shatters the gold ornaments of his enemies; and 'gold-prince', because kings reward warriors with gold. A woman may be called 'gold-dealer', because a high-born woman will reward warriors with gold; and 'sun-pillar', for gold shines like the sun and a woman stands slender and fine like the pillar in a hall; and 'coin-oak', for coins may be made of precious gold (given in reward by a high-born lady) and, like an oak, a noble woman stands fair and tall.

12

The sayings of Odin

THESE SAYINGS EXPLORE what, in pre-Christian Norse society, constituted 'wisdom'. This relates to human wisdom, the use of runes, mysteries and spells. Many of these refer to the advice and conventions that dictated behaviour in the lord's hall or between neighbours. Others, though, refer to matters of religion, belief and mythology. These are the ones recounted here. These are found in the collection of traditions known as the *Poetic Edda*.

Wisdom poetry is written throughout the *Poetic Edda* in a form called in Old Norse *ljodahattr* (literally: song-metre), which consists of stanzas in two sections, with each composed of a long line with four stresses and up to three alliterative syllables, and a shorter line with two stresses and two alliterative syllables. It was a form reserved for wisdom and dialogue poetry. Poems within the *Poetic Edda* do not have to necessarily conform to just one of the forms and styles of verse. This means that while there are whole poems within the *Edda* that are solely composed in *ljodahattr*, there are others that contain only sections of gnomic observations (consisting of short maxims or aphorisms).

Odin, as the Norse god of wisdom, is a tie that binds all the wisdom poetry in the *Poetic Edda* together. It is Odin who instructs Sigurd in battle omens in the poem called *Regin's Sayings*. He also displays his compendious knowledge in *Grimnir's Sayings*, when he disguises himself in order to test the giant Geirrod and ultimately to teach him the true meaning of wisdom. It is only after he has imparted this knowledge that he reveals himself to Geirrod. Within the collection known as *The Sayings of the High One* (examples are given below), it is the figure of Odin who unifies the poem and draws together all the separate strands of wisdom. It is the appearance of Odin half-way through the poem that provides the identification of a narrative voice and adds validity to the wisdom that has preceded it. Wisdom is portrayed in the poetry as Odin's gift to mankind and, as such, his presence as the originator and original acquirer of wisdom is felt throughout all of the wisdom poetry in the *Poetic Edda*.

Wisdom poetry has no prescribed form, no narrative or chronological principle, and the collections of sayings (gnomes) are linked by theme. These poems are often not progressive but rather pick up a theme, explore it and then move on. The themes discussed include a wide range encompassing drunkenness, folly, moderation in food and drink, the behaviour of foolish men, mockery, friendship, limitations of wisdom, wealth and women.

* * *

Odin speaks of how he gained the mead of poetry

I once visited the old giant and have since returned from
there.

Keeping quiet there did me no good, so I spoke out and
there

in Suttung's hall I gained things to my advantage.

I was given by Gunnlod a drink of rare and precious mead.

She gave it to me from her golden throne.

She was generous to me but got little back in return.

I bored my way into the mountain to find where Gunnlod
lived.

I risked my head when I slipped through that passageway,
with giants close at hand.

There I found a vat of mead; that vat was called Odrerir.

I would never have come back from Giantland, had I not
been helped

by the good woman named Gunnlod. The woman that I
embraced.

The next day the frost-giants came to the High One's hall
to ask for advice.

They sought out Odin by the name that he had taken for
himself when disguised

as a slave: that name was Bolverk.

They desired to know whether Bolverk was among the gods
or whether he

had been killed by Suttung the giant.

Odin had sworn a sacred oath on a ring but, despite this, he
betrayed Suttung at his feast and left Gunnlod weeping.

Now wisdom is proclaimed by Odin from his high-seat,
beside the well

from which flows the fate of all.

At that place in the High One's hall, there was talk of men
and runes and good advice.

Odin speaks again, of how he gained wisdom and rune-knowledge

I hung on a tree with the wind blowing round.
I hung there for nine long nights.
I was wounded with a spear.
I was thus sacrificed to Odin; myself to myself.
And it was on that tree, the one whose deep roots are
unknown to any man.
As I hung there I was given no food; I was given no drink.
I stared downward from where I hung.
Then I seized the runes; screaming with pain I seized them.
Then I fell back, but I had gained them.
Nine powerful spells I learned from Bolthor's famous son
(Odin's mother's brother).
As well as this I got to drink of that precious mead that was
poured out
of the vat called Odrerir.
After that drink I revived and became wise.
I grew and I prospered.
One word grew into another and one deed grew into
another.

Runes need to be sought out and the most significant one
found:
a letter that is great and powerful.
Such a letter is one made by the powerful gods and carved
by the one
who is rune-master to the gods.

Odin carved the rune for the Æsir.
Dain carved the rune for the elves.
Dvalin carved the rune for the dwarfs.
Asvid carved the rune for the giants.
Each had a rune that stood for their kind.

And how is such wisdom gained?
It is gained by knowing how to carve, how to interpret the
    meaning,
how to test the meaning, how to ask, how to sacrifice and
    how to kill.
Better not to pray at all, than to sacrifice more than is
    necessary.
Better not to kill at all, than to engage in too great a
    slaughter.
In this way Odin, when known by the name Thund, carved
    runes before
the history of nations was written.

Odin speaks again, of magic spells

I know spells better than the wife of a king; better than the
    son of any man.
I know a spell that brings help against any accusation, any
    sorrow.
It will help defeat fear.

I know another, which will help those who heal the sick.

I know another, which will bind the strength of an enemy.
It will blunt the edge of their swords.
No weapon of theirs will strike home and cut.

I know another, that will free me from chains that men
  might place on me.
When I chant it, I can walk away.
Chains fall away and feet and hands become free.

I know another, that will stop an arrow in flight.
When warriors join in battle and the arrows fly,
then they can be stopped, no matter how fast they fly.
If I see it, I can stop it.

I know another, that I can use if I am wounded in a fight.
Though a wooden weapon is raised against me, it will fail.
And if a man tries to ensnare me with magic then that will
  rebound on him.

I know another, to use if fire threatens to burn down the
  hall.
No matter how wide and fierce it burns, this spell will stop
  it.

I know another, which I can use if disharmony threatens to
  divide warriors.
This one will bring a settlement of peace where there was
  once strife.

I know another, that will protect a ship at sea.
It will quieten the waves and calm the sea.

I know another, to defeat shape-shifting witches.
It will prevent them returning to their human form.

I know another, to protect friends in battle.
This one will protect their journey to the fight, their times
   in the battle,
and their journey away from the field of war.

I know another, for when I see a dead man hanging from a
   tree.
By carving these runes and colouring them rightly, that
   man will walk and speak again.

I know another, to recite when pouring water over a warrior.
That warrior will then be invincible in battle.
No sword will touch him.

I know another, which will assist me to name all the gods.
With it I can tell the Æsir from the elves.
Only those who are wise can do this.

I know another, which will secure for me a woman's affec-
   tion and her love-making.
With it I can command her thoughts and cause her mind
   to conform to my will.

I know another, that will draw all young girls to me.
These are spells that are useful for all who know them.

I know another, that I will not teach to any woman.
I will not teach it to any girl.
I will not teach it to the wife of any man.
Though I will tell it to the woman that I embrace in love.
Or to my sister.

These are the songs that were sung by the High One in the
hall of the High One.

These are useful to the sons of men.

They are of no use to the sons of giants.

They benefit the one who recites and knows them.

They benefit the one who has learnt this recitation; the one
who has listened.

13

The rivalry of Odin and Frigg over the sons of King Hraudung

FOUND IN THE *Poetic Edda* and in a section known as *Grimnir's Sayings*, this story tells how Odin and Frigg competed with each other through the patronage of two royal children. The story also explores beliefs about the wisdom of Odin.

Grimnir's Sayings tells of a rivalry between Odin and his wife Frigg. Frigg tricks King Geirrod into torturing her husband when he arrives at his hall disguised as Grimnir (which means 'masked one' in Old Norse). This is just one of many times that Odin travels in disguise under a false name in Norse mythology and is a distinct feature of the traditions associated with him. The importance of hospitality to Germanic society is seen in the poem with Frigg accusing Geirrod, Odin's favourite, of stinginess – a serious insult – and Agnar (Agnar-the-younger, not to be confused with Geirrod's brother of the same name) receiving Odin's favour due to him taking on the responsibility of the host by offering Odin a drink.

The poem starts with a lengthy introduction, which sets out the narrative backstory. This is then followed by a fifty-four-stanza monologue delivered by Odin disguised as Grimnir. The poetic monologue is concerned with mythological facts and particularly the topography of the world of the gods. The poem concludes with another prose section, which acts as an epilogue showing the fatal consequences of Geirrod's actions. The prose elements are likely to be later than the original poem and were added to provide context.

This is one of several poems in the *Poetic Edda* – including *The Seeress' Prophecy*, *Vafthrudnir's Sayings* and *Sayings of the High One* – that show the importance of wisdom to Odin. In this poem, however, Odin is imparting wisdom, rather than searching for it in the desperate (and vain) hope of preventing Ragnarok. Held between two fires, Odin begins to reveal his knowledge and wisdom for the benefit of Agnar, Geirrod's son, so he can become king in his father's stead. The gaining of this wisdom is implied as being crucial for the young boy if he is to be a successful ruler. This echoes episodes in the youth of Sigurd the dragon-slayer where the acquisition of wisdom is an important step in him moving from being simply a warrior to being a leader of men; and it highlights a key feature of what was expected of a ruler.

* * *

The sons of King Hraudung are rescued by an old couple

There was once a king by the name of Hraudung. He was king over the Goths. He was a sea-king who was famous for his Viking exploits, although some claim that he was a giant. This

king had two sons. Now, the two sons were named Agnar and
Geirrod. Agnar was the eldest when this story starts and was
ten years old. Geirrod was eight years old. One day the two
children went fishing. They only intended to put out a little
way from the shore in order to catch a few small fish. But the
wind caught the boat and pushed them far out to sea; out into
the deep water. It grew dark and they had no idea where they
were until, at last, the waves carried them onto a strange shore.
There, the boat was wrecked but both the boys escaped with
their lives. Exploring, they came across a small cottage and the
farmer there sheltered them for the winter. The couple living
there were an old man and his wife. Together they acted as
foster-parents to the two lost boys. The old woman became the
foster-mother of Agnar and the old man became the foster-
father of Geirrod.

When winter gave way to spring, the old man made enquir-
ies and sought out a ship that they might use to take them
home. The old man and his wife took the two boys down to the
harbour and settled them on the ship. Before it sailed, the old
man spoke privately with Geirrod, his foster-son. At last, the
ship set sail and eventually took the boys back to the land ruled
by their father. But once the ship had grounded on the shore,
Geirrod leapt out of it. Before his brother Agnar could get off
the vessel, Geirrod turned and gave it a mighty push. He cried
out, 'Go wherever the trolls will guide you.' And with that the
ship slipped away from the shore, carrying Agnar with it. Then
Geirrod went up to the royal hall and was greeted with great
joy, for the king, his father, had died over the winter and the
land had no ruler. Then Geirrod was proclaimed king in succession to Hraudung and he ruled as a powerful king with great
renown.

The true identities of the foster-parents revealed

The old couple who had fostered the two boys were none other than Odin and Frigg. It was Frigg who had acted as foster-mother to Agnar and Odin who had acted as foster-father to Geirrod. One day, Odin and Frigg were at Odin's high seat; the place from which it was possible to see into all the worlds. There the lives of Agnar and Geirrod could be seen.

Odin boasted to Frigg that Agnar was reduced to raising children by a giantess in nothing better than a cave. While this was happening, Geirrod was ruling as a king from a royal hall. In this way, Odin mocked the lowly achievement of Frigg's foster-son in comparison with the success enjoyed by his own foster-son. It was now clear that the secret advice that the 'old man' had whispered to Geirrod was that he should abandon his own brother and take the kingdom of their father and rule it alone.

Frigg was incensed at the way that Odin described Agnar and she sought a way to strike back. As she thought about the duties of hospitality that were expected of a king she decided on what carefully crafted insult she would aim at Geirrod. He was, she asserted, a mean king. There was no generosity in him and guests who came to his hall were not given the hospitality that should be expected of a king. Odin denied this and said that this accusation was a lie. And so the two of them laid a bet on the truth of what Frigg had claimed.

The visit of Grimnir, the 'masked one', to Geirrod's royal hall

In order to try out the hospitality of Geirrod, Odin visited him but did so in disguise. He took the name of Grimnir, which means the 'masked one', because his identity was hidden. But before he reached the hall, Frigg had already acted. She had sent Fulla, her servant, to Geirrod to warn him that a wizard, wearing a blue cloak, was on his way to cast a spell on him. Fulla told Geirrod that this wizard was so fierce that no dog would attack him. It did not matter how fierce that dog might be; it would be afraid of the wizard.

When Odin – disguised as Grimnir – reached Geirrod's hall he was seized and held as a prisoner. Geirrod then interrogated him in order to find out who he was and his business. But the wizard would give no answer. In response to this silence, Geirrod forced the wizard to undergo ordeals. First, he gave him no food. Next, he tortured him with fire. For eight whole days the wizard was forced to sit between two raging fires until his blue cloak smouldered with the great heat. But still he would not speak.

At last, Geirrod's son took pity on the wizard. This boy was named Agnar after the lost brother of Geirrod, and he was ten years old. This was the same age as the elder Agnar had been when the wind blew him and his brother out to sea. Agnar-the-younger went up to Grimnir between the two fires and offered him a drinking horn that was full and which would quench his thirst. As he gave Grimnir the drinking horn, Agnar-the-younger said that it was wrong that the wizard was being so badly treated, given that he had done no wrong.

At this, Odin finally began to speak . . .

'The fire is hot and fierce and I have sat here for eight nights without food. Indeed no one offered me food except Agnar (the-younger). So the day will come when he will rule the Goths instead of his father, Geirrod. He will be blessed by Odin for that drink that he brought me.

'I look out over the different worlds. I see the sacred land of the Æsir and of the elves. I see Thor ruling in strength until that day when all will be torn apart. I see Yewdale, where Ull, the god of archery, lives in his hall. I see the hall of Alfheim which was given to Freyr on the day that he lost his first tooth as a child. I see Odin's hall of Valaskialf, with its roof shingled with silver. I see where Odin and Frigg drink daily from golden cups. And I see Valhalla where Odin welcomes the slain, as they arrive fresh from battle. In that place the rafters are made from spears, the thatch from shields and the benches are covered by coats of mail. A wolf hangs over the door and an eagle flies above it. I see the hall of Thiazi the giant and the hall built for Baldr. I see where Heimdall – the watchman of the gods – sits and drinks his mead. I see where Freyia has rule and where half of those slain in battle go; the others go to Odin. I see the golden pillars of Glitnir and the great wooden hall of Niord.

'Over these wide worlds there fly my two ravens: Hugin (Thought) and Munin (Memory). I fear that one day Hugin (Thought) may not return; but most of all I fear the loss of Munin (Memory).

'I see Valhalla with its five hundred and forty doors. They are so wide that eight hundred warriors can pass through one of these doors. They shall pass through these doors on the day that they go out to fight the wolf at Ragnarok. On its roof grazes the goat named Heidrun. She will produce enough mead to fill a great cauldron that cannot be emptied. On that same roof stands the deer named Eikthyrnir. That deer grazes on the branches there and from its antlers drips the waters that form all the rivers of all the worlds. One of those rivers is the one that Thor will wade across on the day that the bridge to the realm of the Æsir burns. On that day, he will sit as judge by the tree called Yggdrasil.

'Under one root of that tree lives Hel. And Ratatosk the squirrel runs up and down the tree carrying messages between the eagle on the topmost branch and the dragon, Nidhogg, down below. The boughs of that tree are fed on by four deer and beneath it lives an unimaginable number of snakes. That tree is suffering beyond belief because the deer gnaw its top, its trunk rots and, below, the dragon Nidhogg tears at its roots.

'From here I also see the way it is in the sky about the earth; how the steeds Arvak and Alsvid pull the chariot of the sun. And under their saddles are iron bellows, placed there by the Æsir. And a shield, called Svalin, stands in front of the sun and were it not there to shield the sun's heat, then all below, mountain and sea, would be consumed by fire. And yet the sun is pursued: by Skoll the wolf. He chases the sun across the sky to the far forests where it dips to hide. And there is another wolf too: Hati, the wolf who pursues the moon. That wolf is the son of Hrodvitnir (or Fenrir).

'Furthermore, I know how the earth was made from the flesh of Ymir; the sea from his blood; the mountains from his bones; the trees from his hair; and the sky from his skull. Middle Earth, where men live, was fashioned from his eyelashes and clouds were formed from his brain.

'And of all that exists, these are the best: Skidbladnir is best of ships and owned by Freyr; Yggdrasil is best of trees; Odin is best of the Æsir; Sleipnir is best of horses; Bifrost is best of bridges; Bragi is best of poets; Habrok is best of hawks; Garm is best of dogs.

'And I am called by many names. I am known as: Mask, Wanderer, Warrior, Helmet-Wearer, High, War-Merry, Masked

One, Maddener, Very-Wise, War-Father, Father of All, Father of the Slain. Since I went among people, there has never been just one name by which I am known. They called me Grimnir when I visited Geirrod. I was Thror at the Assembly. I was Vidur on the battlefield.

'Now Geirrod, you have drunk too much. And you will lose all you have gained, since you have lost my favour. I have told you much but you have remembered little. You have been deceived and I see a sword covered in blood.

'I know that your life is drawing to its end and now, at last, you may look and see Odin. Come close to me if you dare! Odin is my name. I am the Terrible One. And all the other names by which I am known are rooted in me alone. All those names come from Odin the Terrible One.'

When Odin had finished speaking, Geirrod stood up from where he was sitting and made as if to pull Odin, his foster-father, away from the raging fires. Before he leapt up, Geirrod had been sitting with a half-drawn sword on his lap. As he rose from his seat, the sword slipped from his grasp and fell blade uppermost. At the same time, Geirrod lost his footing and fell forward onto his own sword and died. With Geirrod dead, Odin suddenly disappeared. Agnar-the-younger then became king in his father's place and sat on the royal throne as a boy-king. He ruled for a long time.

14

The conflict at the ferry place

A GAIN FOUND IN the collection known as the *Poetic Edda* is this account known as *Harbard's Song*. In it, Odin is disguised as 'Harbard' ('Grey Beard'). In this guise he engages in a battle of insults with Thor, who despite his strength is bested by Odin's cunning. In the story, Thor never guesses the real identity of the one mocking him. But the by-name 'Grey Beard' alerts the hearer/reader to what is going on. In this way, the original composer of the story further stressed the weakness of the apparently mighty Thor in the confrontation. This is a psychologically brutal poem, which includes Odin telling Thor his mother is dead. It is hard to understand Odin's motivation for the confrontation, and nothing explains it in the story as it has come down to us.

This is a type of poem known as a *flyting*. The term is derived from the Old Norse word *flyta*, meaning 'to provoke'. This is a common type of poem in Germanic literature and consists of two opponents exchanging insults. The winner is usually able to demonstrate his own superior strength and manliness, while demonstrating the inferiority and effeminacy of the other. Effeminacy was one of the greatest insults within the warrior-based Norse society of the Viking Age and later. The poem is much less structured than most Eddic poems and is written in a number of different metres – some of which are unrecognisable – and even sections of pure prose.

Stanza 24 of the poem refers to Odin as having followers who are warriors who die in battle, while Thor has peasants. This may express the class divisions in terms of the cults of the two gods. This is reflected in evidence from Anglo-Saxon England, where Woden (the Old English equivalent of Odin) appears in every royal genealogy but one, whereas Thunor (the Old English equivalent of Thor) appears in none. The same noble association with the cult of Odin clearly influenced Viking Age society too. In contrast, Thor's name is derived from the Germanic word for 'thunder' and, as a weather god, he may have had particular appeal to farming communities. However, while 'Thor's hammer' pendants are frequently found in female graves in Scandinavia, the discovery of a silver one in a warrior grave from Repton in Derbyshire, England, shows that the cult could include elite males too, probably through Thor's association with warfare and defeating giants. Gold filigree decoration on a pendant from Great Witchingham in Norfolk, England, underscores this elite association with the cult of Thor.

Although many of the episodes referred to are unknown from the other existing source material, there are several references that will be familiar, including the night Thor spends in a glove during his trip to Utgarda-Loki. In a similar way to *Loki's Quarrel* (see Chapter 15), the poem refers to the unfaithfulness of Thor's wife Sif; although there are no stories outlining the specifics of her unfaithfulness in the surviving corpus of Norse mythology, other than a reference to Loki being involved.

* * *

Thor was travelling from the east. He was often in the east because that was where trolls were found and Thor was often engaged in battling them. On this particular day, as he travelled, he came to an inlet of the sea. As he looked across the water he could see that on the other side of the inlet was the ferryman with his ship.

When he saw this, Thor called out: 'Who is that weakling who is on the other side of the water?'

To this insulting question the ferryman called back: 'And who is that peasant who is shouting across the water?'

And so there started an exchange of shouts. Some of them were boasts and some of them were insults. Either way, their words rang across that inlet of the sea. Back and forth they called to each other.

Thor offered a great reward if the ferryman would only take him across. The payment that Thor offered was an abundance of food. On his back was a basket full of herrings and oatmeal. And just as he had eaten his fill of these for his breakfast, so now he offered the same to the ferryman – if only he would put out from the opposite shore.

The ferryman was unimpressed with what Thor offered and in reply mocked the pride that Thor showed concerning his ability to offer copious amounts of food. Then, to shock him further, the ferryman declared that while Thor was away from home his mother had died. Furthermore, the ferryman mocked

Thor's wealth, doubting he owned as much as three farms of any worth. More to the point, the ferryman pointed out that since Thor stood bare-legged by the shore, he was clearly little more than a beggar who owned no trousers!

Thor ignored this studied insult and instead asked, 'Who owns this ferryboat?' He then went on to say that if the ferryman would but put out across the water, then he, Thor, would direct him to the best place to tie up on the other side of the inlet.

To Thor's question about ownership, the ferryman replied that the boat's owner was named Hildolf. And Hildolf was a respected warrior who possessed great wisdom since he had instructed the ferryman to never take on board bandits or horse-thieves! The only men who should be transported were good men who were recognised by the ferryman. To this end, he called on Thor to identify himself. Only then would the ferryman consider carrying him across the water.

Then Thor declared his identity to the ferryman, proclaiming that he was 'Odin's son, brother of Meili and the father of Magni'. Furthermore, he assured the ferryman that he was the powerful leader of the Æsir. In short, he declared, 'You are talking to Thor!' Then Thor, in turn, challenged the ferryman to state his own name.

To this the ferryman replied that he was named Harbard (which means 'Grey Beard') and he explained that he rarely concealed who he was. Then he defiantly stated that he would defend himself against Thor. It was clear that he did not fear the powerful member of the Æsir one little bit.

This defiance nettled Thor. 'I've no intention of wetting my balls,' he shouted, 'by wading across to get you! But if I cross this water and get my hands on you then you'll regret your challenging of me!'

Harbard was unmoved and said he would wait where he was. And he reminded Thor of when the hammer-wielding god had battled the giant Hrungnir. (That was the giant whose whetstone fragment was still lodged in Thor's head.)

At this, Thor recounted how he had indeed triumphed over Hrungnir (the whetstone aside). For although that mighty giant had possessed a head of stone, still Thor had laid him low and destroyed him. Then he taunted Harbard, asking where he had been when Hrungnir was falling to Thor?

To this, Harbard replied that for five years he had been in the company of a giant by the name of Fiolvar. And in that time they had triumphed in many battles, had many adventures and had their pick of women.

To this, Thor, who was curious, asked how it was that Harbard had succeeded so well with the women and made them so inclined towards him.

To this, Harbard replied in a riddling style that had the women been loyal, then he would have had lively companions; and had they been faithful, then he would have had wise companions. In similarly obscure style, he recounted how the women had made ropes from sand and dug out the deep valleys. And yet he had succeeded in overcoming them with his stratagems and had slept with no fewer than seven sisters. From them he took their hearts and he took his own pleasure. 'And what were you doing, Thor,' he asked, 'while I was doing this?'

Thor was not to be outdone and told how he had killed the giant named Thiazi, the son of Olvaldi, and had thrown his eyes into the sky to form a constellation of stars. 'And what were you doing, Harbard,' he asked, 'while I was doing this?'

To which question Harbard answered that he was using spells to win over female workers of magic and to seduce them from their husband's sides. And these love-spells were not the only signs of his magical powers for he had been given a magic staff by a giant named Hlebard and had used it against the giant himself.

Now, Thor was unimpressed by this last boast and chided Harbard that he had taken a gift and used it against the one who had generously given it to him.

'Cut down one oak and another springs up,' was how Harbard answered this! And added that at such times one looked out for one's own interests.

Thor then recounted how he, in contrast, had been fighting eastern giants while Harbard was repaying Hlebard's generosity with betrayal. In the same place as his giant-fighting exploits, he had also killed trolls that roamed the wild mountains. And had he not been so engaged, then the race of giants would be huge in number and men and women would be wiped off the face of the earth. Thor was clearly pleased at his achievement in this respect and challenged Harbard with it.

Harbard was not to be outdone and replied with tales of battles in Valland, among the Celtic peoples. For there he had incited the nobles to engage in constant warfare, so that Odin could take his harvest of noble warriors who fell in battle. For, he chided Thor, 'Odin takes the warriors, while Thor takes the peasants!'

To this Thor retorted that if Harbard ruled among the Æsir, then the spoils of war would be unfairly shared.

To which Harbard replied that it was a shame that Thor's courage did not match his great strength. And he recounted how Thor had once cowered in a giant's glove that he had chanced upon, not knowing what it was in the darkness of the night. And in that hiding place, Harbard declared: 'You, Thor, were too afraid to as much as sneeze! You were afraid to as much as fart!'

At this Thor lost his temper and hurled insults at Harbard and declared that if only he, Thor, could cross the water, then he would smash his tormentor.

'But we have no quarrel!' was how Harbard replied. Which only angered Thor the more.

With his courage being mocked, Thor once again recounted his mighty deeds of valour. How in the east he had held the river-crossing against the sons of Svarang. Though they had hurled rocks at him, still he had stood against them to defend the river. And so determined was his resistance that they had been forced to sue for peace. 'And what were you doing, Harbard, while I was triumphing in battle?'

'While you withstood stones, I seduced a white-skinned noblewoman. That too was in the east.' Once more Harbard paraded his sexual prowess. 'She was bright with golden jewellery and I made her happy and she gave me pleasure.' Then, when he saw how the story interested Thor, he went on to say how he might have been willing to accept Thor's assistance in dealing with the girl.

'And I'd have helped you,' Thor replied.

But Harbard retorted enigmatically that Thor had not been called on because he had betrayed Harbard's trust.

This Thor dismissed and told how, while Harbard was engaged with the white-skinned woman, he, Thor, had been in conflict with berserker women. And when Harbard mocked him for fighting women, Thor said how these were she-wolves who had bewitched men, assaulted his ship and threatened him with clubs made from iron.

Then Harbard declared that, in contrast, he led armies with blood-reddened spears and fluttering banners.

To which Thor accused him of threatening war on the Æsir.

Ignoring the suggestion, Harbard taunted him further, declaring that he would offer Thor some recompense for the threat and that would involve Thor's backside.

Offended and insulted at the suggestion, Thor declared that he had never heard such shameful words.

To which Harbard mysteriously replied that he had gained these words from the ancient ones who reside in the burial mounds in the woods back home.

Thor lifted his hammer and promised that Harbard would regret such words if only Thor should manage to wade across the water between them. In such an event, the hammer blows would make Harbard howl like a wolf.

Harbard was unmoved and goaded Thor further with claims that Sif, his wife, had a lover while he was away. And that Thor would be better to enter into a trial of strength with his rival than with Harbard.

This truly upset Thor. 'It's easy for you to talk so lightly of something that you know distresses me,' he said. And he accused Harbard of telling outright lies.

But Harbard just mocked him and said it was the truth that Thor was hearing and that he would be in a better position to check it out if he had only managed to get into Harbard's ferry-boat to continue his journey.

Thor exploded with rage. He called Harbard perverted and an obstruction to his journey. But still, of course, he could do nothing about his rage. For without access to the ferryboat he could neither punish the ferryman nor continue his journey. And Harbard delighted to point this out to him as he mocked the mighty Thor who was impotent in the face of a ferryman's mockery.

This was all too much for Thor who demanded that the boat be rowed across the inlet and that Harbard should meet him, Thor the father of Magni, Thor of the Æsir, face-to-face.

To which Harbard merely replied: 'Walk around the bay! I'll not transport you!'

Stuck as he was, Thor had no choice but to ask the way – the way to walk home.

So Harbard shouted him directions: 'It's not far . . . a short distance to the stone marker . . . take the left-hand road . . . carry on until you reach Verland . . . your mother will meet you there . . . she will point out the way back to the land of Odin . . . if you put in some effort, you should be there before the sun rises, for the land is warming and the snow is melting.'

So Thor set off, shouting back threats to Harbard that if he ever met the ferryman then the grey-bearded one would suffer the wrath of Thor.

And Harbard yelled back: 'Go to hell!'

So ended the confrontation of Thor with Harbard at the ferry place. For all his great strength, Thor of the Æsir could not compel the grey-bearded ferryman to transport him and neither could he punish Harbard for his insults and his mockery. He had been bested in the confrontation and so had to walk the long way home. Furthermore, he did not know that it was Odin who had mocked him.

15

Thor and Tyr fetch a giant cauldron from Giantland, and Loki insults the gods and goddesses in the hall of Aegir

THIS STORY IS found in the collection known as the *Poetic Edda*, in a section known as *Hymir's Poem*. When the gods decide to hold a great feast, they force the giant Aegir to prepare the beer. He, in turn, demands a giant cauldron in which to brew the beer. This belongs to the giant Hymir and so the gods Thor and Tyr set off into Giantland to get it. In this great trial of strength, Thor is helped at crucial moments by a giant-woman. The adventure contains a version of the fishing trip for the Midgard serpent that is also found in *The Tricking of Gylfi*, that is preserved in the *Prose Edda* (for a shorter version, see Chapter 7). It also contains a version of the laming of Thor's goat (also see Chapter 7) but in *Hymir's Poem* this, rather confusingly, is placed at the end of the story and is not fully explained. It is probable that it originally was placed earlier in the poem (as in the version in the *Prose Edda*). To better make sense of this story, that is where it is placed here and it is expanded on (using information from the *Prose Edda*) in order to make better sense of the story than survives in the manuscript of the *Poetic Edda*.

The journey into Giantland is followed by a story called *Loki's Quarrel.* In this poem, the troublemaking trickster-god, Loki, forces his way into the hall of the gods and insults every god and goddess in turn. His insults are only halted when Thor returns from journeying into Giantland and threatens the troublemaker with his great hammer. The story is complex in the original, for the poem suggests that Loki was never invited to the feast and gate-crashed it; whereas a prose introduction (also in the original manuscripts) explains that Loki was expelled for killing a servant but later returned to disrupt the event. It is likely that either there were two traditional stories (that became awkwardly combined) or that the writer of the prose introduction did not fully understand the emphasis in the (possibly earlier) poetic tradition. Here, we reconcile the two accounts.

The quarrelling includes references to many other stories that are found elsewhere in this book.

* * *

Aegir is forced to brew beer for the Æsir

The gods once returned from hunting to eat what they had caught. But before they did so they decided to drink together. But who would provide the great cauldron in which the beer would be mixed and from which the drink would be served? They cast the rune-sticks and looked at what they indicated.

They read them to understand that it would be the giant Aegir who would brew their beer for he had many suitable cauldrons.

They went to the hall of Aegir and there he sat unperturbed by their coming. Thor stared at him in defiance of the calm of that mountain-giant and demanded that he should prepare the meal for the Æsir.

This attitude irritated Aegir and so he pondered how he could punish the gods for their overbearing attitude. At last, he came up with a plan. He called on Thor to fetch him a great cauldron; one that was large enough to brew beer for such a great feast.

At this, the Æsir discussed among themselves just where they might look for such a cauldron. Eventually it was Tyr, god of war, who came up with an answer. He explained the plan to Thor. They would travel to the east, into Giantland. There, a long way off, lived Tyr's father, a giant by the name of Hymir. He owned a cauldron that was so large that it was said that it was a league deep.

Thor considered the plan put forward by Tyr and wondered if indeed it was possible to succeed in this adventure. To which Tyr replied that they could succeed if they relied on their wits. For with trickery they could get hold of the cauldron that Aegir required to brew his vast quantity of beer.

Thor and Tyr set out to fetch the giant cauldron from Giantland

With this encouragement, Thor led the way towards the east, accompanied by Tyr. They travelled far from Asgard until they came to the home of Egill. Egill was the father of Thialfi and

Roskva. It was Thialfi who had once split the bone of one of Thor's magical goats. These were the ones that could be cooked and eaten and yet would be found to be whole the next morning. When Thor's restored goat was found to be lame, Thialfi was punished by being forced to become Thor's servant, along with Roskva his sister. From Egill's home, Thor and Tyr travelled on to Hymir's hall in the east.

At their approach, Tyr was astonished at how ugly his grandmother was, for it had been a long time since he had seen her. She had nine hundred heads. But she was not the only woman ruling over that hall, for Tyr's mother was there too. She was draped in gold as fitting her rank and her forehead glittered with gold. She brought beer forward to welcome her son and Thor.

She feared for the safety of her guests, although they were related to the giants, for her husband – Tyr's father – was mean and bad tempered. In order to protect them from his bad nature, she advised Thor and Tyr to hide beneath one of his cauldrons. And this they did.

They had to wait there some time because Hymir came home late from the day's hunting expedition. He had been a long time out in the cold of the winter's day and his beard was frozen; icicles hung from his face and clattered together as he entered the hall.

Tyr's mother stepped forward and greeted her husband: 'You have returned in a good mood,' she jested, for Hymir was not a giant to joke or laugh. And his misshapen form was a stranger to humour.

She explained that their son had returned from his long journeying and had come to the hall in the company of Thor. That was Thor who had slain the giant, Hrod, of their acquaintance. She pointed towards the end of the hall and explained that the two visitors were there, hidden behind a pillar.

As Hymir's stern and unwelcoming gaze turned towards them, the pillar shattered and the roof beam above it broke in half. That was the measure of the giant's glance. And as the roof beam snapped there fell to the floor eight metal kettles which shattered as they fell. But one thing fell and did not break as it hit the floor and that was a well-made iron cauldron that had been worked by a skilled smith.

Since they had been discovered, Thor and Tyr stepped forward. Hymir looked at them as enemies for as he saw them he remembered the many giants that Thor had killed and the many giantesses that he had widowed.

But still Hymir ordered a feast to be prepared. Servants brought in three bulls which were swiftly despatched as each was made a head's length shorter by the blow of an axe. The bulls were taken to the cooking hearth, which was a pit whose bottom was full of glowing fire. There the meal was prepared.

When it was served, Thor alone ate up two of the bulls himself for his appetite was prodigious. It seemed to Hymir that Thor had eaten a great deal more than he had expected him to. And so the giant decided that the next evening they would go out hunting to replenish the stocks of food. For plenty of food would need to be provided if it was going to be enough to satisfy Thor, Tyr and Hymir. On hearing Hymir's plan, Thor said that he wished to row out to sea and discover what he could catch, if only the giant would supply him with sufficient bait.

The bait is prepared and the fishing trip begins

On Hymir's instructions, Thor went out to the barn where the oxen were kept. There he noticed one fine black ox. He seized the beast and tore off its head. Hymir was not best pleased at what fate had befallen his prize animal and said it would have been better if Thor had just sat in silence in the hall.

Still, despite this animosity, they set out to sea. Thor told Hymir, that ugly giant, to row the boat out further into deeper water. But Hymir was not at all happy about this instruction. However, he did as Thor requested and immediately pulled in no less than two whales that seized his bait. While he was doing this, Thor prepared his own fishing tackle.

Thor – the one who protects people, and who will slay the Midgard serpent on the day of Ragnarok – put the head of the black ox onto his hook. Below the boat, the serpent that encircles the earth, the enemy of the gods, rose to seize the ox-head bait. As the line pulled taut, Thor reeled it in and pulled the serpent on board. There the Midgard serpent, the brother of Fenrir the wolf, was at Thor's mercy. With his mighty hammer he struck that serpent a great blow to the head. The serpent roared with pain and the earth shook at the sound. After this great blow, the serpent sank back below the waves. After this, Hymir rowed them back to shore but he was very unhappy at what had transpired.

When they at last reached the shore, Hymir said that Thor could share in the work by either carrying one of the whales back or seeing that the fishing boat was brought securely onto dry land. Thor undertook the latter task. He lifted the heavy boat, poured out the water that had washed on board and on his own he carried the boat back over the wooded hill to Hymir's hall.

The competition back at Hymir's hall

Hymir was envious of Thor's great strength and challenged him to prove how strong he really was. He dared him to try to break the crystal goblet that Hymir owned. The cup was brought to Thor who tried in vain to break it. He struck it against the wooden pillar that held up the roof but the pillar broke and not the goblet. So it was taken back to Hymir, unbroken.

At this point, Tyr's mother whispered to Thor that the only way to smash the goblet was to strike it against Hymir's hard skull. To this advice Thor responded by seizing the goblet once more and bringing it down on Hymir's head. The goblet splintered!

As Hymir looked down on the shards of crystal on his lap he cried out in sorrow that no longer would he be able to command the beer to be brewed. So he told his visitors that if they could move the great cauldron then they could have it.

Tyr tried to lift the cauldron but could not shift it. Twice he attempted the task but failed each time. But Thor seized the cauldron, rolled it onto the floor and lifted it high so that it was turned upside down on his head. With it there like a hat they left the hall.

As Thor and Tyr walked away, an army of mountain-giants descended on them with Hymir at their head. Putting down the cauldron, Thor took hold of Miollnir, his hammer, and with it he killed the army of giants that was pursuing them.

Eventually Thor and Tyr returned to Asgard with the great cauldron that they had brought out of Giantland. As a result of this adventure, the gods were able to drink beer in Aegir's hall every winter and enjoy the feast that they held there.

Loki insults the gods and goddesses in the hall of Aegir

That was not the end of the feast that was held in Aegir's hall. When the beer and food were ready, a great number of the gods and goddesses assembled there. These included Odin and Frigg his wife; Thor's wife Sif was there but Thor himself was away in Giantland; Bragi was there, with Idunn his wife; Tyr was there, the god who was one-handed since the wolf Fenrir had bitten off his hand; Niord (of the Vanir) was there, with Skadi his wife; Freyr and Freyia (also of the Vanir) were there, as were Freyr's servants, Byggvir and Beyla; Odin's son, Vidar, was there; Loki was also there, along with many others of the Æsir and many elves.

As the feast got under way, the servants of Aegir – Fimafeng and Eldir – brought drink to the guests and the atmosphere was peaceful and all were happy. All, that is, except for Loki. For he hated to hear the way that the guests spoke well of the servants of Aegir and the way that they served the guests. In fact, he was so resentful that he rose and killed Fimafeng!

Then all the Æsir rose in fury from the mead benches. They seized hold of their shields and roared at Loki in their anger. They drove him out of the hall and into the night, into the woods beyond the hall. Then, with him gone, they returned to their drinking.

Loki returns to the hall

Loki came back to the hall and met Eldir the servant outside. He asked him what the gods were talking about as they drank.

Eldir replied that they were talking about their weapons and their skills in warfare. But then he added: 'Among the gods and elves inside, there is not one friendly word spoken about you.'

So Loki determined to get into the hall and stir up conflict between those inside; to mix bitter disputes with their beer.

When Eldir saw what Loki was determined to do, he warned him that if he succeeded in stirring up trouble then in the end it would be worse for him.

But Loki was unmoved by the warning and went into the hall anyway. When he entered and those inside recognised him, they fell silent. The happy talking and drinking stopped.

Loki looked around him at those unwelcoming faces and demanded a drink and a place at the feast. 'Either give me a place or send me away,' he challenged them.

At this, Bragi stood up and told him that there was no room for him there, for the Æsir had already decided who had an invitation and who did not.

Undeterred, Loki looked straight at Odin and reminded him of how they were blood-brothers and how Odin had always assured him that there would be a drink for Loki wherever Odin was drinking.

At this reminder of previous promises, Odin told his son, Vidar, to give up his place to Loki, the father of Fenrir wolf, so that there could be no reproach levelled at his hospitality. So Loki took his place. And that was when the trouble started.

Bragi offered Loki a horse, a sword and a ring if he would only agree to avoid causing dissension among the gods. But Loki replied that Bragi was short of swords and arm rings because he lacked the courage needed to be a warrior. At this, Bragi was indignant and threatened Loki that, were it not for the hospitality offered at the feast, he would have his head. To which Loki replied that Bragi was brave in a mead hall but a coward on the battlefield.

Then Idunn spoke up and asked Bragi not to trade words of anger with Loki. But Loki looked at her and remarked that she was so promiscuous that she had embraced the man who had killed her own brother. But Idunn refused to be provoked and said that she would not trade angry words with him in Aegir's hall.

Gefion, the virgin goddess, then intervened and asked why Bragi and Loki were exchanging angry words for, she added to console Bragi, 'Loki is only joking for he knows that you are loved by all living things.' Then Loki looked at Gefion and accused her of exchanging sex for jewellery offered by a white-skinned boy.

Odin was angry at the way that Loki insulted Gefion and rebuked him. He reminded him that: 'Gefion is a wise goddess who understands what fate has in store for men no less than I do myself.' But Loki was unabashed and just mocked Odin for allowing those he supported to die in battle so that they might join him in Valhalla. To which Odin reminded him that he, Loki, had been dishonoured by taking on the form of a woman and bearing children. To which Loki retorted that Odin was a fine one to speak since he himself had once dressed as a woman to practise cross-dressing magic while beating a magical drum. So Odin was in no position to mock him.

At this, Frigg rebuked Loki and reminded him: 'The things that you two did in ancient times you should keep silent about, as it is not fit talk for others to hear.' But Loki replied that it was Frigg who should keep silent because her past was nothing to boast about either, since she had slept with Ve and Vili, Odin's brothers. Frigg was highly affronted and declared that if her son Baldr was here then he would repay Loki for such an insult. To which Loki reminded her that it was he, Loki, who had ensured that Frigg would never see Baldr again (for it was Loki who had engineered the death of Baldr).

Then Freyia came to Frigg's defence and declared that Frigg was well aware of all these things but just kept silent with regard to her knowledge of the working of fate. But Loki ignored this and instead mocked Freyia with the claim that: 'There's not a god or elf here today who has not been your lover, you are so free with your sexual favours.' And when she accused him of having a lying tongue he humiliated her further, calling out: 'You were riding your own brother, Freyr, when the gods caught you by surprise. And as they watched, you farted for them to hear.'

Then Freyia's father, Niord, spoke up for his daughter and declared that it was harmless if a woman had a lover in addition to her husband. But what was really shameful was for a god to bear children, as Loki had once done. To which Loki reminded Niord that if shame was being discussed then he should recall his time as a hostage of the Æsir, when he had spent time in the hall of the giant Hymir. 'Remember,' Loki asked, 'how Hymir's daughters used you as a chamber pot and pissed in your mouth?' Niord, seeking to regain his dignity, declared that it was true that he had once been held as a hostage but that it was then that he had fathered Freyr who was loved by all, a noble youth. To which Loki spitefully replied: 'That may be, but everybody here today should know that you fathered him on your own sister.'

Tyr spoke up in defence of Freyr and recounted how he was best of the Æsir; he never made a woman cry and he freed men held as captives. But Loki just mocked the one-handed god, saying: 'You're a god who cannot do plain dealing, for even your right hand was consumed by the wolf, Fenrir.' To this Tyr defiantly declared that if he had lost a hand then Loki had lost Fenrir-wolf his son, for he was chained until the day of Ragnarok. But Loki just sneered and claimed that he had another son, fathered on Tyr's own wife.

Freyr then warned Loki: 'If you continue in this manner you too will be bound in chains, just like the wolf is chained until the day of Ragnarok and the destruction of the gods.' The words against Loki had brought to the fore all that would happen on that future terrible day and, with that in mind, Loki reminded Freyr of how he had given away his sword to gain a giant's daughter. So, Loki taunted him: 'On the day that the sons of Muspell ride through Mirkwood, what then will you use to fight with?' In this way he reminded Freyr of how he would die on the day of Ragnarok.

To this Byggvir cried out that he would be proud to have the nobility of Freyr and that Loki should be ground down for he was a trouble-causing crow. But Loki just mocked him for always being so keen to be among the gods but well hidden under the straw on the floor of the hall when the gods went out to fight.

Heimdall rebuked Loki's words as those of a drunkard, but Loki dismissed the watchman of the gods as one who had to sit in mud as he watched out for the day of Ragnarok.

Then Skadi said: 'Loki, you won't be so merry in mischief when we bind you to a sharp rock with the guts of your own dead son.' To this warning, Loki replied that this might be so but Skadi should recall that it was Loki who was at the forefront when the gods killed Skadi's father, Thiazi (the giant who kidnapped the goddess Idunn). 'Then, you'll never hear a pleasant or helpful word from me,' Skadi replied. To which Loki retorted: 'Oh, you were far more pleasant in your speech when you invited me to come to bed with you. These things need mentioning when we are making a list of shameful deeds.'

Sif poured Loki a drink and stated that all present should hear that she at least was blameless of wrongdoing. But Loki was having none of it and reminded her: 'Once you took the wicked Loki as your lover.'

At that moment, the mountains shook. And the goddess Beyla exclaimed that it could only be because Thor was on his way home and would bring peace again to the hall. To which Loki replied that she was nothing more than a 'serving wench of the latrines' and should keep quiet.

However, Beyla was correct, for at that moment Thor strode into the hall, wielding his great hammer and threatening to strike Loki's head from his shoulders.

Even then Loki did not fall silent but mocked Thor: 'You won't cut such a brave figure on the day the wolf swallows Odin. Then you will not be brave enough to face Fenrir.'

'Be silent,' Thor roared. 'With Miollnir, my hammer, I will shut you up and throw you out on the roads that lead to the east.'

'Which is not a direction you should boast about,' Loki suggested. 'Since it was out there that you hid in the glove of a giant, gripped by fear. You were a real hero then!'

Once again Thor commanded silence and threatened Loki with his great hammer. Loki though was unafraid and just reminded Thor of when he had been unable to open the backpack of the giant Skrymir.

Then, as Thor raised his hammer, Loki finally backed down. 'Enough's enough. I would not be quiet in front of the Æsir but I'll be quiet before you. Since I know that you will use that hammer on me!'

So Loki backed down. But before he left he shouted a last bitter word. This one was to Aegir: 'You'll never again hold such a feast here and your hall will be consumed by fire.'

So Loki left. He hid himself under a waterfall as a salmon but the Æsir caught him. They bound him to a rock using the guts of Narfi his son. And his other son was changed into a wolf. Skadi suspended a snake over Loki so that it dripped poison on him. Sigyn, Loki's wife, held out a basin to catch that poison but every time she emptied the bowl the poison dripped on Loki. When that happened, he struggled so much against his bindings that the earth shook. And these are now called earthquakes.

16

Thor dresses as a woman in order to retrieve his hammer from the giants

IN THE STORY found in *Thrym's Poem* in the *Poetic Edda*, Thor and Loki suggest that the promiscuous goddess, Freyia, marries a giant. As we will see, the story recounts her indignation at the suggestion. But there is more of this, almost burlesque style, in this poem. For Thor is forced to dress up as a woman in order to retrieve his hammer from the giants. The story plays upon the characteristics of both of these characters as they are found in Norse mythology. For Freyia, the characteristic focused on is her sexual activities; while for Thor, his rugged manliness is in contrast with the female cross-dressing that is such a feature of this story. The idea was so striking that the story later appeared in a number of medieval folk traditions recorded in Sweden and Denmark, where it was recounted in ballad form. This is a highly entertaining story where we are invited to poke fun at the gods and laugh at their fallibilities.

In this story, Loki acts as a messenger for Thor and helps and accompanies him, using his wit and trickery to benefit Thor. The story shows Loki and Thor working closely together and their personalities complementing each other. That fact that it is Loki that Thor turns to when his hammer is stolen suggests that they have a relatively close relationship and that Thor trusts Loki – this is in contrast with other stories and poems where Loki appears to be universally distrusted. That Loki acts as a messenger for Thor and goes with Thor to recover the hammer is also another indication of this close relationship. In other stories, Loki is so distrusted that he is not even invited to a feast, whereas here he is entrusted with the returning of the hammer, which is incredibly important to the gods in general and Thor in particular. This story also highlights how intelligent Loki is and the fact that Thor needs Loki because, although he is very strong, he lacks the intellect to cope with the situation by himself. In most other stories where Loki's intelligence is apparent he seems to be using it against the gods rather than to help them. Not so here.

* * *

One day Thor awoke to discover that he could not find Miollnir, his hammer. He reached out for it and it was not where he had left it. His anger welled up inside him and his hair stood on end and his beard bristled with fury. He searched for it but could not find it anywhere.

He called out to Loki for help; for the hammer of the mighty Thor of the Æsir had been stolen. It was a secret that only he, and Loki, and the thief were aware of – and Thor was keen to recover it before anyone else could learn of its loss. But there was just one other person who needed to be let in on the secret, and that was Freyia.

Thor and Loki went to the hall of Freyia; it was a place of great beauty that was renowned among all who knew the halls and courts of the gods and goddesses of the Æsir. There they found Freyia, and Thor asked her a favour: 'Please lend me,' he asked, 'your cloak made of feathers. For I have lost my hammer and we need to fly fast, to find out who has it and where.'

At this, Freyia responded generously and said that it was theirs to borrow and, even if it had been made of gold or silver, she would share it gladly with them for such an urgent task.

So Loki took the cloak from her and put it on. With it on he could fly like a bird and so he soared up into the sky and away from the courts of the Æsir, and far off towards Giantland. For of all beings, it was the giants who were most likely to have stolen the weapon of Thor, their old adversary.

Loki flies to the hall of the giant, Thrym

Flying like a bird, with the aid of Freyia's feathered cloak, Loki soon found that he was soaring over Giantland and looking down on the halls of the giants, those enemies of the gods. Down there, far below, Loki could see a giant by the name of Thrym. He was a giant-lord and well known to the Æsir.

He was sitting on a grassed-over burial mound and making collars for his dogs from gold thread and weaving plaits in the manes of his horses. As he did so, he was talking to himself:

'The Æsir are in a panic and so are the elves. And Loki has come alone into Giantland. For what is bad news to them is a joy to me. For I have taken the hammer from mighty Thor and buried it deep beneath the ground. Indeed, it is so deep that no god, man or elf will ever find it. And I shall only return it to him if the gods agree to give me Freyia as my wife . . .'

High above him the circling Loki caught the words and knew that he had found the one guilty of the theft of Thor's hammer. He wheeled and flew straight back to Asgard and the courts of the Æsir.

Swooping down he saw that Thor was waiting for him and any news that he might have of the missing hammer.

As Loki made as if to land, Thor cried out: 'Before you land tell me what you saw. For often when a man relaxes he forgets the detail of his message!'

So, circling above him, Loki called down what he had seen. How he had come upon the giant, Thrym, sitting on the burial mound and how he had overheard that giant boasting of how he had taken possession of the hammer of Thor and hidden it deep underground. And, furthermore, how he would only return it in exchange for Freyia, most beautiful of all the goddesses of the Æsir.

Thor and Loki put Thrym's proposition to Freyia

In haste, Thor and Loki went to find Freyia, for it seemed that she alone could solve the problem that they faced. Before she could say a word, they instructed her to put on her bridal clothes to be driven to the land of the giants.

Freyia was having none of it. In fact, her anger was so great that all the halls of the gods and goddesses in Asgard shook as she exclaimed in fury: 'If I go to Giantland with you and marry this giant, you'll think me the most sex-mad of any woman!' As her fury mounted, the great necklace – known as Brisingamen, the necklace of the Brisings – slipped from around her neck and crashed to the floor.

It was at that point, alerted by the commotion, that all the Æsir assembled to debate the proposition that had been laid before Freyia. Seeing how Freyia felt about it, they discussed what other strategies Thor and Loki could employ in order to regain possession of the hammer.

Finally, Heimdall spoke. Although of the divine race of the Æsir, he had the ability to see into the future in the manner of the divine race of the Vanir. He looked at Thor . . . he looked at where the necklace of the Brisings lay on the ground and he put the two together in his mind. To the amazement of those present he declared that Thor should go . . . dressed as Freyia!

As the others listened, he explained how the deceit would work: 'He will wear a bridal veil; we will take the necklace of the Brisings and place it around his neck; he can carry latch-lifter keys hanging from his belt as a woman does; a dress will cover him down to the knees; jewellery will adorn him; and he'll wear a bride's veil to cover his face!'

Now it was Thor's turn to snort with anger. 'I will be the laughing stock of the Æsir,' he cried, 'for all will think me a pervert!'

But Loki was not impressed by Thor's outrage and reminded him that if they did not act quickly, then the giants would soon be evicting the gods and goddesses from Asgard. And without his skull-crushing hammer, Thor would be unable to stop them.

Thor is dressed as a woman for his wedding to Thrym

So Thor reluctantly consented. The other gods dressed him as a woman. They adorned his hair with a bridal headdress. They put the necklace of the Brisings around his neck and hung latch-lifter keys on his belt as if he was mistress of the hall and its treasures. They draped a woman's dress over him and pinned jewellery on his chest. When they had finished, Thor looked like a woman.

Finally, Loki dressed himself as a maid and said that in this guise – mistress and maid – they should ride on Thor's cart to Giantland.

They harnessed Thor's two goats to the cart. Those goats were well rested from browsing on the pastures of Asgard and were ready to trot off at a fast pace.

Then they set off. And as they rode, the mountains trembled and were shaken; fire flamed from out of the earth as from a volcano: for Thor, son of Odin, was riding to the eastern lands of the giants.

When Thrym heard of their coming he was elated. He called on all the other giants to make ready for the arrival of the beautiful Freyia, the famous daughter of Niord. They took straw and scattered it on the mead benches and all was prepared for her arrival. Golden-horned cattle were assembled in the courtyard, and black oxen were driven there too in preparation for the wedding feast. Thrym brought out his finest jewels, necklaces and arm rings of gold. For, as he declared, the only treasure he was now short of was Freyia herself.

Thor and Loki arrive at the wedding feast

Early in the evening, Thor and Loki, dressed as women, arrived at Thrym's hall. Food and drink was brought out in their honour. Thor (dressed as Freyia) took and ate an entire ox. Then he consumed eight whole salmon. He next picked up and drank three great casks of honey-sweetened mead.

The giants watched in astonishment and Thrym declared that he had never seen a woman eat and drink as much; not ever. He looked suspiciously at his new bride, for nothing from his previous knowledge of women had prepared him for such a prodigious appetite.

Loki saw the surprise on the giant's face and sought to reassure him, explaining that Freyia had not eaten for eight nights. Then he added: 'She could not eat, so excited was she at the thought of her journey to Giantland!'

Then Thrym bent down to kiss his bride. He lifted 'her' veil and stepped back in astonishment at the terrifying fire that burned in 'her' eyes. He exclaimed that, 'It looks as if fire is burning in those eyes.'

To which Loki replied that this was because she had not slept for eight nights. Then he added, 'She could not sleep, so excited was she at the thought of her journey to Giantland!'

It was then that Thrym's sister entered the hall. Seeing her brother's new 'bride', she asked that the newcomer should give up her wedding gifts to her, in order to secure her sisterly favour. For she coveted the rings of red gold that Thrym had brought out to give to Freyia.

The 'wedding' of Thrym and Thor

Then Thrym called for the hammer, Miollnir, to be brought out. He declared that it should be laid on his bride's lap and so sanctify her and also consecrate the marriage. All this would be overseen by Var, the goddess who oversees all pledges made between man and wife.

And so the hammer was brought out. When Thor saw it, a great laugh rose from deep within him. He seized the great hammer and brought it down on the head of Thrym. Then he struck out at all the giants who were assembled there. He killed Thrym's giantess sister too, the one who had coveted the bridal rings of red gold. Instead of coins, she received blows; instead of the red-gold rings, she received the crushing blow of Thor's hammer.

This was how Thor and Loki retrieved the hammer from Giantland and how Freyia avoided being given in marriage to Thrym the giant.

In this way, Odin's son got back Miollnir.

17

The 'history' of gods and people,
The Seeress' Prophecy

T HIS STRANGE AND mysterious account charts the 'history' of gods, people, giants and dwarfs from the beginning of the world to its end, and even beyond. It is found in the collection known as the *Poetic Edda* and in a part known as *The Seeress' Prophecy*. Its structure assumes that it is being spoken by a prophetess, a seeress. The traditions concerning Ragnarok are also found in Chapter 18.

The Seeress' Prophecy is the first and probably one of the most well-known poems contained in the *Poetic Edda*. The poem is recited by a seeress who can look both back to the beginning of the world and forward to its eventual destruction at Ragnarok. It is one of the most important primary sources for the study of Old Norse mythology because of this wide-ranging scope and was almost certainly the basis for much of Snorri Sturluson's work. The poem shows Odin questioning the seeress on what is to come at Ragnarok, to better equip himself for when the time comes. This is one of a number of ways in which we see Odin trying to acquire knowledge through the course of the Norse mythological corpus.

The poem is written in *fornyrðislag*, which is a metre traditionally associated with Eddic poetry and usually used in narrative poems such as this one. *The Seeress' Prophecy* is found in the thirteenth-century *Codex Regius* manuscript and in the fourteenth-century *Hauksbok*. Many of its stanzas are also quoted or paraphrased in the *Prose Edda*. There are a total of sixty-six stanzas, although the order and number of the stanzas varies between the *Codex Regius* and the *Hauksbok* and each also contains stanzas that are not in the other.

Although not recorded until much later, *The Seeress' Prophecy* is thought to date from the late tenth century when the Norse world was beginning to convert to Christianity. The last section of the poem in particular has been viewed as evidence of later Christian influence. The reference to the 'great and powerful one' who will come in judgement has been seen as a reference to Christ and possibly the final judgement. In the final verse, there is a reference to a dragon. It is unclear whether this means that evil was thought to still exist in the new world or whether we have returned to the 'present' with the dragon a reference to the impending doom at Ragnarok.

* * *

I was asked by Odin, the Father of the Warrior Dead, to declare the histories of people and of gods, for my memory goes back to the very beginning of all things. And so I call all to pay attention to me: the gods and all sacred beings; all the nations of people across the world. Listen and I will recount the story of all things.

I was born from the race of giants and I remember the beginning of time and I recall my life when I was cared for by those who were present then. At that time, I first saw the nine worlds and there were then nine giant women and the great tree that is used to measure all things grew with its roots going deep beneath the earth.

The forming of worlds

Time was new and years were few when Ymir set up his home (he from whose body was formed all things within the world). And at that time wherever one looked, there was no sea, no sand, no waves; no earth below and no sky above; there was no grass. And all was the yawning void of chaos . . . nothingness.

Then, first, came the sons of Bur (that is Odin and his brothers Vili and Ve). Their father, Bur, was himself the son of Buri who was licked out of the ice by the ancient cow, Audhumla. These sons of Bur made the earth. These are the splendid ones who created the world between them. As they did so, the southern sun shone brightly on the rocks they piled up and as they did this, the soil formed over it and grass and plants began to grow on it.

In that far distant time the heavenly lights were not in their proper places and fixed courses. The Sun was there with the Moon but did not yet know its course or where it would rest when it had accomplished its task. The Moon did not yet know the power it had to bring light at night. And none of the stars knew their combinations nor how they should move across the sky by night.

The naming of the Sun, Moon, stars and times of the day

It was then that all these ancient beings approached the throne from which destiny and fate is decided. For they needed to know how things should be ordered. And so it was that night, along with the Moon and stars, were given their names and places. Then it was that the stages of the day were established: morning was named and its place was set; midday too was named and its role fixed when the Sun is highest in the sky; the afternoon and the lengthening shadows of evening were established, when the Sun sinks to its home and the Moon and stars appear. It was then stated that, as this daily round was added to daily round, so would years be formed and reckoned over time.

The setting up of the home of the gods

Then the Æsir met together on the great plain called Idavoll. There they constructed the temples and altars of the gods. Work places too were set up: blacksmith forges, tools for making expensive things as well as common things of life. After this, they played board games and rejoiced in the large amounts of gold that they owned. This was until three giant women came to them out of Giantland. It was then that the Golden Age came to an end but we shall hear more about this as the story unfolds . . .

The forming of the dwarfs

Then again the ancient beings approached the throne from which destiny and fate is decided. For they needed to know how things should be ordered. They asked who should have lordship over the dwarfs? For these beings had been formed out of Brimir (that is Ymir); formed from his blood and body. It was then that the greatest of the dwarfs was created. This was Motsognir. Another was named Durin. Then it was that the race of the dwarfs were formed; beings that resemble human beings. They were created from the earth. Those that were formed were given many ancient names, such as Meadwolf, Loamfield, Oakenshield and Fialar. These were those who made up the ancient line of Dvalin, the folk of Lofar. In the earth they established their rocky homes.

The coming of Odin and his companions

Then three gods appeared who were loving in their nature and strong (Odin, Haenir and Lodur). They found ash and elm washed up on the shore. These trees then had no life in them until it was given them in this fashion. Odin gave them breath, Haenir gave them spirit, and Lodur put a living spark within them. The greatest of the ash trees is the one called Yggdrasil. It stands tall and the earth that coats its bark shines. From that great tree the dew drops to the earth and turns the valleys green. Beside that great ash tree stands the well of fate.

The three fates

It is now time to talk again of those three giant women who came to the land of the Æsir. For they had great knowledge and they came from the lake by that great tree. One woman is named Fated; another is named Becoming; the third is named Must-be. They carved their names on slips of wood and set down the laws that must be followed and they selected the fates that would befall all people.

The first war in history

Then it was that the seer and worker of magic, who was named Gullveig (and whose name means 'Gold-Darkness'), was attacked and bristled with the spears that were driven into her. In the hall of Odin they also burned her three times. Yet three times she was reborn and still she lives. They called her the Bright One and her name was changed from Gullveig to Heid (meaning 'Bright'). She was a seer who could see into the future and could charm with spells. She could make magic of the kind called '*seid*' ('sorcery') and with this skill could play with the minds of others (some call her Freyia of the Vanir). Wicked women love her.

The war between the Æsir and the Vanir

Then again the ancient beings approached the throne from which destiny and fate is decided. For they needed to know how things should be ordered. They asked should the Æsir give tribute (to the Vanir) or whether all the gods (Æsir and Vanir) should share in sacrifices?

It was then that war broke out between the Æsir and Vanir over this. Oden raised his spear and threw it over the army in the first war in the history of the world. Then the wall of the stronghold of the Æsir was breached for the unconquerable Vanir marched across the plain on which the Æsir lived.

War between the Æsir and the giants

Then again the ancient beings approached the throne from which destiny and fate is decided. For they needed to know how things should be ordered. They asked who had polluted the air with wicked talk and had given Freyia, wife of Od, to the giants. (For after the war with the Vanir and the establishment of peace between the Æsir and the Vanir, the broken walls of the Æsir were repaired by a giant who claimed as his price the Sun, the Moon and Freyia.)

It was then that Thor in his great anger struck a blow against the giant who had demanded such a high price. He cannot stay still when he hears such talk by giants. In that act of violence, oaths were broken and words and promises shattered. Solemn pledges had been made (to reward that giant with the fee he demanded) but these pledges were broken by Thor when he acted in anger.

The gaining of wisdom

I know how much has been offered in order to gain wisdom. Heimdall (watchman of the gods) gave his ear to have a taste of it, and he left it as payment in the well of fate by the ash tree called Yggdrasil. There it is hidden deep beneath that tree.

I see in the torrent pouring down that tree that which came about because of the wager made by the Father of the Warrior Dead (Odin who gave up an eye to gain rune-knowledge and placed it in that well of fate).

I sat alone when the old man (Odin) came to see me. He is the member of the Æsir known as the Terrible One. He looked directly at me but I told him that I know everything and that I cannot be tested and found lacking. For I knew that he gave up one eye and threw it in the well of fate. He threw it into the water where Mimir (the one whose name means the 'Rememberer'), the wise one, drinks every morning. For to him the water from that well is better than any mead. It was to fulfil his wager that Odin did such a thing, in order to gain wisdom.

To me the Father of Many offered golden rings and necklaces of fine workmanship. I in return granted him wisdom in his speech and a magical staff to use in telling the future. He asked it from me because I see far and wide, into every world that exists.

The seeress sees the fate of the gods

I saw valkyries approach from every direction and from great distances. They were ready to ride to the nation of the Goths. There was Skuld with one shield; Skogul with another shield; there was Gunn, Hild, Gondul and the one known as Spear-carrying-Skogul. They were assembled and were ready to ride down to the earth below.

I saw Baldr and I saw his blood. Though he was Odin's son, I could read his concealed fate. For, as well as him standing there, I could also see the mistletoe standing tall, slim and fair out on the plain where the Æsir live. For it was from that plant – that seemed lovely – that a killing arrow was fashioned. And it was Hod who fired it and killed Baldr. Then was Odin's son (Vali) born swiftly and he could fight at one day old. He did not comb his hair, he did not wash, until he had avenged Baldr and punished the one who killed him. Then was that one (Hod) brought to Baldr's funeral pyre. It was over all of this that Frigg wept. She wept because of the sadness that it brought to Valhalla.

It was then that the guts of Loki's son were used to bind Loki as punishment. These bound him as punishment for what he had done (for he had organised the killing of Baldr). Then I saw where Loki was held prisoner, bound beneath hot springs for his love of evil. There his wife sits, sorrowful for her captive husband.

The road to Ragnarok

From the eastern lands there falls a torrent of swords and knives that sweeps out from poisonous valleys. North of that was the dwarf-hall of Sindri, made of gold; and the hall of the giant Brimir where he drinks beer.

I see another hall. It stands out of the sunlight and faces the north. Poison drips from its roof and it is made from the bodies of serpents.

More I see. Men who murder and break oaths wading through the rivers. Men who seduce the wives of other men. And in that place the dragon, Nidhogg, feasts on the corpses of the dead. A wolf too tears at those corpses.

In the east, in Iron-wood, there is an old woman. She raised the children of Fenrir the wolf. One of these will be the wolf that will eventually devour the Moon.

Dead men fall ... the halls of the gods are red with blood ... the Sun succumbs to darkness ... the weather is sharp and cruel. A golden-combed cockerel wakes up Odin's warriors and another one crows beneath the earth in the realm of Hel. Garm, the terrible hound, breaks loose and the ravening one runs free (he who will fight Tyr at Ragnarok). For I have much wisdom and I can see far; I can see the destruction of the gods.

Brother will kill brother; brother and sister will violate each other and break kinship's bonds; it will be a hard time and a time of much adultery. It will be an axe-age, a sword-age, when shields are splintered. It will be a wind-age, a wolf-age, when the world collapses and none are spared.

Then will the sons of Mim be seen to play and fate itself will catch fire. Heimdall, the watchman of the gods, will sound his warning horn. Odin will consult with the head of Mim (who was beheaded by the Vanir and whose head was sent to the Æsir). That head speaks wisdom.

The ash tree Yggdrasil will shake and the giant will break loose and the road to Hel will be consumed with fire. Garm, the terrible hound will howl as his rope snaps and he is set free. I look further and I can see the destruction of the gods.

The frost-giant, Hrym, comes from the east with his shield before him. The great serpent (the Midgard serpent) twists his body in his great anger and he churns the waves in his fury. Above that, the eagle cries as it awaits the time for feasting on the slain; that pale-beaked one rips the bodies on the battle-field. Naglfar (the ship fashioned from the uncut nails of the dead) will break from its moorings. And from the east ride the people of Muspell (meaning 'World's End'). That ship cuts through the waves, with Loki at the tiller. He is in the company of all those monsters bringing destruction.

And what will become of the Æsir? What will become of the elves? All is in turmoil. The land of the giants is deeply troubled; the Æsir assemble to decide their strategies; the dwarfs cry out in distress in their mountain fortresses.

Then Surt the giant will advance from the south with fire to consume all in destruction; flames will be reflected on sword blades. Mountains will shake and splinter as troll-women, monsters, walk the land. Then the sky will be torn open and people will be made to walk the pathway that leads to hell.

The deaths of the Æsir

On that day, Frigg will not only mourn for her son Baldr, for Odin himself will fall. As he advances against Fenrir the wolf, he will meet his fate. Beside him will be Freyr, the one who slew Beli the giant. Freyr will advance on Surt. But Odin will be avenged by Vidar, his son. He will advance on the wolf, that beast of slaughter, and stab it to the heart. Then shall the wolf, Loki's son, fall and Vidar's father will be avenged.

The Midgard serpent shall open its terrible jaws as it rises from the depths into the air. And Odin's son, the brother of Vidar (that is Thor), will advance to meet that serpent-son of Loki. In anger he will strike the beast. At this time, all farms and villages will empty of their inhabitants. Once he has struck the serpent, then Thor, son of Fiorgyn (by Odin), will walk away no more than nine steps, for that serpent is terrible.

Then the Sun will cease to shine, earth will be consumed by the sea, stars will fall from the sky and all will be destroyed by fire that reaches to the very sky. Garm, that terrible hound, will break loose. Then will that beast of destruction run free, for I see the destruction of the gods.

And after Ragnarok?

Then I see a second earth rising from the great sea. It will be green, with waterfalls and eagles flying over it as they hunt for fish within the mountain rivers. And then the Æsir (who survive) will meet on Idavoll plain and talk of what has come to pass: the Midgard serpent and the great events that they have seen. And they will recall the runes from ancient times that Odin the Mighty One once gained.

After that they will find the golden gaming pieces, lost in the grass by those who played there in ancient times.

Then crops will grow in the fields without being sown and all that is broken will be made whole. Baldr will live once more and he and Hod (once divided by conflict) will live together in peace. Wooden slips that foretell the future shall be made once more and Haenir (who once relied on Mimir for his knowledge) will himself choose the slips to interpret them as the world once again is settled by people.

I see a fine hall that is brighter than the sun and has a roof of gold. It will be there – at Gimle – that the lords of this new world will live in happiness and peace.

Finally, the great and powerful one will come: he who rules over all. He will come from above to the place where once the gods gave judgements.

Then the dragon will come flying; he will rise up from the hills that are dark as when the moon is down. Nidhogg will carry the bodies of the dead on his wings as he flies over the plain.

Now I lie down and am silent.

18

Ragnarok and the end of the world

FOUND IN The *Tricking of Gylfi* section of the *Prose Edda*, this story tells of the end of the world. Traditions about this event are also found in Chapter 17.

Ragnarok means the 'Doom of the gods' in Old Norse. The Norse word *rok* (doom), though, has sometimes been confused with the word *rokkr* (twilight) leading to the alterative 'Twilight of the gods' or *Götterdämmerung* (as used by Richard Wagner in the name of the final part of his Ring Cycle).

Ragnarok is a series of events including a great battle where almost all of the major Old Norse gods will die. This is accompanied by a series of natural disasters ultimately leading to the flooding of the world. After this, the world will start anew with a younger generation of gods and the humans who have managed to survive by hiding in Yggdrasil (the mythical tree that connects the nine worlds in the Old Norse cosmos). It is unclear whether the mythological new world is free from evil or whether the same mix of good and evil is retained.

The events of Ragnarok are inevitable and there is nothing the gods can do to prevent them happening. This is despite the strength of Thor and Odin's continuous quest for wisdom and knowledge. This presents the gods in a strangely vulnerable light as beings who, despite their supernatural powers, are as bound by the same power of fate (Old Norse *urðr*) as humans. The only comfort appears to be that the world will start anew – albeit with a new generation of gods.

* * *

The breaking loose of the forces of chaos

The end of the world will be heralded by three winters in which the world will be torn by conflicts. War will rage across the land and brother will kill brother. The bonds of family will be shattered and son will kill father and father will kill son. It will be an age of axes and an age of swords, an age of winds, an age of wolves. It will lead to the ruin of the world.

Then will come a strange and cold winter that is called Fimbul-winter. The deep snow will cover the land and there will be bitter winds and deep frosts. The sun will lack the heat needed to thaw that deep cold. Of these winters, three will follow one after the other and there will be no summer between these times of great cold.

After these six winters, the wolf named Skoll, that pursues the Sun, will finally catch up with her and he will swallow the Sun, which will bring disaster on all people. And the wolf, named Hati Hrodvitnirsson, that pursues the Moon, will also catch up with her and swallow the Moon. At that time, the stars will disappear from the sky. The earth will be shaken and mountains will fall and trees will be uprooted. All restraints that now hold fast the forces of chaos will be broken in this shaking and so Fenrir the wolf will be set free. But that is not all . . .

The Midgard serpent in its rage will fling itself against the shore and the sea will flow across the land. As the sea sweeps across the land it will tear from its moorings the ship named Naglfar that is constructed from the fingernails and toenails of dead men. This is why the nails of the dead are trimmed; otherwise they will contribute to the building of that terrible ship. For that is a ship that both gods and men wish was never finished, for it will bring destruction. As Naglfar is carried along in that great flood it will be commanded by a giant, called Hrym, as its ship's captain.

While this is happening, the wolf Fenrir will open his great jaws so that the upper part of his jaws touches the sky, while the lower part rests on the earth. From his eyes and nostrils flames will flare and burn.

At the same time, the Midgard serpent will spit its poison across both sea and sky and it and Fenrir will be side by side as they advance to battle.

As the Midgard serpent and Fenrir cause havoc, the sky will tear open and from it will ride the sons of Muspell, from the place of fire. Riding on horses, they will advance from Muspell, and will break the bridge, Bifrost, that connects heaven and earth. Of these riders the first is named Surt. As he rides, he spreads fire before and behind. In his hand a sword will flash with great brightness that exceeds the brightness of the sun itself. The sons of Muspell will ride to the field of battle that is called Vigrid. They will ride there at the head of their assembled warriors. There they will meet the Midgard serpent and

Fenrir. With them will be Loki (no longer in chains) and with him the people from Hel. All the frost-giants will be there too, under the command of the giant named Hrym. That field of battle is very large – three hundred miles in every direction – because so many will assemble there.

The destruction of the gods

When all these enemies of the Æsir gather together they will threaten the very existence of the gods. Heimdall will blow on his horn to summon the gods to decide the order of battle in response to the threat. But first Odin will ride to the well of Mimir to seek guidance and the ash tree Yggdrasil will shake with such movement that fear will spread to all living things. Then the Æsir will arm themselves for battle and will advance to meet their enemies on the field of Vigrid.

At their head will ride Odin, wearing a golden helmet and a mail shirt and wielding his spear. He will attack Fenrir, with Thor beside him to assist him; but Thor will not be able to aid him because he will have enough to do battling the Midgard serpent. Freyr will battle Surt, the son of Muspell, and the conflict will be fierce before Freyr falls before the weapon of Surt. He will be defeated because he lacks his sword, the one he gave to his servant Skirnir when that servant travelled into Giantland to seek out a wife for Freyr. Tyr too will fall in battle but his adversary will be the evil dog, named Garm, who has broken free from his shackles. But as Tyr falls he will also slay Garm. Thor, though, will be victorious over the Midgard serpent and will at last destroy it. But his victory will be short-lived, for he will walk away no more than nine paces before he falls dead from the poison that has been spat at him. Odin will also die; swallowed by Fenrir the wolf. But that wolf will not have long to enjoy his victory. For soon will come the god Vidar and place one foot on the lower jaw of the wolf and with one hand will seize the upper jaw and tear the wolf's mouth apart. And so Fenrir will die. The foot that Vidar uses to hold down the wolf's lower jaw will be shod with a shoe fashioned across all time from the pieces of leather cut from the toe and heel of people's shoes. These pieces of leather should always be thrown away, for in this way those that do this will give assistance to the Æsir in their war against the forces of chaos. Loki and Heimdall will kill each other in battle and Surt will throw out fire that will consume the whole world. At the end of this battle the gods, giants and all mankind will have died and all created things will be destroyed by fire.

Despite this destruction, some things will remain. Those who are secure within Gimle, in the hall called Brimir, will find plenty of drink there. Another good hall is the one named Sindri, made from red gold. However, oathbreakers and murderers will be condemned to live in the hall on Nastrands, with its doors facing the cold north and its walls made from snakes that spit their poison into the hall, so that those condemned to be there must wade through it as their punishment. Worse, though, will be the punishments meted out at Hvergelmir. There the dragon Nidhogg will torture the bodies of the dead.

The world after Ragnarok

Despite all the destruction, all will not be lost. Earth will once more rise from the sea and will be green again, with crops growing without being sown. The gods Vidar and Vali will survive the slaughter and will live on Idavoll, where once Asgard had stood. To that place will come Thor's sons, Modi and Magni, and they will bring Miollnir, their father's hammer. To that place will also come Baldr and Hod, having escaped from the confines of Hel. Together they will talk of the mysteries that they know and of old times; tales of the Midgard serpent and of Fenrir the wolf. At that time, they will find scattered in the grass the golden playing pieces that had once belonged to the Æsir.

In addition, in Hoddmimir's wood two people will hide themselves from the fire of Surt that destroyed the rest of the world. Named Life and Leifthrasir, they will drink the morning dew and repopulate the earth. Over this new earth the daughter of the Sun – no less beautiful than her mother – will shine and will trace her way across the sky as once her mother did before her. And of what happens next, nobody knows, for knowledge stretches no further than this.

The Æsir reflected on all these tales and were determined that they should not be forgotten. To ensure that they were recalled, they gave the names of characters and places in the stories to people and places in Sweden. In this way, the names of ancient gods and stories of old were retold into later times. Those given the names were attributed with the adventures of the ancient gods and their deeds, that they would not be forgotten among people.

Part Two: Norse Legends

19

The Saga of the Volsungs and the story of Sigurd, the dragon-slayer

IT IS CLEAR that many Norse myths include some pieces of information drawn from the actual history of Scandinavia. These might include a reference to a famous battle, the name of a heroic king or the lineage of great rulers. However, the main focus of the stories (the *myths*) that we have explored so far deal with other worlds and the gods. Where the *legends* that we will now be exploring differ from these is that they add more human traditions, snippets of history and fragments of real events to the stories of gods, elves, dragons and magical rings. So, while they certainly are not referring to real events, they tend to add more 'echoes of real events' to the mix than exist in the kinds of mythologies that survive from the *Prose Edda* and the *Poetic Edda* that we have explored so far. They are often described as *fornaldar-sagas* (sagas of the ancient times) or 'legendary sagas'.

In many ways, they act as something of a bridge between the myths and the non-supernatural world of politics, family quarrels and ambitions, travel and revenge that we find in the so-called 'family-sagas' for which Iceland is famous. These family-sagas, we should recall, are also works of literature and should not be read as straight historical accounts, but they can seem to have that characteristic in their accessible and credible tales of the lives of men and women. They certainly feel 'historical' and are definitely not 'myths' recounting the worlds of the gods.

The writings that form the basis for this 'legendary section' – even though some have the word 'saga' in their title – are of a different order to these family-sagas. As we shall see, in *The Saga of the Volsungs*, for example, the human world and echoes of real fourth- and fifth-century events *are* present but, very noticeably, they are intermingled with mythological features; and this gives them a character that reminds us of the myths that we have explored so far. They are mythologically informed 'Norse legends'. The reforging of the sword once-broken is reminiscent of a similar motif in Tolkien's *The Lord of the Rings*. The stories of the otter-pelt covered with gold, Fafnir and Sigurd also appear in Chapter 11.

The journeys to Vinland that we explore finally in this section are not mythological, but they are still included because they explain the past through the adventures of larger-than-life characters and it will be seen that they still contain supernatural features. In short, they are rather less mundane in their focus than the 'historical' family-sagas and have something of that 'explaining how things have come to pass' quality of the myths and other legends.

* * *

How Sigi became king of the Huns

There was once a man named Sigi and it was said that he was the son of Odin. One day he went out hunting with a slave named Bredi. This Bredi was the slave of the goddess Skadi (who was once wife of the Vanir god, Niord). At the end of the day, Sigi compared his hunting kills with Bredi and was angry and embarrassed to find that Bredi's kills were more impressive. In fact, Sigi was so angry that he murdered Bredi and buried his body in a snowdrift. When Sigi returned home, he told Skadi that Bredi had ridden off and left him and he had no idea where he had gone.

Now Skadi did not believe him and sent men out to search for Bredi. Eventually they found his body buried in the snowdrift. From that day onwards, people have called deep snowdrifts 'Bredi's drift' in memory of that terrible event. Because it was clear that Sigi had murdered the slave he was declared an outlaw, a 'wolf against the sacred'. As a result, he had to leave home and flee for his life.

Now, Odin guided Sigi on his long journeying; he and the warriors that had gone with him. Eventually they reached the coast and turned to a life of raiding, at which they were very successful. In time, he became so successful that he gained a kingdom (that of the Huns) and a noble wife. His son was named Rerir and the son grew tall and strong.

In time the brothers of Sigi's wife grew jealous of Sigi. They plotted against him and laid an ambush for him, which succeeded in killing him and all his bodyguards. He was succeeded by Rerir, his son, and when Rerir was strong enough he gathered an army and slaughtered those relatives on his mother's side who had been responsible for the death of his father. After this act of vengeance, Rerir grew to be a wealthy and powerful king. But he had no heir to succeed to the kingdom of the Huns after him. Of the location of that Hunnic kingdom, some say it lay among the Franks by the River Rhine, others that it lay far to the east.

Odin grants King Rerir a son: Volsung

King Rerir and his wife prayed to the gods for a child and their pleas were heard by Frigg. She, in turn, relayed their request to Odin. On hearing this, he summoned one of his chosen maidens (a valkyrie) and she dropped an apple into Rerir's lap. Although Rerir did not understand the nature of this gift, he soon found that his wife was pregnant.

However, things did not go well with the royal family. Firstly, the king died while on campaign. Secondly, the queen did not give birth in the normal timespan and her pregnancy lasted for six years! In the end, she realised that she would not live long enough to give birth and ordered that the child should be cut from her body. This was done and that was how Volsung, who became king of the Huns in place of Rerir, his father, was born. He became a famous warrior who was renowned for his victories in battle. He built a great hall and in the centre of that royal palace a huge tree grew; it stretched up to the roof and its branches grew through the roof and its blossom spread over the top of the roof. The tree was named Barnstock, which means 'Child-tree' or, some say, 'Hearth-tree'.

In time Volsung married the valkyrie who had dropped the apple in his father's lap. Her name was Hljod and she was the daughter of a giant named Hrimnir. Together they had no less than ten sons and a daughter. Their eldest son was named

Sigmund. He was one of twins and his twin was the daughter and her name was Signy. In time, Signy's hand was requested in marriage by King Siggeir of Gotland, in southern Sweden. This was the land of the Goths or, as they are also known, the Geats. Signy was not in favour of the match but her father decided that it should go ahead. As a consequence, King Siggeir of Gotland came to the hall of King Volsung to celebrate the royal wedding.

A hooded one-eyed stranger and a magical sword

While the feasting was underway a stranger entered the hall. He was tall and wore a hooded cape that overshadowed his features. But it could still be seen that he had only one eye and that his hair was grey with age; and he entered the hall barefoot. In his hand he carried a sword, which he plunged into the great tree that stood in the centre of the hall. Then to the astonished assembly he declared that whosoever could draw the sword from the trunk would have it as a gift and could own no better sword. Then, as all eyes were fixed on him, he turned and left.

All tried and failed – starting with the noblest there – to pull out the blade. Then, at last, Sigmund, the son of King Volsung, came forward. He clutched the hilt and easily drew out the sword where others had utterly failed.

At the sight of this, King Siggeir of Gotland offered him three times the sword's weight in gold if Sigmund would give it to him. To which Sigmund replied that if Siggeir had been meant to have the sword then he would have been able to pull it from the tree!

Siggeir was angry and felt slighted by the reply but resolved to have his revenge by stealth. And in this decision is the measurement of this man. In the morning, King Siggeir announced that he was returning to Gotland with his new wife. All who heard this were astonished for it was a discourtesy to leave so soon after a royal wedding. On hearing of his intention, Signy (who was now his queen) begged her father to end the marriage for she was unhappy with her new husband and feared that only tragedy would result from the match. But Volsung said that he could not do this, for it would be a great insult to the king of Gotland and it would cause conflict between their two nations. So, King Siggeir of Gotland left with Signy and travelled north, back to his kingdom.

King Volsung is betrayed and Sigmund alone survives the attacks of a terrible she-wolf

Three months later, King Volsung and his sons set off in three ships to visit King Siggeir in Gotland. They arrived off the coast one evening. That night Signy warned him that disaster awaited him if he stepped on shore and begged him to return home. But King Volsung would have none of it, for he feared neither fire nor iron. And so the next day he and his sons went ashore. There they were attacked by King Siggeir and, though they resisted with tremendous courage, Volsung was killed and his sons taken prisoner.

Signy pleaded with her husband not to kill her brothers but instead to imprison them in stocks made from a tree trunk. This, at last, he consented to do. But that night at midnight a terrible she-wolf came and killed and devoured one of the brothers. This happened every night at midnight until only Sigmund, the twin brother of Signy, was left alive.

Then Signy sent one of her servants to smear honey on Sigmund's face and put honey in his mouth. That night when the she-wolf padded up to him, she smelled the honey and licked it from his face. Then she pushed her tongue into his mouth to eat what was held there. At this, Sigmund clamped down on the wolf's tongue with clenched teeth. The she-wolf leapt backward and as she did so her tongue was wrenched from her mouth and she died. At the same time, as she pushed her paws against the stocks, she broke them apart and Sigmund was set free. It is said by some that the terrible she-wolf was none other than the mother of King Siggeir and that she had taken on this form through magic.

Then Signy hid her brother in the woods and there Sigmund lived in hiding for some time, since King Siggeir thought that he was dead. Eventually Signy sent her eldest son by King Siggeir to be Sigmund's companion. But Sigmund found the boy to be timid and afraid to knead dough that seemed to have something living in it, and so Sigmund told his sister that he had no wish to have the boy as a companion in the woods. To which Signy said that he should kill the lad. And so he did. The next winter, Signy sent her youngest son by King Siggeir and the same thing happened and Sigmund killed him too, on the advice of Signy.

Signy has another son, who becomes the companion of Sigmund in the woods

One day, a sorceress visited Signy and Signy reached an agreement with her: the two would change shape and the sorceress would sleep with King Siggeir in place of Signy. And so this is what they did. The sorceress slept with King Siggeir and Signy went to visit her brother in the woods. She asked him for shelter and Sigmund agreed. That night he asked her to share his bed, because she was an attractive woman and, in her changed shape, he did not recognise her. This she did for three nights.

After this, she returned to Siggeir's hall and there she gave birth to a son. He had the look of the Volsungs and she named him Sinfjotli. As with her other sons, she tested his manliness by stitching his garments to his hands but whereas they had cried out in pain, Sinfjotli made no sound. When the boy came to Sigmund in the woods, he too was told to knead the dough and this he did although there was a poisonous snake within the flour! It did not bother him one bit.

Sigmund took him as a companion but decided to toughen him up before seeking vengeance against King Siggeir. So through the summers they wandered the forest and killed men for what they could take from them. And all the time Sinfjotli reminded Sigmund of his debt of honour that called for the death of King Siggeir. But Sigmund did not fully trust him because he thought that he was King Siggeir's son.

During their time in the woods they came on two sleeping men that magic had turned into wolves but who, every tenth night, could shed their wolfskins. So Sigmund and Sinfjotli took the skins and put them on, becoming wolves and unable to resist the magic. In this form they roamed the woods, killing men. In time, they fought and Sigmund injured Sinfjotli in the throat but brought healing to the wound because he saw a weasel do the same to an injured companion with a certain leaf.

Thinking that Sinfjotli was finally hardened enough for vengeance, Sigmund took him to the hall of Siggeir. They hid in an outer room but were discovered by Siggeir's two little sons. On Signy's instructions, Sinfjotli killed the children, but

Sigmund refused to do so. Then Sinfjotli threw the bodies into the hall in full view of Siggeir. A great fight ensued and Sigmund and Sinfjotli were captured and chained.

The revenge of Sigmund and Sinfjotli

King Siggeir determined that the manner of their deaths would be slow and painful and so he resolved to bury them alive in a cairn of stones that was covered with earth and turf. They were chained either side of a great rock within the cairn so that they would be denied any comfort in each other's company. In this manner, they were left to starve to death. However, Signy ordered her slaves to pile straw into the mound and within this she had hidden a joint of pork and also Sigmund's magical sword. With that sword Sigmund cut their chains and together they used the sword to saw through the rocks of the cairn.

Once free they made their way to the hall of King Siggeir and set it ablaze. Signy came out and declared to her brother that she too had striven to take revenge for the death of Volsung, their father; when her sons by King Siggeir had been slow to avenge their grandfather's murder she had told Sigmund to kill them; and then she explained how Sinfjotli was their son and so a Volsung by both his parents.

Then, declining Sigmund's offer of freedom and honour, she walked back into the flames to die with her husband, King Siggeir.

After this, Sigmund and Sinfjotli returned to their country and deposed the man who had ruled it since the death of King Volsung. Sigmund became a famous and wealthy ruler. He married a woman named Borghild and they had a son named Helgi. Norns (the female beings who rule the destiny of gods and men) came at his birth and declared he would be the most famous of kings. Helgi went to war when he was only fifteen years old and was a great warrior.

King Helgi finds a warrior-wife

One day, while returning from battle, King Helgi came upon a group of beautiful noblewomen. The most beautiful was named Sigrun. When Helgi discovered that she was on her way to marry a king that she did not love, he resolved to defeat that king so that he could marry her himself. And the king they set out to fight was named Hodbrodd.

Then Helgi summoned his warriors and a great fleet and they sailed to Gnipalund (in Denmark) along with Helgi's half-brother, Sinfjotli. And there Sinfjotli entered into a battle of insults with the brother of Hodbrodd who was named Granmar.

First, Granmar accused Sinfjotli of killing family members and sucking blood from corpses . . .

Then Sinfjotli replied by saying that Granmar had acted like a woman to be the passive sexual partner of a man and, while living as a valkyrie, he had given birth to nine wolves . . .

Next, Granmar accused Sinfjotli of being castrated by a giant's daughter and living in the forest with wolves . . .

Then Sinfjotli retorted that Granmar was the mare that the stallion, Grani, mated with and that after that he was a herder of goats . . .

After this battle of insults was over, the two armies eventually fought and King Helgi killed Hodbrodd. As he did so, Sigrun and her female companions arrived, like valkyries at the battlefield. So Helgi married Sigrun.

Sigmund: his wives and his death at the hands of Odin

Now, Sigmund was married to Borghild but her brother was killed by Sigmund's son, Sinfjotli, for they were rivals in love for the same woman. At his funeral feast, Borghild came to Sinfjotli three times with a poisoned drink (in revenge on her stepson for her brother's death). But twice Sinfjotli suspected her and, instead, Sigmund took the drink; for no poison could harm him. The third time that Borghild brought a drink to Sinfjotli, Sigmund was too drunk to help his son and advised him to filter the drink through his moustache! This Sinfjotli did but the poison killed him. And for this act, Borghild was driven from the kingdom.

Sinfjotli's body was carried by Sigmund to the fjord where a ferryman offered to carry the body across the water. But once the body was placed in the boat, the ferryman and the boat vanished with the body of Sinfjotli.

After this, Sigmund sought the hand of another woman. Her name was Hjordis. He travelled from the kingdom of the Huns to seek his bride. And though he had a younger rival, Hjordis chose Sigmund for he was the most famous warrior of the two.

As a consequence, the rejected suitor – who was named King Lyngvi – came against Sigmund with a great army, but in the battle that ensued, Sigmund was shielded by the norns who decide the fates of men. And so he conquered and his arms were covered in the blood of the men that he killed.

Then it was that a stranger appeared on the battlefield. He was cloaked and wore a broad-brimmed hat but still it could be seen that he had but one eye . . . And he raised his spear against Sigmund. When Sigmund struck at him with his mighty sword, the blade snapped against the spear. It was then that the battle turned against Sigmund and he was mortally wounded. As a result, King Lyngvi prevailed over him.

That night Sigmund's wife, Hjordis, tended him on the battlefield for it was clear that Odin willed his death in battle. Before he died, he gave the broken pieces of his sword to Hjordis and told her to give them to their son when he was born (for she was carrying a child). The sword – when reforged – would be called Gram (meaning 'wrath').

In the morning, a Viking fleet landed and the warriors from it searched the field of carnage for wealth and precious things lying among the slain. When they sailed again they took with them Hjordis and her maid-servant, although the two had exchanged roles. In time, the true identity of Hjordis was discovered and she married the Viking king, who was named Alf. After this marriage the warrior Sigurd, Sigmund's son, was born. He was to become the most famous of warriors and his name is still spoken of among the poets of the northern world.

The beginning of the adventures of Sigurd

Sigurd's foster-father was a man named Regin. (Among Norse nobles it was common for young men to be raised in the household of allies and become foster-children, to strengthen the bonds of loyalty among the warrior families.) Regin taught Sigurd the use of runes; how to write poetry and play chess; and the speech of several languages. But Regin also tried to make Sigurd dissatisfied with his lot. He questioned the wealth allotted to the young man by the king and said that he should ask for a horse. To this Sigurd replied that he would do so when he was ready. And when he finally did so, the king said that he could take any horse of his choosing from the herds.

The very next day Sigurd went out to choose a horse from the herds that grazed by the edge of the forest. As he approached the place where the herds grazed, he met an old man who had a long beard. Sigurd did not recognise the man but asked him for his advice in choosing a horse from the herd.

The old man agreed to help him and said that they should drive the horses down to the Busiltjorn river. This they did and the horse-herd plunged into the deep water. At once, all the horses – but one – swam for the shore. But Sigurd chose the horse that stayed in the deep water. This horse was a handsome grey colour; it was young and a fine animal. The bearded old man told Sigurd that it was descended from Sleipnir, the eight-legged horse of the god Odin. He advised Sigurd to raise the horse carefully because it was the finest of all horses. And then the old man vanished. It was Odin himself that Sigurd had met. Sigurd named the horse Grani.

Sigurd was pleased with the horse that the king had allowed him to take for himself but still Regin encouraged him to be dissatisfied. To this end, he told Sigurd that there was fabulous wealth for the taking; it was guarded by a great serpent or dragon, named Fafnir. The treasure could be found on Gnitaheath and this was not far away.

As Sigurd reflected on what Regin told him, he recalled how previously he had heard of Fafnir and his ferocity and strength. To which Regin replied that Fafnir was no greater than any other snake that might be found in the meadow. And that Sigurd's Volsung ancestors would have willingly taken on such a beast and conquered it. To this, Sigurd asked why it was that Regin was so keen that he should face the dragon . . .

Then Regin told him the story of Fafnir. It soon became clear why Regin was so keen to have Sigurd confront the dragon. For Fafnir was none other than the brother of Regin. And there was yet another brother, named Otter, who caught fish since he took on the form of an otter by day. He would lie on the bank with his eyes shut and there he would consume his catch. It was in this form and in such a state that the gods Odin, Loki and Haenir chanced upon him and Loki killed him with a stone. They took the dead otter to the hall of Hreidmar (who was father of Fafnir, Otter and Regin) who recognised his dead son and had the surviving two brothers seize the three gods and threatened them with destruction if they did not cover the otter-pelt with the finest red gold. Loki set out to do this and went to Andvari's Waterfall to catch the famous pike that lived there. This pike was actually the dwarf Andvari, in fish form. And that dwarf was fabulously wealthy. Loki succeeded in netting the wily pike and forced the dwarf to hand over all his gold, down to his very last ring. Taking the gold back to Hreidmar they covered the otter-pelt with gold; the final whisker being covered by the ring that Loki took from Andvari. But later Fafnir killed his father and in so doing not only committed this horrendous crime but also robbed his brother, Regin, of his share of the compensation for the death of Otter, their brother.

When he heard this account of the crimes of Fafnir, Sigurd at once offered to kill the dragon and asked Regin to fashion a sword that was capable of the deed, for Regin was a skilful worker in iron. So Regin fashioned a fine sword but it shattered when Sigurd struck the anvil with it. He made a second sword and it too shattered against the anvil. At last Sigurd went to his mother and asked her for the sword that had once belonged to

King Sigmund, his father. That sword was named Gram and its pieces were taken by Sigurd to Regin with instructions that the skilful smith should make a new sword from the broken pieces. And so he made an incomparable sword. It was so strong that when Sigurd struck the anvil the blade sliced it in two; it was so sharp that when wool was carried by the current of a river against the blade then the wool parted in two. Sigurd was satisfied.

Equipped with the sword, Sigurd went out to kill Fafnir and so fulfil the vow that he had made to Regin to do this brave deed.

Sigurd's fortune is foretold by Grithir and King Sigmund is avenged

Sigurd's mother had a brother named Grithir. He had the ability to see into the future. After the sword had been reforged, Sigurd went to meet him and ask if Grithir could see the shape of Sigurd's life. Eventually Grithir told him what he saw; and Sigurd found that it all came to pass in time. Then Sigurd returned to Regin and said that before he killed Fafnir, he would kill those who had been responsible for the death of his father, King Sigmund. It was against King Lyngvi that Sigurd swore vengeance.

So he set out and his fleet sailed before a fair wind. Even when a storm arose, Sigurd would not allow the sails to be shortened for he was in an urgent hurry to destroy those who had been responsible for his father's death. When they reached that land, they spread fire and death before them until at last King Lyngvi raised an army and came against them. The battle was terrible and many men died, but at last Sigurd prevailed over King

Lyngvi. With the reforged sword, Gram, he cleaved King Lyngvi through his helmet, head and body. And around King Lyngvi fell all those who had been party to the death of Sigmund.

Sigurd slays Fafnir

Regin and Sigurd rode out to where the dragon Fafnir was accustomed to go to drink. When they got there, Sigurd was astonished to see that the cliff was so high that Fafnir had to be huge in order to stoop down to drink from there. Furthermore, the tracks of the dragon were so large and deep that Sigurd realised the great size of the beast was more than Regin had told him. Regin advised him to dig a ditch and lie in it, in wait for Fafnir. When Sigurd asked how he should avoid the blood of the dragon, Regin chided him for lacking the courage that was associated with his ancestors. Then Sigurd rode onto the heath and Regin withdrew, for he was afraid.

Sigurd began to dig a ditch and, as he did so, an old man with a long grey beard appeared and advised him to dig several ditches in order to channel away the blood of the dragon. This Sigurd did.

At last Fafnir appeared. He slithered his great bulk towards the edge of the cliff and, as he did so, he breathed out poison ahead of himself. As he passed over the ditches, Sigurd plunged his sword upwards and into him and the wound was mortal. For Gram was a mighty sword. As Fafnir writhed in pain, he demanded to know the name of his assailant and Sigurd declared that he was the son of Sigmund. Then he declared that it was with determination, strength and a mighty sword that he had come against Fafnir and that this had carried him to his goal when others would have hung back in fear.

As they spoke, Fafnir foresaw that the gold that Sigurd would win from him would be the cause of his death. But Fafnir declared that this death would not be caused by the sea so long as Sigurd bore in mind his advice to never travel that way unwarily. And there on the wild heath, Sigurd questioned Fafnir about the norns (of which some are of the Æsir, some of the elves and some are dwarfs). Then Fafnir told Sigurd that it was his own brother, Regin, who had caused his death and that Regin would be the cause of Sigurd's death also. Finally, he advised Sigurd to ride away, lest he fall to the final blow that Fafnir laid on him as he died. But Sigurd knew no fear and said that he would go to Fafnir's treasure store instead, and seize hold of all his gold, for he knew that all men die and so fear of death would not cause him to lose hold of such a treasure hoard!

Sigurd drinks the blood of Fafnir and eats his heart

With Fafnir dead, Regin returned and declared that Sigurd had won a great victory that would never be forgotten but that he, Regin, mourned the loss of his brother. Sigurd mocked Regin for running away and Regin replied that had it not been for the sword that he had forged, then Sigurd would never have had the victory. To which Sigurd declared that without a brave heart the sword would not have sufficed to kill the dragon.

Then Sigurd cut the heart from Fafnir and Regin asked that he would roast it for him. This Sigurd did but, when he burned his finger, he put it in his mouth and, as soon as the dragon's blood touched his tongue, he found that he could understand the speech of the nuthatches calling from a nearby tree. They warned him to kill Regin or else he would betray Sigurd and they spoke of how Sigurd should help himself to Fafnir's gold-hoard. So this is what Sigurd did. He struck off Regin's head with his sword. Then he rode to Fafnir's lair and laid hands on the gold there and took it away. That gold-hoard was enormous. Afterwards, whenever anyone sought to measure courage or treasure, they would compare it to Sigurd of the Volsungs and the killing of Fafnir and the winning of the dragon's treasure-hoard.

Note: The life of Sigurd after he gained the gold of Fafnir

The stories in this chapter form a large part of *The Saga of the Volsungs*. Some of this has already appeared, in part, in Chapter 11 because it also appears (in a shorter form) in *The Prose Edda*, in the part known as *The Language of Poetry*. However, *The Saga of the Volsungs* contains a great deal more detail in terms of the background to these events and how they form part of the mythical/legendary origins of the 'heroic' family of the Volsungs. After Sigurd's victory over Fafnir, *The Saga of the Volsungs* goes on to give a more detailed version of his relationships with the women in his life and of the tensions, violence and revenge that flowed from these complex connections. To recount all of this would be to enter into too much repetition of Chapter 11 and so readers are referred to that chapter for the abridged version of the rest of the story (based on the evidence in the *Prose Edda*).

20

Legendary rulers of men

FOUND IN THE *Prose Edda* and in *The Language of Poetry* are stories of heroic rulers of men and the lineages of heroic kings.

The battle of the Hiadnings is a never-ending battle, which is documented in a number of sources including the *Prose Edda* and the *Gesta Danorum* (*Deeds of the Danes*, a twelfth-century history of Denmark by the Danish author Saxo Grammaticus). Battle scenes carved onto a stone at Stora Hammars (Stora Hammars I image stone) on Gotland, Sweden, have been interpreted as representing it, and there are allusions to it in the Old English poems *Deor* and *Widsith*.

Hild is a valkyrie and has the power to raise the dead, using this power to prevent her loved ones from ever truly dying. Hild is a figure who appears elsewhere in Norse literature, including in the list of Valkyries in *The Seeress' Prophecy* and other Old Norse poems. Identifying her, though, is not always straightforward as the word *hildr* in Old Norse means 'battle' so it is not always clear when the poets are referring to her specifically or when they are using the name as a personification of battle.

King Hedin is described as the son of Hiarrand (hence 'Hedin Hiarrandason'). Hiarrand is listed as one of the names of Odin in the *Prose Edda*. This adds additional mythological significance to the events described.

Halfdan the Old is a legendary Norse king from whom, as outlined below, many legendary families and characters were descended. This includes some of those referred to in the previous chapter on the Volsungs.

* * *

The abduction of Hild by King Hedin Hiarrandason and the unending battle of the wolf-warrior Hiadnings

There was once a king whose name was Hogni and he had a daughter by the name of Hild. While he was away at a meeting with other kings, his land was raided by King Hedin Hiarrandason and his daughter was abducted. When the news reached Hogni that his land had been attacked and his daughter seized, he set off in pursuit of King Hedin Hiarrandason. His scouts reported that King Hedin Hiarrandason had sailed north along the coast towards Norway. And so King Hogni set off in hot pursuit.

When King Hogni's fleet reached Norway, he discovered that King Hedin Hiarrandason had turned west and sailed out to sea towards the Orkney Islands. King Hogni followed him and eventually caught up with him at the island of Hoy. There he found the whole raiding army gathered. On his arrival, King

Hedin Hiarrandason sent Hild to negotiate on his behalf with her father. She gave her father a very mixed message. On one hand, she conveyed to him how King Hedin Hiarrandason offered him a fine gold neck ring as compensation for the abduction of his daughter. On the other hand, Hild confided in her father that King Hedin Hiarrandason was in no mood for further negotiations and was prepared to do battle. On hearing this, King Hogni's answer was short and to the point: there would be no settlement, so prepare to fight. So this is the message that Hild took back.

Then both sides took up positions on the island and prepared to settle the matter with weapons. It was then that King Hedin Hiarrandason sent another message to King Hogni. He sent it as a son-in-law would to his father-in-law for he had abducted Hild to make her his wife. The message was one final chance to avoid bloodshed and reach an agreement. And in order to achieve this, King Hedin Hiarrandason offered him a huge amount of gold as compensation for what he had done.

King Hogni's reply was not designed for reconciliation. He declared that it was now too late to make amends, for he had drawn his great sword, which was named Dainsleif (that means 'legacy of Dain', who was a dwarf, although some say he was a king of elves). This sword was forged by the dwarfs and when drawn had to cause the death of an enemy before it could be sheathed once more. This is fitting because Dain's name means 'dead'. Furthermore, one sweep of that sword never failed to inflict a wound that would never heal. And that was the message that King Hogni gave to King Hedin Hiarrandason's offer.

Hearing this, King Hedin Hiarrandason replied that while the boast might hold true of the sword, it was no assurance of ultimate victory in a battle.

And so the two armies closed to fight. The battle is known as Hiadnings' battle. The Hiadnings were wolf-warriors, who went into battle wearing hoods of wolfskin. They were great warriors. All day long the two armies were locked in battle. At nightfall, the kings retired to their ships. But that night, while they slept, Hild walked the battlefield with its carpet of dead men and worked her magic on the slain, so that those who were dead revived. The next morning the two kings returned to the field and the battle recommenced. There on the battlefield and engaged in the fighting were all those who had died the previous day, alongside those who had survived. Day after day this took place: those who died were revived at night by Hild's magic and the next day the battle was fought again. Those who died turned to stone as did their shields and weapons but at daybreak they returned to their former condition: men to men and weapons to weapons. And so it is said that these wolf-warriors will fight in this way until the end of the world, until the day of Ragnarok.

Halfdan the Old and his sacrifice

There was once a king named Halfdan the Old. He was a famous king and his deeds were well known. Once he held a great sacrifice at the time of midwinter, when days are short and cold. He sacrificed in the hope that he would reign for three hundred years. The reply he received from the gods was that this would not be granted but that, instead, for three hundred years all in his line of descent would be men of noble birth. There would not be a woman and there would not be a man below the rank of noble.

This Halfdan was a warrior of great renown and he travelled far in the eastern lands. In those lands, he faced in single combat a king whose name was Sigtrygg. And in that single combat he killed him. In those eastern lands, he married a woman named Alvig the Wise. She was the daughter of King Emund of Novgorod in the Russian lands.

Together they had eighteen sons. Nine of these sons were born at the same time. These nine were great warriors and since their deeds are so famous their names have become used as titles to be remembered by those who have come after them. So Gylfi means 'roarer or sea-king', Gram means 'fierce', Hilmir means 'helmet', Iofur means 'prince', Raesir means 'ruler', Thengil means 'prince of men', Tiggi means 'noble', Skuli means 'protector' and Herra means 'lord'. None of these nine warriors had children and each died in battle.

Halfdan and Alvig the Wise had nine further sons. These were: Hildir, from whom are descended the Hildings; Nefir, from whom are descended the Niflungs; Audi, from whom are descended the Odlings; Yngvi, from whom are descended the Ynglings; Dag, from whom are descended the Doglings; Bragi, from whom are descended the Bragnings; Budli, from whom are descended the Budlungs; Lofdi, from whom are descended the Lofdungs, one of whom was Sigurd who slew the serpent Fafnir, and his warband was called the Lofdar; finally there was Sigar, from whom are descended the Siklings and they are related to the Volsungs. These are families of great warriors. Other kings' lines that descended from them are the Skioldungs in Denmark and the Volsungs among the Franks. Another – but in eastern lands – is the family of Skelfir (the Skilfings). These royal and noble families are so famous that their very names appear in poetry as titles of honour.

Kings and kingdoms named after Odin

There was once a Swedish king of the island of Gotland by the name of Goti. In fact, 'Gotland' is named after him, as is the tribe of the Gautar or Gotar, who live on this island. And he in turn was named from one of the names used by Odin. This name means 'father'.

In the same way, the name of Sweden itself is derived from Svidur, another name used by Odin. This name means 'wise one'.

21

Ynglinga Saga and the 'history' of gods and kings

*Y*NGLINGA *SAGA* IS the first part of the Icelandic historian Snorri Sturluson's history of the ancient Norwegian kings, which is called *Heimskringla* (*Circle of the World*). It is a legendary saga, which was originally written in Old Norse in about 1225. *Ynglinga Saga* covers the period from the mythical origins of Norwegian kingship, through legendary rulers and then into the historic period. It ends in 1177, with the death of Eystein Meyla, who was one of the rival kings of Norway during a period of civil war.

The earliest part of the saga purports to deal with the 'arrival' of the Norse gods in Scandinavia. It explains how they originated in a part of Asia to the east of the Tana-kvísl river, which from Snorri's explanation is what we now call the River Don. Snorri knew it as the Tanais river (Tanais being a settlement in the delta of the River Don). This river flows from south of Moscow to eventually reach the Sea of Azov, which is linked to the Black Sea. This region is now in southern Russia, east of Ukraine, and borders the Caucasus to the south. Here, according to Snorri, the original city of the gods was called Asagarth (Asgard in other myths) and it was the capital of an area known as Asaland (literally 'Land of the Æsir' or 'Asia Land').

The 'geography' of this account was clearly inspired by knowledge of strange lands to the east that had actually been explored by Viking Age traders but which had later been reinvented in twelfth- and thirteenth-century Norway and Iceland into a fabulous never-never land that was situated far, far away. This is revealed by the fact that, in Snorri's account, Odin's journey to Scandinavia is described as being via the Don and Volga rivers and through Garðaríki (the Old Norse name for Kiev-Rus); a route that, in reverse, was the historic Viking routeway to the Byzantine Empire and Serkland, which was the Norse name for the Islamic Abbasid Caliphate.

Ynglinga Saga explains that the ruler of this area was Odin but he is described in what is known as a *euhemerised* way. This means that a mythological figure is presented as if he/she was once a *real* heroic person, who was later regarded as divine. In this way, Snorri – who wrote in Christian thirteenth-century Iceland – presented the traditional stories of the Norse gods as if they had been human ancestors whose real identity was obscured and distorted by later writers. The mythological tradition of a conflict between the divine Æsir and Vanir is presented as if it was a *real* war between those led by Odin out of Asaland and the rulers of Vanaland, which suffered invasion. The eventual truce and exchange of hostages (which in Norse mythology explains the presence of Vanir among the Æsir, such as Niord with his children Freyr and Freyia, and Æsir among the Vanir, such as Haenir and Mimir) is partly written as if it was a reflection of the kinds of political compromises found in the real Viking Age. The confused nature of this is revealed in the fact that Odin is presented *both* as a magical figure and *at the same time* as a mortal who dies and is cremated.

The saga goes on to explain how Freyr founded the Swedish Yngling royal dynasty at Uppsala. Then the storyline follows the line of Swedish kings until Ingjald. His descendants settled in Norway and were thus the ancestors of the Norwegian kings. Snorri is particularly careful to identify this as the line of the famous Norwegian king, Harald Fairhair (died *c.*933).

* * *

Odin, the ruler of Asaland

To the east of the river Tana-kvísl there is a land that was once called Asaland, that is the 'Land of the Æsir' or 'Asia Land', though some remember it as Asaheimr or the 'World of the Æsir'. The capital city of that land was called Asagarth. In that city the ruler was named Odin.

A great temple was located there and the custom of the place was that twelve temple priests presided over its rituals, sacrifices and judgements. They were known as the *diar* ('lords'). Odin was a famous warrior and travelled far and wide, conquering other nations. He won every battle he fought and so his people came to believe that it was him who decided who would win and lose. Whenever his own people went to war, he blessed them and they believed that this would assure them of victory. And whenever his people were in trouble, they called out his name and believed that he would help them and protect them. They did this on land and sea.

Odin had two brothers and one was called Ve and the other was called Vili. They acted as his regents when he was away. Once it happened that Odin was away for so long that the people thought he would never return. Then Ve and Vili divided up the land and its wealth between them but held Odin's wife, Frigg, in common. However, Odin did eventually return and took back the land and his wife.

The war between the Æsir and the Vanir

Odin and the people of the Æsir were in conflict with a rival people known as the Vanir. Odin took an army of the Æsir and invaded the land of the Vanir, but they defended their land determinedly and neither side could gain the victory. Eventually both sides grew tired of this conflict and they arranged a meeting, which aimed finally to put an end to the war. As part of this they gave each other hostages in order to safeguard the peace and ensure that each side kept to the agreement. As part of this arrangement, the Vanir offered up their noblest members: Niord, who was very rich, along with his son Freyr. The Æsir did likewise and gave as hostages Haenir, who was strong and good-looking and who the Æsir said was a fine leader; and Mimir, who was very wise. The Vanir too offered one of their wisest members: he was called Kvasir.

Things did not turn out as expected, though, for Haenir was totally dependent on Mimir for advice. However, if Mimir was not present then he would always reply: 'Let others decide.' After this had happened many times, the Vanir decided that the Æsir had cheated them and that Haenir was not at all wise. In their anger, they beheaded Mimir and sent his severed head to the Æsir. But Odin took Mimir's head, covered it with herbs that stopped it from decaying and, furthermore, he recited spells over it. This gave the severed head magic power and it was able to speak to him and tell him secrets.

Things turned out better for the Vanir hostages among the Æsir. For Niord and Freyr were appointed by Odin as priests, who were to carry out sacrifices. Among the Æsir they were considered to be gods. Niord's daughter was named Freyia and she was a priestess. It was Freyia who taught the Æsir the magic known as *seithr*, which enabled her to connect with the spirit-world; for this was common practice among the Vanir. Now, Freyr and Freyia were Niord's children by his own sister. However, among the Æsir it was forbidden to have sexual relations with close family members.

Odin leads the Æsir from Asaland to Scandinavia

A great range of high mountains runs from the north-east to the south-west in the vicinity of Asaland. South of the mountains lies Turkland. Odin held land there. It was at that time that the Rumverjar (Romans) became powerful, ruled many peoples and drove their leaders into exile.

Since Odin had magical powers, he could foresee that his descendants would inhabit the northern regions of the world and would rule them. As a result, he appointed his brothers, Ve and Vili, to rule from Asagarth; however, he and all of the gods with him and a host of people left Asaland and travelled to a new home. At first, they travelled to the west into Garthariki (Russia); from there they turned south to Saxland (Germany). Odin became the king over large areas of Saxland and placed his many sons there to hold the land. After this, he led his people north towards the coast and took up residence on the

Danish island of Funen, at the place later called Odinsey ('Odin's sanctuary'). After this, Odin sent Gefion north over the sea in search of more lands. She came to King Gylfi of Sweden and he gave her one 'plough-land'. After this, she travelled into Giantland and there she had four sons with a certain giant. Eventually she changed them into oxen and harnessed them to the plough. These giants/oxen pulled the land out into the sea and that is called Zealand. It was there that she made her home and married a son of Odin. A lake was left behind. It is called Logrinn or Mälaren. The fiords in Logrinn correspond to the headlands in Zealand.

When Odin heard tell of the good and fertile land to the east of his home he went there in search of it. It was then that Gylfi came to terms with Odin because he decided that he was not strong enough to resist the Æsir. Despite this, Odin and Gylfi often competed over who was more skilled in the art of tricks and illusions. But the Æsir always won. Odin set up his hall at the place that is now called Old Sigtunir. It was there that he constructed a large temple and carried out sacrifices in the manner of the Æsir. He gave dwelling places to the various priests who served in his temple: Niord lived at Noatun, Freyr at Uppsala, Heimdall at Himinbjorg, Thor at Thrudvangar, Baldr at Breidablik.

The shape-shifting of Odin and his victories in battle

When Odin went into battle he always terrified his enemies: for he could change his appearance and speak in a way that all believed his words. He spoke always in rhyme, which gave rise to what we now call poetry. It was with Odin and his priests that poetry originated in the lands of the north.

As well as this, Odin could make his opponents blind or deaf or fall into a panic. When this occurred, their weapons were no better than pieces of wood. In contrast, his own men did not wear mail and acted as wild as if they were dogs or wolves. They bit the edges of their shields, and became as strong as bears or bulls. They slaughtered many – but nobody could touch them. That is the wild anger of warriors that is called berserk-fury.

As well as this, Odin could change his shape. It was then that his body appeared as if he was asleep or dead. But while this occurred, Odin had actually taken on the form of a bird or a fish or a snake, and had been transported, in an instant, to far-off lands. In addition, he could also put out fire, calm a stormy sea or change the wind direction. He could achieve this with words alone. Furthermore, he owned a ship which, although it was large enough to carry Odin and his warriors, could also be folded up and carried in a pocket.

Odin also kept Mimir's head by his side, for from it he learned secrets from across the various worlds. More than this, he sometimes woke up dead men; at other times, he sat beneath the gallows with the bodies of hanged men swaying above him. For this reason, he was sometimes called '*draugadrottinn*' (the 'lord of ghosts') or '*hangadrottinn*' (the 'lord of the hanged').

He had two ravens, who flew far and wide and brought him the news. As a result, he became very knowledgeable and wise. He was skilful in the use of runes and magic spells. As a result, the Æsir are called '*galdrasmithir*' ('magic makers'). In addition, Odin practised what is called *seithr*, a form of magic that enabled him to connect with the spirit-world. And from that he was able to predict the fates of men and to foresee things that had not yet happened; it also enabled him to cause the death of men or cause calamity and disease; he also used it to take the ability to think and take the strength from some men, and give it to others of his choosing. It was this form of magic that Freyia of the Vanir had introduced to the Æsir.

The laws established by Odin

The laws of the Norse people originated in the laws established by Odin. For it was Odin who decreed that all the dead must be cremated along with all their possessions. He decreed that those dead warriors who come to his hall at Valhalla would come with as much wealth as was piled on their funeral pyres and burned with them. However, their ashes were to be deposited in the sea or buried under burial mounds. And memorial stones were to be raised up to record the deeds of the famous dead. This was a custom that carried on for a great many years after that.

Odin's laws also decreed that there would be three times for sacrifice in the year: one sacrifice was to occur as winter approached for a good winter season; another sacrifice was to take place in the middle of winter to ensure success in next year's crops; and a third sacrifice was to take place in summer and that final one was to ensure victory in war.

The death of Odin

When Odin was on the point of death he had himself marked with the point of a spear. From this he claimed for himself all men who died in battle. He said he was going to Gothheimr ('Home of the gods') and there he would be reunited with his old companions. The people of the Svear (that is, in Sweden) believed that he had gone back to Asagarth, from where he had journeyed long before. There, they believed, he would live for ever.

The Svear thought he appeared to them before great battles occurred. It was then that he granted victory to some; and others he allowed to die so they would join him in Valhalla.

When Odin died, he was cremated in a magnificent ceremony. It was believed that the higher the smoke rose into the sky, the higher up in the realm of heaven would be the one whose funeral smoke was rising. And he would be richer in Valhalla if his wealth was burned with him.

After Odin died, Niord became ruler over the people of the Svear and continued the manner of worship established by Odin. He received payments of tribute from across Sweden. During his reign, there was peace and good harvests, so that the Svear believed that he had power over the harvest and could assure prosperity to the kingdom.

It was during Niord's reign that most of the gods died and were all burned in the same manner as Odin before them. Afterwards, they too were worshipped. Eventually, Niord himself fell sick and died. Before he died he caused himself to be marked for Odin as Odin had done with the spear point. Then the Svear burned his body and mourned him greatly.

Freyr establishes the royal line of Sweden

Freyr ruled the Svear after Niord. He was popular among the people and, like his father, the harvests were good during his reign. Freyr built a great temple at Uppsala and made Uppsala his capital. He ruled from there and it was to Uppsala that taxes and tribute were brought. Freyr was also known as Yngvi and this title came to be used after him as a title of honour; and his descendants were called the *Ynglings* (meaning 'the descendants of Yngvi').

Eventually Freyr fell ill and, as his health faded, the leading people decided how to respond: few were allowed to approach him and the leaders built him a great tomb. In it they constructed a doorway and three windows.

When Freyr died, they placed him in the tomb and told the Svear that he was still alive. They kept up this pretence for three years. During this period of time, they poured all the tribute brought to Uppsala into the mound: the gold was poured through one window, the silver was poured through the second window, and copper was poured through the third window. The prosperity and peace associated with the reign of Freyr continued. And his sister, Freyia, continued the traditional sacrifices, for she was the only one of the gods left alive. As a result, she became the best known of the deities, and all noblewomen came to be called by her name as an honorary title.

The sacrifice of a king to bring prosperity to the land

There was once a king of the Svear who was named Domaldi. He succeeded his father, Visburr, and ruled over Sweden. In his time, though, misfortune came on the land and there was famine. People grew very hungry.

It was then that the Svear came together and held great sacrifices at Uppsala. They did this in the autumn over three years. In the first year, they sacrificed oxen, but there was still no improvement in the situation and the crops continued to fail. The second year, they carried out a human sacrifice, but still the crops failed; indeed, some said the situation worsened. The third year, the Svear once again came in the autumn to Uppsala, and they came in great numbers. For it was the time when the sacrifices were to occur and there was much suffering in the land.

It was then that the Swedish nobles held a great council. They discussed the crisis and they came to an agreement among themselves. They agreed that their king, Domaldi, must be the one who was the cause of the terrible famine. In consequence, they resolved that they should sacrifice him in order to restore the prosperity of the land. And this is what they did. They killed him and his blood ran red on the altar at Uppsala.

A king sacrifices his own sons in order to extend his own life and reign

There was once a king of Sweden named Aun and he ruled from Uppsala. When he reached sixty years of age he held a great sacrifice that he might have a long life. He sacrificed his own son to Odin. Then Odin told him that he would live for another sixty years.

Aun was king for another twenty years until he was driven from his throne by a rival and he was in exile for twenty years. Then, when that rival died, King Aun returned to Uppsala and reigned there for another twenty years. That completed the sixty years that he had been promised by Odin.

At the end of this time, he held another great sacrifice and sacrificed his second son. After this, Odin told him that he would live for ever but that this would only be so if he sacrificed a son of his to Odin every ten years. At the same time, he was to give a name to a region in his land which reflected the number of sons that he had sacrificed to Odin.

This continued until he had sacrificed seven of his sons; and then he lived for ten years without being able to walk. His servants carried him around on a chair.

After this, he sacrificed his eighth son to Odin; and then he lived for another ten years, but he was confined to his bed.

Then he sacrificed his ninth son and, after this, he lived for ten more years, but he had to drink from a feeding cup like a baby.

Finally, King Aun had just one son left. He determined to sacrifice him, and was going to give Odin all the region of Uppsala and it would be called Tiundaland ('Tenth land').

But the people of the Svear stopped him from doing this. So, no sacrifice was held. As a result, King Aun died, and he was buried at Uppsala.

It was from these ancient kings of the Svear that the line of the kings of Sweden and Norway were descended. These kings traced their lineage back to the Æsir and Vanir.

22

The magic sword called Tyrfing

THIS IS THE story of a magical sword. Different manuscripts and traditions render its name as 'Tyrfing', 'Tirfing'
or 'Tyrving'. The name is obscure and may be related to that of
the Terwingi: these were a part of the Goth tribe. Roman
sources in the fourth century record this tribal name in the
form 'Tervingi'. By the fourth century AD this group were living
on the Danubian plains west of the Dniester river, which today
rises in Ukraine and then flows through Moldova, before finally
returning to Ukrainian territory and flowing into the Black
Sea. The accounts of this magic sword are preserved in stories
known as 'the Tyrfing Cycle'. These are a collection of Norse
legends, which have the magic sword Tyrfing as a common
feature. Two of the legends are found in the *Poetic Edda* (which
includes a poem called *Hervararkviða*) and in the *Hervarar
Saga*, which contains other traditions about this sword. The
name of the sword is also used in this saga to indicate the tribal
group of the Goths. This may indicate a Norse tradition that

these eastern lands of 'Kiev-Rus' (through which Norse adventurers had travelled and some had married into the ruling dynasties) were places of mystery.

The dwarfs too have names attested in a number of traditions. That of Dvalin is found in both the poem *Grímnismál* in the *Poetic Edda* and also in the story called *Gylfaginning* in the *Prose Edda*.

With regard to Princess Eyfura, the twelfth-century book entitled the *Gesta Danorum* (*Deeds of the Danes*), compiled by Saxo Grammaticus, identified her as a Danish princess and said that she was the daughter of a king whose name was Frodi. This may indicate that the character had a tradition apart from the sword legend and may have been incorporated into that account in order to enhance its local Scandinavian colour.

These features of these traditions are very much in keeping with the 'legendary' material found in these stories, where some material that would be at home in the Norse 'myths' is intermingled with the doings of real (or probably real) tribes and peoples. In these legendary accounts, we also hear garbled echoes of real conflicts that occurred between the Gothic tribes (of Norse origin), living north-west of the Black Sea, and invading Hun tribes in the fourth century. These conflicts occurred in the period of 'folk wanderings' (the so-called *Völkerwanderung*) in the 'migration period' that accompanied the end of the Roman Empire. Because of the Scandinavian origins of the Goths, and because of later Scandinavian exploration of the eastern lands as they travelled towards the Byzantine Empire and the Caspian Sea, these ancient conflicts became woven into later Norse legends. In this way, magic swords and migration-period tribes are brought together in a curious blend of fiction and history.

Myrkvithr (Mirkwood) was later to make an appearance in Tolkien's *The Lord of the Rings*.

* * *

King Svafrlami and the sword that was forged by the dwarfs, Dvalin and Durin

There was once a king whose name was Svafrlami. He was the king of the people known as the Gardariki. The name of this people means something like 'the tribe of cities', or 'the tribe of towns'. Svafrlami was the son of Sigrlami, who was the son of Odin. So, this Svafrlami was the grandson of Odin. By cunning he managed to trap the two dwarfs named Dvalin and Durin.

Dvalin's name means 'the sleeping one' and some use his name for one of the four stags who feast on Yggdrasil, the world tree. It was Dvalin who led the host of dwarfs from the mountains to find a new home. They travelled from the mountains, through the marshes to the fields of sand. Some say that it was Dvalin who taught the dwarfs how to write in runes, in the same way that it was Dain who taught the elves and Odin who taught the runes to the gods. Some poets call the sun 'one who deceives Dvalin', for the sun turns a dwarf to stone if one is caught out in it. Other poets call mead by the name 'Dvalin's drink' as the mead of poetry was originally created by the dwarfs. Some of the norns (who decide the destinies of men) are known as 'Dvalin's daughters'.

Durin too is famous for he was the second dwarf created after Motsognir, the father of the dwarfs, in the distant times when the worlds were first created.

Now Dvalin and Durin were trapped because they left the rock within which they lived and so were exposed to the trickery of Svafrlami. It happened in this fashion. One day, Svafrlami was out hunting on horseback and chanced on these two dwarfs. They were standing near a large rock; this was the home within which they lived. Svafrlami raised his sword over them so that they could not disappear back into the rock and so they were trapped. With them in his power, he forced them to forge a magical sword for him. It had a hilt made from pure gold and when wielded it never missed its intended victim. It would never rust and, when it came to sharpness, it could cut through stone and iron just as if these were mere cloth.

Forced by Svafrlami, the two dwarfs forged the sword, and Svafrlami saw how it glowed like fire. However, in revenge for their imprisonment, the two dwarfs cursed the sword that they had made, so that it would kill a man every time it was drawn from its scabbard. In addition, it would be the cause of three great evils. As if this was not enough, they completed their vengeance by cursing it so that it would lead to the death of Svafrlami himself.

When Svafrlami realised what the dwarfs had done, he was furious and he tried to kill Dvalin. But the dwarf disappeared into the rock from which he had originally emerged. Svafrlami drove the magic sword deep into the rock but Dvalin escaped the cutting blade and so survived Svafrlami's anger.

The sword becomes the property of Arngrim, the berserker

The sword was indeed the undoing of Svafrlami. In time, he was killed by a berserker (a wild warrior) who was named Arngrim. At first, all seemed well for Svafrlami when he battled Arngrim. The sword Tyrfing sliced through Arngrim's shield but, so great was the force of the blow, that it dug deep into the earth. Svafrlami was caught by surprise and found that his sword was caught fast in the ground. As a result, Arngrim was able to cut off Svafrlami's hand. Then he seized Tyrfing from him and killed him.

After his triumph, Arngrim forced Svafrlami's daughter (whose name was Eyfura) to marry him. After she had married Arngrim, they had twelve sons. They were all berserkers. These twelve sons were later all killed by the Swedish warrior Hjalmar and his companion Orvar-Odd, as we shall shortly see. Some say, however, that the sword came into Arngrim's possession by a different route and that Arngrim fought for King Frodi of Denmark and only gained the hand of the princess after he had defeated the Finnish tribes of the Samis and the Bjarmians. Arngrim thus became the warrior champion of King Frodi and, as a result, he was later granted both the sword, Tyrfing, and the princess, Eyfura, as rewards for his service.

After Arngrim died, the sword passed to Angantyr, his son by Eyfura, who was one of twelve brothers. With regard to these twelve brothers, one Yule they were back home on Bolmsö, in Lake Bolmen, in Småland, in southern Sweden. It was then that the next eldest son, Hjorvard, declared that he wished to marry Princess Ingeborg, who was the daughter of Yngvi, the king of Sweden. To this end, he swore an oath declaring his intention and his determination.

As a result of this oath, these twelve brothers set off for the Swedish royal court at Uppsala. When they reached Uppsala, Hjorvard proposed to Princess Ingeborg. But things soon turned sour. For, at that point, Hjalmar – who was one of the Swedish king's champions – claimed that he had a better right to the princess than the berserker, Hjorvard. This placed the Swedish king in a very difficult position, for he greatly feared that if he opposed the brothers – who were infamous berserkers – then terrible violence would overwhelm his royal court. As a way out of his dilemma, he suggested that Ingeborg herself should decide the man that she wished to marry.

She chose Hjalmar, as she knew him and preferred him to the threatening stranger. Hjorvard was furious and challenged Hjalmar to a duel on the Danish island of Samsø. He underscored the challenge when he declared that Hjalmar would lose his honour if he was too frightened to appear. But Hjalmar was unafraid and decided to accept the challenge and to sail there in the company of Orvar-Odd, his trusted friend who was his Norwegian sworn-brother.

The first evil deed of the sword

When the twelve brothers arrived on the island of Samsø, they worked themselves up into a frenzy of berserk-rage. As was their habit, they bit the edge of their shields, they screamed out loud and obscene curses; they fell on the crewmen of the ship of Hjalmar and Orvar-Odd and cut them to pieces. The bloodshed was terrible.

However, when the Swedish warrior Hjalmar and Orvar-Odd the Norwegian arrived at the scene, the tide of battle turned. Angantyr's eleven brothers were swiftly slaughtered by Orvar-Odd, who despatched them with a war-club. Orvar-Odd then went to assist Hjalmar. On reaching him, he saw that Angantyr was dead but that Hjalmar had been mortally wounded by Tyrfing. This mortal wounding of Hjalmar was *the first evil deed of Tyrfing*.

Orvar-Odd realised that the sword had both dealt out death and, at the same time, had brought destruction on its owner, too. It was, indeed, a cursed weapon.

As a result, Orvar-Odd buried the twelve brothers in earthen barrows there on the island of Samsø. With them he buried the cursed sword, Tyrfing. In this way, he hoped that it would no longer cause any harm. After this, Orvar-Odd carried the body of Hjalmar, the Swedish champion, to Uppsala where he gave the body to Princess Ingeborg, daughter of King Yngvi.

But the plan of Orvar-Odd was thwarted because Angantyr's daughter – who was named Hervor – later travelled to Samsø and retrieved Tyrfing and took it as her own possession. This is remembered as the 'awakening of Angantyr'.

The second evil deed of the sword

Hervor was raised as a slave girl and had no idea who her parents were. When at last it was revealed to her, she took arms as a female warrior (a shield-maiden), as if she was one of the valkyries. Learning of her father's death, she travelled to the island of Samsø to search for the sword that the dwarfs had cursed and which had caused the death of her father in battle. There she found it beneath the burial mound and took it for herself.

After this, she married the son of King Gudmund, who lived in Jotunheim in north-eastern Norway. He ruled over a land called Glaesisvellir, which was renowned for its warriors and warfare. This was the area known as the 'Finnmark' or 'Finnish borderlands', for it was on the edge of Norse and Finnish territory. Some say that Gudmund was a giant and some later called him 'Gudrun *faxi* ('horse mane') and thought him a god who roamed the dark countryside at Yule collecting the dead.

The man that Hervor married was named Hofund. Together, they had two sons, whose names were Heidrek and Angantyr (junior). Hervor decided that the magic sword should go to one of these sons. Without telling anyone else she gave it to her son Heidrek. But, once again, the sword Tyrfing was to be the undoing of those who owned it.

One day Angantyr (junior) and Heidrek were out walking. As they walked, Heidrek wanted to have a look at the sword that his mother had given him. To do so he drew it from its scabbard. But once unsheathed it was doomed to kill a man. This was the curse that the dwarfs had put on the sword. And so, as a result of this curse, Heidrek killed his brother Angantyr (junior). This was *the second of Tyrfing's three evil deeds.*

The third evil deed of the sword

After he had killed his brother, Heidrek became king over the Goths. He embarked on an adventure and while travelling he camped in the Carpathian mountains. Now Heidrek was travelling in the company of eight slaves. And while Heidrek was asleep one night, these slaves broke into his tent, stole Tyrfing, his sword, and killed him. This was *the last of Tyrfing's three evil deeds.* Heidrek's son – who was also named Angantyr (ruling as King Angantyr II) – hunted down, captured and killed the slaves who had murdered his father. In so doing, he reclaimed the magic sword; then the curse had run its course.

The magic sword in the ownership of King Angantyr II

After he had avenged himself on the slaves who had killed his father, Angantyr II became the next king of the Goths. However, he was challenged by his illegitimate half-brother. This brother was half-Hun and was named Hlod (or Hlothr). He was illegitimate by a Hun slave-girl, but was, nevertheless, a son of Heidrek. Hlod had grown up with his grandfather; this was Humli, the king of the Huns. It was his daughter who had been taken by the Goths as a slave and by whom Heidrek had a half-Hunnish son. Hlod was handsome and brave. Even while he was a baby he had been given weapons and horses, as was the custom of the Huns, for they were fierce warriors.

Hlod demanded half of the kingdom from his half-brother, King Angantyr II. To enforce his claim, he rode to his court at the heart of the kingdom of the Goths.

The Battle of the Goths and the Huns

When Hlod reached the court of Angantyr II, he was admitted but found that Angantyr awaited him dressed in mail, carrying his shield and the magic sword. Nevertheless, Angantyr invited Hlod to drink to the honour of their dead father.

However, Hlod rejected his offer of hospitality and demanded half of the kingdom: its treasure, herds, mills, slaves, the forests of Myrkvithr (Mirkwood) and the land as far as the carved stone that stood beside the River Dniepr.

Angantyr refused Hlod's demands and declared that he had no right to inherit land that had legitimately come to Angantyr. But he sought peace by offering Hlod compensation: weapons, cattle, treasure and a thousand each of slaves, horses and armed retainers. Furthermore, one third of the Gothic lands would be his.

Whether this would have satisfied Hlod no one was to discover because the offer was soon overshadowed by an insult against Hlod. Staying with Angantyr II was Gizur Grytingalidi, the grey-haired king of the Geats. He had come to attend the funeral of Heidrek, who was his dead foster-son. Listening to the demand and offer, he thought that Angantyr had been far too generous to his Hunnish half-brother. As a consequence of this, Gizur dismissed Hlod as a bastard and the offspring of a slave-girl. As such he should not be given the riches offered him by the king of the Goths.

Hlod was furious at being called a bastard and the son of a slave and so he rejected Angantyr's offer and, instead, he returned to the land of the Huns and to Humli, his grandfather. He recounted to Humli how Angantyr had refused to share the kingdom with him, and that Gizur Grytingalidi had dismissed him as the mere son of a slave!

At this, his grandfather was as offended as he was and set about gathering a vast Hun army. By the spring, it was ready and warriors were summoned from across the vast grasslands ruled by the Huns. Every male older than twelve years of age was summoned to come equipped for war.

In spring, the assembled Hun host rode through Myrkvithr, which bordered the land of the Goths. Pouring out of the forest onto the plains beyond, they reached a fortress which was held against them by Hervor, the grandmother of Angantyr II.

In the battle that took place before that fortress, Hervor was killed and the news of her death was taken to Angantyr. The Huns then burned and destroyed the borderlands. Angantyr pondered what to do against such a vast invading army. It was then that he was reminded of a law declared by Heidrek of the Goths that if the king was to mark out a battlefield with hazel poles then no invading army could pillage until it had settled matters by the sword on that battlefield.

The message declaring this was carried to the Huns by Gizur Grytingalidi, the king of the Geats. And the marked-out battlefield was to be on the plains beside the River Danube. When Gizur informed the Huns of this, he added that Odin was against them and that they would fall to the weapons of the Goths.

So it was that the two great armies met on the plains beside the Danube, at the place marked out by hazel rods. There the battle raged for eight long days of death and destruction. For the Goths, it was a war to defend their freedom; for the Huns, it was a war to prevent them being annihilated by a victorious Gothic army. And this added urgency to the way both sides wielded their weapons.

The Huns greatly outnumbered the Goths but still the Goths triumphed, because Angantyr used Tyrfing against them and they were vanquished by its powerful death-dealing strokes. At the sight of this great blade dealing out death, the Huns lost heart. The Goths broke the lines of the Hun army and drove them back. With this sword, Angantyr killed his half-brother Hlod in battle and went on to rout the Huns. Humli too died in the middle of that great slaughter. So great was the slaughter of the fleeing Huns that the bodies of their slain warriors and their dead horses filled the rivers, causing a flood that inundated the valleys.

After the battle, Angantyr went back and searched among the bodies on the battlefield until he eventually found the body of his half-brother. Looking at one who had fallen to the edge of Tyrfing, he declared that it was a cruel fate when the norns decreed that a brother would kill his own brother.

This ends the story of the sword that was named Tyrfing.

23

The Saga of King Hrolf Kraki

THE STORY OF King Hrolf Kraki and the characters associated with him is one of the most important and influential of the *fornaldar-sagas* (sagas of the ancient times) or 'legendary sagas'. As with these others stories, it recounts legendary traditions associated with (possibly real) pre-Viking Age kings. In this case, the king in question is the sixth-century King Hrolf of Denmark. His nickname 'Kraki' refers to his face being 'long and thin like a pole-ladder'. So, when his Old Norse nickname is translated, it is something like 'Thin-faced Hrolf'.

The original story of King Hrolf Kraki was first written down *c.*1400 in Iceland but drew on much earlier traditions that are found in other Germanic literature (there are echoes of some of it or its concerns in an incomplete tenth-century poem called *Bjarkamál* and in the late-twelfth-century *Saga of the Skjoldungs*). Its structure reveals that it is really a collection of stories and subplots. There are five of these subsections and each revolves around a different set of characters but all are linked in some way to Hrolf Kraki and other members of his family and his royal court. In the first four subsections, Hrolf Kraki's role is a relatively minor but unifying one; in the fifth story, he is centre-stage. Interestingly, it is often women characters who connect the stories as much as Hrolf Kraki, and women generally play a major part in the stories. However, the abuse suffered by Olof and by the mistress of Hjalti reminds us of the vulnerability of women to male violence in the Viking Age.

Overall, its most striking parallel is with the Old English (Anglo-Saxon) story of *Beowulf* that was put into written form in England somewhere between the eighth and eleventh centuries and was itself based on even earlier traditions. Both refer to legendary 'events' that were thought to have occurred in the Danish kingdom of the Skjoldungs (*Scyldinga* in Old English). Both stories were inspired by the warriors of the past (the family name itself was derived from *skjold*, shield); similarly named characters appear in both accounts although their roles sometime differ; most strikingly, both stories include the actions of a bear-like warrior. In *The Saga of King Hrolf Kraki*, the character is named Bodvar Bjarki (*bjarki* meaning 'little bear') and in *Beowulf* it is Beowulf himself (whose name, 'bee-wolf', is a poetic term for a 'bear' named from its love of honey). The stories of both heroes start in Götaland in southern Sweden (in Old Norse the land of the *Gautar*, in Old English the land of the *Geatas*). Until the later consolidation of Sweden, starting from the tenth century, it was a separate political unit from the kingdom of the Svear (early Sweden). In both stories, the hero crosses water to the Danish court of the Skjoldungs and kills a monster ravaging the land.

The supposed geography of the collection of stories is centred on the royal court at Hleidargard, on the Danish island of Sjælland (Zealand). However, it ranges far and wide, from arctic Lapland to northern England. And its relationship to Norse mythology is shown in the stories of Odin (disguised as the character named Hrani), an elf-woman, magic spells, sorceresses, a monstrous boar and Bodvar Bjarki who appears in Hrolf Kraki's final battle in the form of a giant bear unstoppable by weapons. The later negative references to Odin and the statement about Hrolf Kraki not worshipping the old gods reveal the outlook of the Christian writer(s) who recorded the story in its current form.

The stories associated with King Hrolf Kraki clearly fascinated later Icelanders. In the twelfth- to thirteenth-century Icelandic *Landnámabók* (*Book of Settlements*) is recounted how (in *c*.900) one of the early settlers of Iceland – named Skeggi – broke into the Danish burial mound of King Hrolf Kraki and took his sword, called Skofnung, along with an axe and treasure. When he went on to attempt to steal the sword of Bodvar Bjarki, he discovered that this long-dead warrior was still keeping watch over the treasure and rose up against him. It was only when King Hrolf Kraki himself came to Skeggi's aid that he managed to escape with the treasure. According to later Icelandic tradition, the sword was last heard of in the 1070s when it accompanied the Christian Icelander, Gellir, on a pilgrimage to Rome.

* * *

The exile and eventual triumph of the princes Hroar and Helgi

There were once two royal brothers and their names were Halfdan and Frodi. Halfdan was kind and generous, while Frodi was cruel and greedy. They both ruled kingdoms but that of Halfdan – Denmark – was the more desirable of the two. This caused Frodi to resent him deeply. In time, this resentment grew so great that Frodi invaded Denmark and killed Halfdan.

However, he was unable to capture the sons of Halfdan. They were named Hroar and Helgi. Their foster-father was named Regin (it was common then to place children with other nobles in order to strengthen bonds of loyalty). At great risk to himself, he took the boys to an island where lived a man named Vifil, who was both a great friend of King Halfdan and well versed in ancient magic. There the boys were hidden.

Now Frodi hunted high and low for the young princes and offered rewards to those with information and threats to those concealing them. In the end, he turned to his own workers of magic and they said that he should search the island home of Vifil but that his home was protected by magic mist for they could not see into it. So Frodi sent men to search.

Early one morning, Vifil woke with a sense that his island had been visited by the magic of others and so he warned the boys to hide. It was not a moment too soon, for Frodi's men arrived, although they were unable to find the boys. When they returned to Frodi he was angry and told them to search again – but still they could not find the boys.

At last, Frodi himself visited the island but even he could not find the boys for they had been well hidden by Vifil.

After this, Vifil sent them to seek shelter with their brother-in-law Jarl (Earl) Saevil. He was the husband of Signy, their sister. This they did and they went in disguise and always wore their hoods up. It was three winters since they had first fled into exile and still Frodi could not find them. But he suspected they might be hiding with Saevil so he summoned him to court to a feast. When the jarl refused to take the boys they followed him anyway. The youngest – Helgi – was the bravest and rode his horse facing backwards, making himself look like a fool. His older brother – Hroar – rode after him. As they rode they were recognised by their sister. She told Jarl Saevil who warned the boys to return to his hall but they would not.

When they reached the royal hall of Frodi, he summoned a seeress to foretell where the boys were. She began to speak but when Signy (the sister of Hroar and Helgi) threw her a gold ring she stopped revealing secrets. At last, when pressed by Frodi to continue, the seeress warned the boys to escape and she and they ran from the hall. It was then that they were recognised by Regin, their foster-father. He followed them to the woods and, by careful communication (so that he did not break his oath of loyalty to Frodi but still gave them advice), he advised them to set fire to the hall. This they did and Frodi and his supporters were trapped inside and died. But Regin escaped, as did Jarl Saevil and Signy. However, their mother, Sigrid, died in the hall because she refused to leave.

The reigns of Hroar and Helgi

Hroar went to live in England, where he married Ogn, the daughter of King Nordri of Northumbria. Helgi ruled in Denmark. It was at that time that Regin, their foster-father, died.

Meanwhile, Helgi heard that in Saxland, in northern Germany, there ruled a beautiful but proud and arrogant queen named Olof. She carried weapons as if she was a man and was a strong ruler. Helgi decided to marry her whether she liked it or not. Sailing to her land, he caught her by surprise and she had no choice but to invite him to feast in her hall. There, he insisted on marrying her and, despite her protestations that she was not willing for such a swift match, he prevailed. But Helgi had drunk too much and passed out on the bed. Olof placed a magic thorn in his ear so he could not awaken; then she shaved him, tarred his body and rolled him into a sack. Her men then carried the sleeping king to his ship. When his men, on being told that their king had returned to his ship, went after him they found him in the sack. Helgi was furious and set on revenge but could do nothing as Olof had rallied her army. So he sailed away.

Helgi got his revenge in this way. He sailed again to Olof's land and there hid a great treasure in a forest. Disguised as a beggar he persuaded one of Olof's slaves to tell her that he had found treasure in the forest but that she must come alone lest anyone else claim it. She was so greedy that she did this and so was caught by the angry Helgi. At once she offered to marry him but he would have none of it. His revenge on her was to take her captive to his ship where he slept with her for many nights.

When Helgi had finished with her, he let her go and she returned to her court. Helgi, though, went raiding and conquering.

Back in Saxland, Olof found that she was pregnant with Helgi's child. She hid her condition and gave birth in secret to a girl. Olof hated the child and named her Yrsa after one of her dogs. When she turned twelve, Yrsa was sent to tend cattle and her parentage kept from her.

Next year, Helgi returned to Saxland to see what had happened there since his last visit. Again, he did so in disguise and met Yrsa in the woods. He did not know she was his daughter and he fell in love with her, for she was very beautiful. Against her will, he took her back to Denmark and married her. When Olof heard, she was glad for she knew that in time this would lead to the dishonouring of Helgi.

It was at this time that Hroar and Helgi settled the matter of the Danish inheritance. At first, Hroar had kept an interest in the kingdom of Denmark but in time he decided to remain in England and give up his claim to any land elsewhere. He sailed to Denmark to tell Helgi and, in return, Helgi gave him a magnificent ring that Hroar desired.

It was at that time that Jarl Saevil died and his widow, Signy (sister to Hroar and Helgi), advised her son, Hrok, to claim a reward from his uncles for assistance given them by Saevil. So he went to Helgi and demanded either one-third of Denmark or the great ring. But Helgi *would not* give him the one and *could not* give him the other. So Hrok sailed to England and asked Hroar for the ring. Hroar would not do so, so Hrok asked if he could see and handle the ring. When Hroar agreed, he took it and flung it into the sea. For this crime Hroar had Hrok's foot cut off.

In time, Hrok returned to England and killed Hroar in battle. He then demanded to marry Hroar's widow. This was Ogn, the daughter of King Nordri of Northumbria. King Nordri was old but still willing to fight to defend his daughter who had no wish to marry her nephew, the killer of her husband. Since she was carrying Hroar's child she asked for the marriage to be delayed and sent to Helgi for assistance. When Helgi heard that Ogn had given birth to a son, named Agnar, he decided it was time to act. He sailed to England, captured Hrok and had his arms and legs broken. Crippled, he was sent home.

Agnar grew up to be a strong warrior and, in time, he sailed to where the great ring had been lost to the waves. He dived three times and at the third attempt he surfaced with the ring!

Back in Denmark, Helgi became renowned for the success of his summer raiding. He and Yrsa loved each other and they had one son. So it was that Hrolf, later surnamed Kraki, was born.

Their happiness was brought to an end when Queen Olof visited Denmark and at last had her revenge on Helgi when she revealed to Yrsa the truth of her parentage: that her mother was Olof but that Helgi, her husband and father of her son, was none other than her own father. In her distress, Yrsa decided she could not remain with Helgi but returned to Saxland with Olof. Helgi was devastated. He took to his bed in deep depression and could not rule the land. Olof had taken her terrible revenge.

In time, King Adils of Sweden sought the hand of Yrsa in marriage. She had no enthusiasm for the match but still it went ahead. After this, Olof no longer plays a part in this story.

When Helgi heard that King Adils had taken Yrsa to Sweden as his wife, he sunk even deeper into depression. One night, at Yule, he saw a poor beggar outside his door and invited her into his chamber. She asked to sleep in his bed and he agreed. But when he turned to her in the night he discovered that she had turned into a beautiful woman, released from a spell by his acceptance of her. He desired her and slept with her. In the morning, she left but told him to go, a year hence, to where the ships tied up and collect their child. But he forgot and three years later the child – a girl named Skuld – was brought to him at midnight by the elf-woman with whom he had slept three years before. She told Helgi that he would gain from releasing her from the spell but that his family would suffer because he had not gone to collect the child as instructed. The child grew up with a mean and dangerous character.

Helgi himself returned to his summer raiding but left Hrolf (who was later known as Kraki), his son, at home. Eventually, Helgi sailed to Sweden where he visited King Adils at Uppsala. He was received by the king and by Yrsa who was now queen of Sweden. When Adils saw how much Helgi still loved Yrsa he set a trap for him. When Helgi returned to his ship he was ambushed by the twelve berserkers who acted as King Adils' bodyguard. Trapped between them and Adils' army, Helgi died in battle. So ended the reign of King Helgi of Denmark.

After this, King Adils considered himself a famous and powerful king. He was a devoted follower of the Norse gods and practised magic. Yrsa was reluctantly reconciled to Adils by compensation for the death of Helgi, her father, but inside she longed to kill the king's berserkers and she desired to free herself from the rule of Adils.

Svipdag fights the berserkers of Adils of Sweden and enters the service of King Hrolf

There was once a wealthy farmer named Svip. He lived in the mountains of Sweden and he had three sons. One of these was named Svipdag. He grew tired of living far from people and from action and so he resolved to go to the court of King Adils and become a warrior. His father armed him with a great axe and mail and a fine horse and he set out for Uppsala.

When he reached the defended royal residence, he broke down the gate to make his entrance and all were astonished. He was greeted by the king who asked who he was and he told him. But the berserkers of King Adils wished to fight him because they were provoked by his arrogance. The king, though, told them to wait. It was then that Queen Yrsa welcomed him for she wished him to kill the berserkers who had ambushed her father. She wanted them dead and sent to Hel. The berserkers knew this but defied her hatred for they were confident in their strength and skills.

In the morning, a series of single combats occurred until Svipdag had killed four of the berserkers. King Adils would have set his remaining men on Svipdag but Queen Yrsa arranged a truce that lasted until nightfall. It was then that the remaining berserkers set upon Svipdag as he left the hall on his own. They had been sent to attack him by the king. Svipdag killed another of them before the king stopped the fighting. He then banished the surviving berserkers for he was no longer impressed by their fighting skills. At this they left but threatened revenge. In this way, Svipdag replaced the berserkers at the court of King Adils and the queen was pleased at this turn of events.

Eventually, the berserkers gathered an army and returned to threaten King Adils. At his request, Svipdag was sent as leader of the king's army to confront the invaders. Before battle was joined, Svipdag had spikes scattered on the chosen site to injure the horses of his enemies. When the battle commenced, one of the berserkers was killed along with many in the invading army and they returned to their ships in disarray.

After they had gathered more warriors, the berserkers returned once more and again Svipdag was sent against them but with a smaller army than that of the invaders; although the king promised to assist him with his bodyguards. So battle commenced and it was a hard fight.

Nearby was where Svip was living with his remaining two sons. He awoke from sleep and called his sons to him. He told them to go to the assistance of their brother for he knew that

Svipdag had lost an eye and had suffered many wounds. And although he had killed another three berserkers, there were still three ranged against him.

At this instruction, the two brothers went to his aid, for the king had not come to his assistance. It was this that saved Svipdag and doomed the remaining berserkers. All the time, King Adils was watching from the edge of the forest, unsure of who he wanted to win.

So it was that Svipdag survived and was nursed by the queen. But when he recovered, he resolved to leave Sweden since its king had offered him such poor support. Instead, he and his brothers went to Denmark and offered their services to King Hrolf. He accepted them and gave them places on his mead benches. At the end of summer, the twelve berserkers of King Hrolf returned to the hall. As was their custom they confronted every man there, but only Svipdag stood up then. There would have been battle but Hrolf parted them and reconciled Svipdag and the leader of the berserkers. From that moment onwards they were equals in battle and close friends.

It was after this that King Hrolf established his hall at Hleidargard in Denmark. It was then that Skuld – the half-elven half-sister of Hrolf – was married to King Hjorvard. (Some say he was king of Öland in Sweden and others that he ruled among the Germans.) A little while later, Hrolf tricked Hjorvard into becoming his tributary king. He did it in this way. While undoing his belt, he asked Hjorvard to hold his sword. This Hjorvard did and then Hrolf took back his sword. He then reminded Hjorvard that whoever held another man's sword while he fastened his own belt accepted being of lesser rank. Hjorvard was angry but duly delivered tribute to Hrolf, as did all the other tribute-paying kings.

This is the end of the story of Svipdag, who killed the berserkers of King Adils of Sweden and became a warrior at the court of King Hrolf.

Tales of magic in Norway and Lapland: Bjorn the bear-man and his sons

Far away in the north of Norway there was a king named Hring and he had a son named Bjorn. When the queen died, King Hring sent southwards for a new wife. However, storms drove his messengers far to the north where they spent the winter among the Lapp people who lived in the frontier regions that the Norse call Finnmark ('Finn borderlands'). There, in that isolated land, they chanced on two beautiful women in a small house. When questioned, it turned out that the older woman was the mistress of the king of the Lapps and the younger was her daughter, named Hvit. They were hiding because a powerful king had demanded to marry Hvit but she had refused him and they feared that he would take her by force.

The messengers of King Hring were sure that Hvit would be a suitable bride for their king. They persuaded her to accompany them south and the old king was pleased to marry such a beautiful young woman.

Now Hring's son, Bjorn, loved a girl named Bera who was the daughter of a wealthy farmer. One day, when King Hring set out to war, Queen Hvit asked that Bjorn might stay with her and help her govern. To this request King Hring agreed because he thought that Hvit was becoming arrogant and the people did not like her. So Bjorn remained at home, although Bjorn was not happy at this decision.

After Hring had gone, Queen Hvit came to Bjorn and tried to console him but he sent her away. But she returned and offered to share her bed with him. This she said would be better than what she experienced being married to a man as old as Hring. At this suggestion, Bjorn struck her and threw her out. In revenge, Queen Hvit slapped him with her glove that was made from wolfskin and cursed him so that he turned into a bear. At this, he left the court, for he was trapped by her magic.

After that a great grey bear attacked the king's cattle and killed many of them. One evening, while Bera the farmer's daughter was outside, the bear approached her but did not threaten her. She followed it to its cave and there it became Bjorn once more. By day he was a bear but a man by night. One night Bjorn told her that the king's hunters would kill him in the morning but she would give birth to three sons after his death. When he was killed, she was to ask the king for whatever was under his left shoulder but she was not to eat any of the meat offered her by the queen, who was really a troll. After their sons were born, she was to read the runes inscribed on a wooden chest in the bear's cave. It would reveal what weapons each son was to have and each weapon would be embedded in rock.

And so it came to pass. The next day Bjorn the bear-man was hunted down and killed. Bera was allowed to take his ring from under his left shoulder though none saw what she took. But afterwards the queen forced her to eat a tiny piece of the bear's cooked flesh, and declared that eating this tiny piece would be enough for her to work her magic.

In time, Bera gave birth to three boys: one was like an elk below the waist and was named Elk-Frodi; one had feet like a dog and was called Thorir Dog-foot; a third appeared fully human and he was named Bodvar. Eating even a tiny piece of bear-meat had affected the children.

Elk-Frodi grew up violent and resentful. At twelve years old, he left the company of people, took the smallest portion of the treasure and a small sword and became a robber and murderer in the mountains. When Thorir Dog-foot left home he took an axe from the cave and his share of the treasure. As with Elk-Frodi, only the appropriate weapon would allow itself to be drawn out of the rock by him. He travelled to the mountains to stay with Elk-Frodi a while and then, on his advice, he made his way to Götaland in southern Sweden, where he was made king.

To Bodvar, Bera revealed all that had happened to his father at the hands of Queen Hvit. Together they went to King Hring to demand vengeance. But Hring asked that for the sake of his love for Hvit they should leave her be and then Bodvar would be compensated with treasure and the rule of the kingdom when Hring died. However, Bodvar wanted vengeance and the king could not stop him. He surprised Queen Hvit and trapped her head within a leather bag that he carried. He beat her and dragged her through the streets and so she died. The king was greatly distressed and soon after this he too died. It was then that Bodvar became king.

He was not content as king, though, and decided to leave. First, he took his weapon – a magic sword – from the rock in the cave. Its nature was such that it would kill a man every time it was unsheathed; and only three times could it be used by any one owner. He made it a sheath from birch bark and travelled until he reached the home of Elk-Frodi, who did not recognise him since his hood was up. They fought and wrestled until at last Elk-Frodi recognised him. He asked him to stay but Bodvar would not. Elk-Frodi gave him a little of his own blood to drink in order to increase his strength. And he promised to avenge him if Bodvar was killed by another man.

When Bodvar reached Götaland, King Thorir Dog-foot was away but Bodvar was so similar that even the queen thought he was her husband. At night, they slept together but Bodvar kept a blanket between them. When Thorir Dog-foot returned, he was overjoyed to see his brother. But Bodvar would not stay for he desired to join the warrior companions of King Hrolf, at Hleidargard in Denmark.

On his way, he was given shelter by an old couple. The mother was weeping because Hott, her son, was cruelly treated by the champions of King Hrolf at Hleidargard. Each evening they pelted him with bones at their feast. Bodvar resolved to save the boy in gratitude for the hospitality the old couple had given him. So it was that when he reached Hleidargard and saw that Hott was hiding behind a shield of bones, he pulled him out and made him sit at the mead bench beside him. When a great bone was thrown, it was Bodvar who hurled it back and killed the man who had thrown it. After this, King Hrolf – who had earlier told his men to desist from their bullying and had been ignored – asked Bodvar to join his champions. But Bodvar would only do this if Hott could accompany him!

Once he had joined the champions, Bodvar learned that each Yule a huge winged troll attacked the land. That Yule-eve, Bodvar and a very reluctant Hott went out to meet the beast. Drawing his mighty sword, Bodvar killed the animal. Making Hott drink its blood and consume its flesh made him strong and courageous. Then, to demonstrate this transformation to all, they propped up the beast as if it was still alive. Later, as others came to investigate, only Hott would approach it and, taking King Hrolf's sword named Golden Hilt, he struck the beast, which fell to the ground. In this way, King Hrolf gained two champions: Bodvar and Hott, whose name was changed to Hjalti in honour of his personal transformation.

This is the end of the story of Bodvar and his brothers.

The reign of King Hrolf: conflicts with King Adils of Sweden, Bodvar Bjarki the bear-man, Odin disguised as Hrani, the death of Hrolf

It was the custom that whenever the berserkers of King Hrolf returned from campaigning, they challenged every man in the king's hall – from the king himself downwards! They believed none was their equal. But the next time that the berserkers returned, things were different: for Bodvar and Hjalti (who was once called Hott) were sitting on the mead benches! When Bodvar was challenged, he called the berserker who did so a son of a mare and would have killed him had not King Hrolf restored order! Hjalti did the same. Now that the two new champions were there, things were different in the hall. On the king's right-hand side sat Bodvar and Hjalti; on his left sat Svipdag and his three brothers; next were the twelve berserkers. So prominent was Bodvar that he married King Hrolf's only daughter, Drifa.

One day, while King Hrolf and Bodvar sat feasting, they talked of the greatness of kings and it was then that Bodvar advised the king that his greatness would be diminished so long as King Adils of Sweden held the treasure of Hrolf's father, Helgi, in Uppsala. King Hrolf agreed but said that it would not be easily regained for Adils was skilled in the dark use of magic. So it was that they set out to travel to Uppsala. On the way, they stayed three nights with a farmer named Hrani and each night they were tested: by cold, by thirst and by heat. Hrani advised King Hrolf to send home those who had failed the test. No one knew it at the time but this farmer, who called himself by the name Hrani, was really Odin in disguise. In the end, only twelve companions rode with the king towards Uppsala.

When they reached there, Svipdag led the way, for he knew the hall of King Adils and there were many obstacles set in their way that they had to overcome to reach where he was sitting. Pits were dug as traps and wall hangings concealed armed men. They battled through them all. At last King Adils called his men to order and – remarking on how few men King Hrolf had with him – bade them sit. Then a fire was lit to warm them but it blazed so fiercely that it threatened to burn them, for King Adils wanted to separate Hrolf from his men since he assumed he would not endure the heat as easily as his champions. However, Bodvar, Svipdag and Hjalti threw King Adils' retainers into the fire and Adils himself only evaded them by using magic to escape through a hollow tree at the centre of the hall.

Then it was that Queen Yrsa sent a servant to attend to the needs of King Hrolf. When he saw the king, he remarked how his face was long and thin like a ladder carved out of a tall pole. In Norse such a carved ladder is called a *kraki*, and this is how King Hrolf became known as Hrolf Kraki! The servant warned the king that Adils would use magic to cause a troll in the shape of a boar to attack them and that is what occurred. It only retreated when attacked by the hound of Hrolf Kraki. Then King Adils set fire to the hall and the companions only escaped by breaking through the walls. Outside a fierce battle ensued and Hrolf Kraki and his champions were victorious; even his hawk slew all of King Adils' hawks in the royal mews. Then it was that Adils fled and the victorious warriors took their seats in the surviving part of his hall. Queen Yrsa brought Adils' treasure to them, including the finest ring that King Adils owned; and she gave them twelve fine horses, for Adils had ordered the maiming of their mounts. Then they left and Hrolf Kraki bid his mother a fond farewell.

As they rode away they were pursued by King Adils but Hrolf Kraki scattered gold on the road and those pursuing slowed to pick it up! Even Adils stopped when he saw his finest ring on the ground. As he bent to pick it up, Hrolf Kraki mocked him for grovelling like a pig and sliced his buttocks with a sweep of his sword. Then the closest of Adils' men were killed and the two kings finally parted.

That evening they came upon a farm and once more they were greeted by the farmer named Hrani. The farmer offered weapons to the king but the king turned him down. At this, Hrani grew very angry and, though it was dark, Hrolf Kraki and his champions had no choice but to leave. Neither Hrolf Kraki nor Hrani bid farewell to the other. When they were on the road, Bodvar reflected that they had been mistaken not to accept the farmer's gifts and would be defeated as a result. And Hrolf Kraki agreed, saying that he now knew that they had met Odin the Old and that was why the farmer had only one eye. They turned back and found that the farm and the farmer had vanished. Hrolf Kraki declared that it would be futile to search further, for the farmer was an evil spirit.

When they reached home, Bodvar advised Hrolf Kraki to no longer go into battle for he feared that the king's battle-luck had run out due to the encounter on the road. But the king said that fate decided a man's life and not the evil spirit that was Odin.

It was soon after this that Skuld – the half-elven half-sister of Hrolf – incited her husband, King Hjorvard, to deny tribute to King Hrolf Kraki. It was this tribute-paying that had been tricked out of him by the incident involving the belt and the sword. Then Skuld used her magical powers to summon elves, norns and many horrible creatures to join the army she was assembling. King Hrolf Kraki was unaware of these preparations even as Skuld and Hjorvard arrived outside Hleidargard with their army; he was too confident in the strength of his rule and his champions, and too concerned with enjoying life at Hleidargard. It is not said that he and his warriors worshipped the old gods; rather, they put too much trust in their own abilities and valour.

It was then that Hjalti (who was once called Hott) went to lie with his mistress outside the fortress and saw the assembled enemies. At the same time, he bit off her nose (some say for her unfaithfulness) and declared how treachery can fool anyone for a while. Then he raised the alarm. Hrolf rallied his champions, including Bodvar, who men also called Bjarki ('little bear') because he had defeated the berserkers.

The king and his champions drank deeply and then went out to battle. And terrible that battle was: corpses piled up and Hrolf Kraki's sword, Skofnung, sang as it shattered bones. All the time a huge bear fought on the side of Hrolf Kraki. It tore and crushed men and horses and no weapon could harm it.

It was then that Hjalti saw that Bodvar Bjarki was missing and summoned him from the hall, chiding him for remaining there. But when Bodvar Bjarki appeared on the battlefield, the great bear vanished and the battle turned against Hrolf Kraki. For now Skuld could work her magic and a terrible boar appeared and slaughtered Hrolf Kraki's men. Bodvar Bjarki saw too that the dead warriors in the enemy army were being brought back to life. He called to Hjalti that, even as he had hacked apart King Hjorvard, the man had not fallen and that this was clearly all the work of Odin, son of the devil, although he could not see him. It was then that King Hrolf Kraki fell, surrounded by his enemies and overwhelmed by magic. He could not prevail because he did not know the true God.

So it was that Skuld prevailed but little good did it do her. For Bodvar Bjarki was avenged by his brothers, Elk-Frodi and King Thorir Dog-foot and a Swedish army sent by Queen Yrsa. They overcame Skuld and her magic, tortured and killed her and returned Denmark to the rule of the line of Hrolf Kraki through his daughters. Then a great burial mound was raised over the grave of Hrolf Kraki and his sword, Skofnung, and mounds were raised over the graves of all the champions.

So ends the story of King Hrolf Kraki and his champions.

24

Journeys to Vinland

THESE STORIES OF the journeys to Vinland, in North America, end this section of 'Norse legends'. They are more firmly rooted in later historic times than the *fornaldar-sagas* (sagas of the ancient times) that we have just been exploring. Even so, they still contain some mythic features and even the most apparently 'historic' of them contain legendary larger-than-life characters that remind us of Arthur in his more 'historic' forms, Robin Hood or the more legendary aspects of Robert the Bruce's exploits, in British traditions.

The accounts in this chapter are found in two thirteenth-century sagas from Iceland: *Eric the Red's Saga* and *The Saga of the Greenlanders*. The account here of these western voyages and the discovery of North America is a composite made by combining information from both of these sagas. This works remarkably well as often one source adds detail to something that is only recorded in outline in the other or does not form part of its tradition at all. At points, though, they offer distinctly different versions of the same traditions. For example: *Eric the Red's Saga* says that it was Eric's son, Thorstein, who purchased a ship from Gudrid's father, with which to sail west; whereas *The Saga of the Greenlanders* says that the ship was purchased from Bjarni Herjolfsson by Eric's son, Leif. In these cases a decision has to be made; the more detailed account is usually followed in order to provide the best 'story'. Occasionally another factor may come into play, such as the account chosen dovetails more exactly with another aspect of the story. *Eric the Red's Saga* contains a lot of information about the settlement of Greenland but is used here mostly for the information it provides about the female explorer, Gudrid Thorbjornsdottir (who plays a significant part in the settlement of Vinland) and the additional information it provides concerning the journeys to Vinland.

The lands 'discovered' in these medieval accounts were, for a long time, regarded as legendary and the products of medieval Norse imagination. However, more recent study of the medieval texts, comparison with North American geography and, finally, archaeological evidence of Norse settlement at L'Anse aux Meadows on the northern tip of Newfoundland in Canada, have meant that we are now sure that these accounts are based on real events, albeit interwoven with some legendary material. The site at L'Anse aux Meadows may correspond to the camp known as Straumsfjord (Old Norse: *Straumfjörð*) that is mentioned in *Eric the Red's Saga*.

As a result, the lands mentioned in these thirteenth-century sagas are now identified as follows:

Helluland is named from the Norse word for 'flat stones' and today many experts believe that it refers to Baffin Island in the Canadian territory of Nunavut.

Markland is named from the Norse word for 'forest' and probably refers to the coast of Labrador.

Vinland is named from the Norse word for 'grapes' (or 'wine') and probably refers to the area from Newfoundland to the Gulf of Saint Lawrence and, perhaps, as far south as north-eastern New Brunswick since wild grapevines are found there.

* * *

The settlement of Greenland

Bjarni Herjolfsson and his father, Herjolf, sailed with Eric the Red to Greenland and settled there. They sailed in the company of a Christian Hebridean who was a poet.

On Greenland, Herjolf and his family settled at Herjolfsnes and Eric the Red settled at Brattahlid. Eric's children were Leif, Thorvald, Thorstein, and his (illegitimate) daughter was named Freydis and she was a domineering woman. She was married to Thorvard who was rich but had little else going for him.

One of those famous in the story of the settlement of Greenland and Vinland was a woman named Gudrid. She travelled to Greenland from Iceland with her father in a group of thirty settlers. It was a hard time that they had, since half of them fell sick and died but those who survived were eventually rescued.

It was then that a woman who could foretell the future told Gudrid her fortune. It came about in a strange way, for that woman – a seeress by the name of Thorbjorg – visited the farm on which Gudrid lived and asked if any women there could join her in chanting the songs needed if she was to foretell the future. Gudrid said that she had been taught them as a child, but could not take part because she was now a Christian. But she was asked to do it to help the people on the farm and so she joined in the traditional chants. After this, Thorbjorg thanked her and said that due to Gudrid's chanting the spirits had revealed to Thorbjorg that the time of hardship on Greenland would soon end; illness troubling Gudrid would soon cease; and that Gudrid would make a good marriage in Greenland, travel to Iceland to put down roots there and be the one from whom an illustrious family would descend.

Later, Gudrid travelled to the hall of the famous adventurer, Eric the Red. It was at this time that Eric's son, Leif, was ordered by King Olaf of Norway to convert the settlers on Greenland to Christianity. This was because the settlers there at that time were heathen. Both Leif and Gudrid played their part in the settlement of Vinland, as we shall shortly see.

The finding of land to the west of Greenland . . . the discovery of Vinland

The ancient tales tell of two accounts of how the land of Vinland was discovered. One account tells of how Bjarni Herjolfsson was blown off course on a sea voyage to Greenland and saw a strange land far to the west. It was a land of small hills and forested; it was located where no land was known to exist. He saw that land but he did not anchor his ship there or go ashore. He kept the land on his port (left-hand) side and then sailed away from it for two days before once more seeing land. He realised that this too was not Greenland for it had no glaciers; this land was flat and wooded. The crew wanted to put ashore for wood and water but Bjarni Herjolfsson would not do it. Instead, they sailed away from that land for three days, until they came to a third land. This third land had high mountains and glaciers. Once more they did not land and, instead, they sailed around it and saw that it was an island. They then sailed away from it for four days. At the end of this time they came on a fourth land. This was Greenland and they made landfall at the place where Bjarni Herjolfsson's father had settled.

The other tale tells how Leif Ericsson too was blown off course on a sea voyage and he too came upon an unknown land far to the west of Greenland. He found it to be a land of self-sown wheat and vines, where maple trees grew. Some say that he got lost while sailing to Greenland from Norway, while others say that Leif sailed to the west directly from Greenland.

Those who say most about it tell that it came about in this way. Leif had bought a ship from Bjarni Herjolfsson and asked Eric, his father, to accompany him on an exploration, sailing from Greenland to the west. But Eric decided that he was too old for such adventurers. After this he changed his mind, buried all his gold and rode down to where Leif had moored his ship. But on the way Eric fell from his horse, breaking several ribs and hurting his shoulder, and so he decided that it was time to go back home to his farm; consequently, Leif sailed without him.

Leif discovered the land that had earlier been seen by Bjarni Herjolfsson. He passed new lands that he named *Helluland* ('Stone-slab Land'), *Markland* ('Forest Land') and eventually *Vinland* ('Vine Land' or 'Wine Land').

Leif rowed ashore to explore the first land that they reached. Helluland had no grass and glaciers covered the high ground. Between them and the sea the land was a flat sheet of rock. They decided that such a barren land was of no use to them.

So they sailed on until they reached a second land. Once more they went ashore. Markland had white sandy beaches and was flat and wooded, and this was why he called it Markland ('Forest Land') because it was so different to the barren shores that he had come across so far as he sailed past Helluland.

They sailed on for a further two days. And then he came to the most fertile land of all. North of it was an island on which they landed. There was dew on the grass, which was sweet to the taste. Returning to their ship, they sailed into the sound that was between that island and the mainland. After sailing along the coast their ship beached in the shallows, and the sea seemed far off. They wanted to explore this new land and so they left their ship stranded near where a river flowed into the sea from a lake. At last, the returning tide lifted their ship and they returned to it and sailed it up the river and into the lake. There they dropped anchor.

They went ashore and built shelters. They decided to spend the winter there and built proper houses. There was plenty of salmon in the lake and river and these were larger fish than they had ever seen before. They were of the opinion that livestock would not need fodder stored in order to survive the winter months since the weather remained mild and the grass hardly died back. Compared with both Greenland and Iceland, the days and nights were of more equal length; even in midwinter the sun was clearly visible by the middle of the morning and could still be seen in the middle of the afternoon.

It was at this spot that they built shelters and began to explore the surrounding territory. In order to keep safe they divided into two groups: one always remained at the camp and those out exploring always kept together. It was on one of these explorations that Leif's foster-father became separated from the others and, when they eventually found him, he excitedly told them that he had discovered grapes and grapevines growing. It was from that discovery that the land became known as 'Vinland'. As a result, the settlers picked the grapes and felled wood to carry back with them onto their ships.

Later explorers also reached this point and called it 'Leif's Camp'. From that base these later travellers explored further.

The next spring, on his way home to Greenland, Leif rescued the Norwegian Thorir and his crew who had been shipwrecked and were surviving on a skerry: a low rock island. There were fifteen trapped there when Leif arrived. After this, people called him 'Leif the Lucky'. Thorir then spent the winter (along with Gudrid his wife) at the farm of Leif. That winter, Thorir fell ill and died, as did Leif's father, Eric the Red. Gudrid would later be one of the first settlers in Vinland.

Another account of the exploration of Vinland . . . the voyage of Thorvald

Leif the Lucky's brother was named Thorvald. He too sailed to Vinland and reached 'Leif's Camp'. There they settled for the winter and fished.

From there, in the spring, he explored to the west. They were impressed by the well-forested land (on Greenland there was a great shortage of wood) and the white-sand beaches.

The second summer they explored the land to the east. After some time of exploring, his ship was driven ashore in a storm and badly damaged. This happened at a place that he named Kjalarnes ('Keel Point').

While they were there they came across nine of the natives (whom the Norse call 'skraelings', meaning 'barbarians' or 'yelling ones') hiding under three boats made from animal hide. Thorvald and his men killed all but one, who escaped. He sounded the alarm and many more appeared and attacked the Norse with bows and arrows.

Thorvald and his men had fallen asleep and were woken by a voice warning them of danger. It was then that they saw huge numbers of hide-covered boats coming towards them. Warned by the mysterious voice, they defended their ship against attack. After a while, the attackers withdrew. But one of their arrows had mortally wounded Thorvald and he was buried at a place that his companions named Krossanes ('Cross Point'). It was named from the crosses that Thorvald ordered to be placed at the head and foot of his grave. Thorvald was a Christian but his father, Eric the Red, had died before the conversion of Greenland had occurred.

The next spring the surviving settlers sailed back to Greenland and brought the news of Thorvald's death to Leif, his brother.

Another account of the exploration of Vinland . . . the voyage of Thorstein and Gudrid

Thorstein (son of Eric the Red) married Gudrid, who was one of the early settlers of Greenland with her first husband, the Norwegian who was named Thorir. It was this Thorir who had been rescued from the skerry by Leif the Lucky.

Together, Thorstein and Gudrid set up home on Greenland at Lysufjord in the area of Greenland known as the Western Settlement. They had been forced there by bad weather when attempting a voyage to Vinland in order to retrieve the body of Thorvald. There they settled at a local farm for the winter. Now Thorstein and Gudrid were Christians but the people with whom they stayed were still believers in the old gods such as Odin and Thor.

It was there that Thorstein fell ill and died. After that he briefly rose from the dead and told Gudrid's fortune. It came about in this way. Disease struck down many on the farm at which Thorstein and Gudrid were staying for the winter. Even before they died, the spirits of the dead were seen standing outside the door, in the yard between the farmhouse and the outhouse. In this way, those who were soon to die were seen as if they were already dead. When Thorstein eventually died near sunset, Gudrid went to sleep while the farmer kept watch over the dead. But during the night he called Gudrid to tell her that her dead husband had risen and wanted to speak with her. Because Gudrid was a Christian she put her trust in God for her protection and went to where her husband was. There he spoke privately to her and asked that he and the dead from the farm should be buried in consecrated ground at a church. At that time, it was the practice on Greenland to bury the dead in unconsecrated ground and drive a pole down onto the chest of the dead. Then, often much later, the pole was pulled out and holy water poured down the hole and the burial service recited. But Thorstein asked for immediate burial in church ground for all the dead. All, that is, except Gardi the farm foreman who had been the first to die. For Thorstein told Gudrid that it was down to him that the dead were haunting the living; his body should be burned on a funeral pyre. Then Thorstein counselled her not to marry a Greenlander, and to donate their money to the church or the poor. After this, he sank down and was at peace.

This was the second time that Gudrid had had her fortune told. After this, Thorstein's body was taken to the churchyard at Brattahlid (though some say it was to the church at Ericsfjord) and Gudrid lived there as a widow afterwards.

After this, she eventually married Thorfinn Karlsefni who arrived in Greenland. All were talking of going to Vinland and so Gudrid and Thorfinn Karlsefni set off there in the company of Freydis, the (illegitimate) daughter of Eric the Red, and Thorvard, her husband. They were also joined by Eric's son, who was named Thorvald. They took livestock with them since they intended to settle in Vinland. They passed Helluland and saw many foxes there. Sailing on for two days they passed the forested land of Markland and discovered a bear on an offshore island that they called Bjarney ('Bear Island'). After a further two days of sailing, they passed an area that they called Furdustrandir ('Wonderful Beaches') because of its long stretches of sand. It was then that they put ashore two Scots who had been given to them by Olaf Tryggvason, the king of Norway. These were a man named Haki and a woman named Hekja. They could run faster than a deer and were given the task of exploring the country. After three days, they returned with grapes and self-sown wheat. And so Thorfinn Karlsefni pronounced that the land was good for settlement.

They took the Scots back on board and sailed on and into Straumsfjord and eventually they settled at Leif's Camp, where some say that there was plenty of food in the form of a freshly beached whale and grapes growing and game to hunt. But others say that the winter caught them by surprise and that they went hungry at first. So they prayed to God for food as they were Christians but still they were hungry. It was then that one of their number – Thorhall the huntsman – went missing. He was a difficult man and had little regard for Christianity. He was, though, a close companion of Eric the Red. After

Thorhall went missing, it took three days to find him and Thorfinn Karlsefni discovered him on the edge of a cliff in a disturbed state. It was soon afterwards that they found a beached whale of a type that they had never seen before and ate its meat, although it made them ill. It was then that Thorhall the huntsman declared that the discovery of the whale was his reward for reciting a poem to Thor, who was his guardian, and that 'Old Redbeard [Odin] had been more use to them than Christ'. When they heard this, the others threw the whalemeat off the cliff and cried out to God for mercy. Then it was that the weather improved, they could go fishing and had plenty of food. Moving further along the fjord they found plenty of game to hunt, eggs to gather and fish to catch.

With regard to Thorhall the huntsman, he continued to recite poems to Odin, whom he named 'the helmet-god'. Eventually he and his ship set out on their own but they were driven by a storm far away and onto the shore of Ireland where they were badly treated and forced into slavery.

Back in Vinland, one of the remaining ships went north around Kjalarnes where they discovered the keel of a ship that had been abandoned at Kjalarnes. Their ship was blown off course and ended up further south at a place they called Hop ('Tidal Pool'). This was so called because there a river flowed out of a lake into the sea. But the sandbars at the mouth of the river meant that they could only sail into it at high tide. This ship was the one under the command of Thorfinn Karlsefni. At Hop they discovered fields of self-sown wheat, vines growing on the hills and rivers full of fish. By digging trenches along the high-water mark they caught flatfish in them when the tide receded. That winter there was no snow and their livestock could graze outside.

It was at Hop that Thorfinn Karlsefni and Gudrid first met *skraelings*. These people were short in stature, with threatening looks and hair that was wild and tangled; they had large eyes and broad cheekbones. The Norse traded with them. The Norse gave them milk and dairy products and red cloth and the *skraelings* traded animal hide. The *skraelings* also wanted to trade for weapons but Thorfinn Karlsefni would not allow his men to do this. The *skraelings* were afraid of the bull that Thorfinn Karlsefni and Gudrid had brought with them, and so Thorfinn Karlsefni decided that, if need be, he would use the bull to frighten off the *skraelings*.

While they were there, Gudrid gave birth to a son and she named him Snorri. He was the first of the Norse who was born in Vinland. Soon after this, Gudrid saw a ghost. It was a woman with huge eyes. The strange woman said that her name too was Gudrid. But before they could speak further they were disturbed by a loud noise as one of the *skraelings* attempted to steal a weapon and was killed.

Eventually the *skraelings* attacked the settlement. Many were killed and one of them was killed by one of his own companions who had seized an iron axe – which he had found embedded in the head of a dead *skraeling* – and used it on him to see what it would do to him. At this, the chief of the *skraelings* took the axe and hurled it into the sea. Another tale tells this as being used by the *skraelings* on wood, but thrown away when they tried it on stone and the blade shattered.

During the fight there was a point at which the Norse men fell back in the face of the attack by the *skraelings* but the situation was saved by Freydis, the daughter of Eric the Red. Though she was pregnant, she frightened the attackers off by baring her breast and slapping it with the flat of a sword blade.

After this, Thorfinn Karlsefni decided that they could not remain there, for they would be under constant danger of attack. So they sailed back up the coast and killed five of the *skraelings* that they discovered sleeping in animal-hide sleeping bags.

They sailed back around Kjalarnes to a point where a river flowed into the sea. There he and his crew were attacked by a one-legged creature who killed Thorvald, the son of Eric the Red, with an arrow. Thorvald pulled the arrow out of his body and joked with his companions about how fat his stomach was, into which the arrow had sunk. After this, he died.

Once back at Straumsfjord, the men fell out over women. Those men who had no wives tried to take those of the married men. By this time, they had been in Vinland for three years, for that was the age of Thorfinn Karlsefni's and Gudrid's son, Snorri (the one who was the first Norse born in Vinland). Sailing on, they reached Markland, where they came upon five of the *skraelings*: a bearded man, two women and two children. They caught the children, taught them the Norse language and baptised them; so these were the first of the natives of Vinland to become Christians. There, they lost another of their ships.

Next spring, Thorfinn Karlsefni and Gudrid decided to return to Greenland. With them they took a heavy load of wood – for there was none but driftwood on Greenland – wild berries and animal skins.

From there, they went on back to Iceland and then on to Norway to sell the things they had brought back from Vinland. This included the carved wooden prow of their ship. It was purchased for a good price in gold by a trader from Bremen in Saxony who had travelled to Norway. The prow, it was later said, was made of maple wood from Vinland, although at the time Thorfinn Karlsefni did not know what kind of wood he had brought back with him.

From Norway they returned to Iceland. There, in Iceland, Thorfinn Karlsefni and Gudrid eventually settled at Reynines in Skagafjord, northern Iceland. At first, Gudrid was not accepted by her mother-in-law as she felt that Gudrid's family was not worthy of her son. In the end, though, she came round and accepted her.

From Thorfinn Karlsefni's and Gudrid's son, Snorri, are descended many Icelanders, including three who became bishops in the Icelandic church. Most of what we know of the voyages to Vinland comes from the reports of Thorfinn Karlsefni.

Gudrid herself later travelled to Rome as a pilgrim. Returning to Iceland, she built a church at Glaumbaer and became a nun and lived there as a hermit, an anchorite, until she died.

Another account of the exploration of Vinland . . . the voyage of Freydis Ericsdottir with Thorvard her husband

It was later that Freydis, the daughter of Eric the Red, returned to Vinland along with Thorvard her husband. She travelled in the company of two brothers, Helgi and Finnbogi, who came from the eastern fjords of Iceland and owned a ship that they had sailed to Greenland. It was this woman who had terrified the *skraelings* by beating her naked breast with the flat of a sword. But this expedition ended very badly indeed, for Freydis was devious and could not be trusted.

They reached 'Leif's Camp', but there the members of this expedition fell out with each other. Freydis refused to allow Helgi and Finnbogi to use the longhouses at 'Leif's Camp' for she said that Leif – her brother – had loaned their use to her and not to them. So they set up camp further from the sea, beside a lake.

In the winter, the two groups of settlers competed in sports but disagreements soon divided them and that continued through the winter.

Incited by the actions of Freydis, they fought each other. Freydis lied to her husband, telling him that she had been badly treated by Finnbogi and inciting him to revenge. This he and his men did and fell on the other settlers – Helgi and Finnbogi and their followers – while they slept. The men they tied up and these were then killed on the orders of Freydis. But nobody in the group led by Freydis was willing to kill the five women among the followers of Helgi and Finnbogi. In the end it was Freydis, herself, who killed the women who had travelled there with them. She did so with an axe.

After this, the survivors returned to Greenland and Freydis told them to be silent about what had happened or be killed. They were to tell others that the remaining members of the expedition had stayed behind in Vinland.

However, news of the atrocity that Freydis had committed in Vinland leaked out. She was condemned by Leif the Lucky, her own brother; but, as she was of his family, she escaped punishment for the killings that she had caused and had also personally carried out in Vinland.

Notes

Chapter 1: Who were the 'Norse'?

1 C. Balbirnie, 'The Vikings at home', *BBC History Magazine*, vol. 13, no. 9 (September 2012), p. 25.

2 An overview of the use of the term 'Viking' can be found in: M. Arnold, *The Vikings: Culture and Conquest* (London: Hambledon Continuum, 2006), pp. 7–8; A. Somerville and R. A. McDonald, *The Viking Age: A Reader* (Toronto: University of Toronto Press, 2010), p. xiii.

3 K. Kunz, in Ö. Thorsson (ed.), *The Sagas of Icelanders* (London: Penguin, 2000), p. 640.

4 For an accessible account of this discovery, see: H. Ingstad and A. Stine Ingstad, *The Viking Discovery of America: The Excavation of a Norse Settlement in L'Anse aux Meadows, Newfoundland* (St John's, NF: Breakwater Books, 2000).

5 P. B. Taylor, 'The Hønen runes: A survey', *Neophilologus*, vol. 60, no. 1 (January 1976), pp. 1–7. See also: C. Cavaleri, 'The Vínland Sagas as Propaganda for the Christian Church: Freydís and Gudríd as Paradigms for Eve and the Virgin Mary', Master's thesis, University of Oslo, 2008.

6 For modern translations of these, see: Snorri Sturluson, *Edda*, ed. and trans. A. Faulkes (London: Everyman, 1987) – often known as the *Prose Edda* – and *The Poetic Edda*, trans. C. Larrington (Oxford: Oxford University Press, 1996).

7 For an accessible overview, see: M. L. Colish, *Medieval Foundations of the Western Intellectual Tradition, 400–1400* (New Haven, CT, and London: Yale University Press, 1997), ch. 8: 'Varieties of Germanic literature: Old Norse, Old High German, and Old English'.

8 See: G. Nordal , *Tools of Literacy: The Role of Skaldic Verse in Icelandic Textual Culture of the Twelfth and Thirteenth Centuries* (Toronto: University of Toronto Press, 2001), p. 58.

9 For an overview of the Norse saga literature, see: M. Clunies Ross, *The Cambridge Introduction to the Old Norse-Icelandic Saga* (Cambridge: Cambridge University Press, 2010).

10 J. Jesch, 'The Norse gods in England and the Isle of Man', in D. Anlezark (ed.), *Myths, Legends, and Heroes: Essays on Old Norse and Old English Literature in Honour of John McKinnell* (Toronto: University of Toronto Press, 2011), pp. 18–19.

11 M. Osborn, 'The ravens on the Lejre Throne', in M. D. J. Bintley and T. J. T. Williams (eds), *Representing Beasts in Early Medieval England and Scandinavia* (Woodbridge: Boydell & Brewer, 2015), p. 104; A. Andrén, K. Jennbert and C. Raudvere (eds), *Old Norse Religion in Long-term Perspectives: Origins, Changes, and Interactions: An International Conference in Lund, Sweden, June 3–7, 2004* (Lund: Nordic Academic Press, 2006), p. 128.

12 Feminae: Medieval Women and Gender Index, https://inpress.lib. uiowa.edu/feminae/DetailsPage.aspx?Feminae_ID=31944 (accessed 17 March 2017).

13 L. Hedeager, *Iron Age Myth and Materiality: An Archaeology of Scandinavia AD 400–1000* (Abingdon: Routledge, 2011), Figure 4.21, p. 76.

14 P. Parker, *The Northmen's Fury: A History of the Viking World* (London: Vintage, 2015), p. 130.

15 See: J. D. Richards, 'The Scandinavian presence', in J. Hunter and I. Ralston (eds), *The Archaeology of Britain: An Introduction from the Upper Palaeolithic to the Industrial Revolution* (London: Routledge, 1999), p. 200; J. Jesch, 'Speaking like a Viking: Language and

cultural interaction in the Irish Sea region', in S. E. Harding, D. Griffiths and E. Royles (eds), *In Search of Vikings: Interdisciplinary Approaches to the Scandinavian Heritage of North-west England* (Boca Raton, FL: CRC Press, 2015), p. 58.

16 Anglo-Saxon Chronicle annal for 878, D. Whitelock (ed.), *English Historical Documents, Volume I, c.500–1042* (London: Eyre Methuen, 1979), p. 195. Referring to this event, the later *Annals of St Neots* (early twelfth century) records the tradition that the banner fluttered prior to a victory but hung down before a defeat.

Chapter 2: The impact of Christianity on Norse mythology

17 P. Meulengracht Sørensen, 'Religions old and new', in P. Sawyer (ed.), *The Oxford Illustrated History of the Vikings* (Oxford: Oxford University Press, 1997), p. 206.

18 See: J. Lindow, *Handbook of Norse Mythology* (Santa Barbara, CA: ABC Clio, 2001), p. 10.

19 A. Faulkes, 'Pagan sympathy: Attitudes to heathendom in the Prologue to *Snorra Edda*', in R. J. Glendinning and H. Bessason (eds), *Edda: A Collection of Essays* (Winnipeg, MB: University of Manitoba Press, 2014), p. 285.

20 In the same way, many experts have argued that the Norse mythological scenes found on stone crosses in Britain represent the use of Norse pagan motifs to communicate a Christian message. See: J. Jesch, 'The Norse gods in England and the Isle of Man', in D. Anlezark (ed.), *Myths, Legends, and Heroes: Essays on Old Norse and Old English Literature in Honour of John McKinnell* (Toronto: University of Toronto Press, 2011), p. 12.

21 He states: 'Now there shall be told more of the underlying stories from which those kennings just listed have originated', M. Clunies Ross, 'Quellen zur germanischen Religionsgeschichte', in H. Beck, D. Ellmers and K. Schier (eds), *Germanische Religionsgeschichte* (Berlin and New York: Walter de Gruyter, 1992), p. 647.

22 It has been argued that the Icelandic material 'may give a picture of pagan mythology that is rather too systematic and learned'. A. Mills, *Mythology* (Cape Town: Struik Publishers, 2006), p. 233.

23 Adam of Bremen, *History of the Archbishops of Hamburg-Bremen*, trans. F. J. Tschan (New York: Columbia University Press, 2002), Bk IV, p. 207.

24 Tacitus, *Germania*, trans. M. Hutton and W. Peterson, rev. R. M. Ogilvie, E. H. Warmington and M. Winterbottom (Cambridge, MA: Harvard University Press, 1914), p. 144.

25 See: A. A. Somerville and R. A. McDonald, *The Vikings and Their Age* (Toronto: University of Toronto Press, 2013), ch. 2: 'Society and religion in the Viking Age: Conversion'.

Select Bibliography

The selection of myths and legends freely retold in this book can also be found, academically translated from Old Norse in the context of other traditions, stories and accounts, in these translations.

The Poetic Edda, trans. C. Larrington (Oxford: Oxford University Press, 1996).

The Saga of King Hrolf Kraki, trans. J. L. Byock (London: Penguin, 1998).

The Saga of the Volsungs, trans. J. L. Byock (London: Penguin, 1999).

Sturluson, Snorri, *Edda*, ed. and trans. A. Faulkes (London: Everyman, 1987). Often known as the *Prose Edda*.

Sturluson, Snorri, *Heimskringla: History of the Kings of Norway*, trans. L. M. Hollander (Austin TX: University of Texas Press, 2007).

'The Vinland Sagas', trans. K. Kunz, in J. Smiley et al., *The Sagas of Icelanders* (London: Penguin, 2000).

Index